SABOTAGE IN THE SECRET CITY

SABOTAGE IN THE SECRET CITY

A Libby Clark Mystery

Diane Fanning

This first world edition published 2018
in Great Britain and the USA by
SEVERN HOUSE PUBLISHERS LTD of
Eardley House, 4 Uxbridge Street, London W8 7SY
Trade paperback edition first published
in Great Britain and the USA 2018 by
SEVERN HOUSE PUBLISHERS LTD

British Library Cataloguing in Publication Data
A CIP catalogue record for this title is available from the British Library.

ISBN-13: 978-0-7278-8782-5 (cased)
ISBN-13: 978-1-84751-905-4 (trade paper)
ISBN-13: 978-1-78010-960-2 (e-book)

All Severn House titles are printed on acid-free paper.

Severn House Publishers support the Forest Stewardship Council™ [FSC™],
the leading international forest certification organisation.
All our titles that are printed on FSC certified paper carry the FSC logo.

ONE

I dreaded going to work in the rain. The facility was no longer the shoe-sucking morass it had been when I first arrived at Oak Ridge, but still wet weather posed hazards. I traveled the sidewalk alternating between surging forward when the road was clear and pausing my progress when a vehicle was about to hit a mud puddle up ahead.

I made it to Y-12 with a sigh of relief, suffering no more than a few small brown spatters on my skirt. Shaking off my umbrella, I stepped past security. A sense of dread still clung to me like mud but I couldn't put my finger on any reason for it. All in all, it seemed to be a normal Thursday at work.

I got to the lab early, hoping to have the preliminaries ready before anyone else walked through the door. I moved quickly from one work bench to another, handing out samples for testing at multiple stations. I hoped to have another full canister of green salt to ship out early next week. The protocol I had established had built-in redundancy to ensure accuracy of results. My final number would be an average of all the others.

I sat down at my assigned space and soon was engrossed in the tasks of the day with only a vague awareness of the shuffles and scrapes heralding the presence of the other scientists in the lab. I passed a couple of hours in deep concentration before looking across the room and seeing, with one exception, that everyone was engrossed in his assigned tasks.

The one anomaly was Tom. He sat as still as his stool – his face blank, his eyes fixed on the wall ahead of him. I smiled at the stray red curl on his forehead that had escaped from his shock of slicked-back hair, giving him the look of a naughty little boy. Assuming he was just taking a break, I bent back down to my work. About an hour later, I looked up again and Tom didn't appear to have moved a muscle. I focused on him for a few minutes and the only sign of life was the lifting and dropping of his shoulders as he emitted one soft sigh after another.

I walked across the room and lay a hand on his forearm. 'Tom,' I whispered, 'are you feeling all right?'

'No,' he said without looking at me.

'Do you need to go back to your room and lie down?'

'No.'

'Tom, what's wrong?' I said and waited for a response. Not getting one, I asked him to look at me. As an afterthought, I added 'please.'

He slowly swiveled his face toward me. His expression was so forlorn, it broke my heart. I waited, but still he said nothing.

'Oh, good heavens, Tom. Please tell me what is wrong.'

'My father . . .' he said and stopped.

'Is something wrong with him?'

Tom scowled and said, 'Pops is dead.'

'Let's go get a cup of coffee.'

'I don't want to talk about it.'

'You need to talk about it. And it wouldn't hurt if you cried about it.'

'I'm not a woman,' Tom shouted, bringing every eye in the lab over in our direction.

'Everyone is staring at us,' I whispered. 'And you leave me no choice. Either we go and talk or I'll be forced to tell Charlie you are not completing your assignments.'

'Dirty woman tricks,' he hissed as he rose to his feet. 'Lead the way.' I bit off the sharp retort that leaped to my tongue and begged for release.

He followed me to the nearest coffee urn without saying a word. As we sat down with our full mugs, he snarled, 'Do you have to win every argument with a man?'

I ignored his question and asked one of my own. 'What happened to your father?'

Tom stared at me for a long time before sighing, shaking his head and opening his mouth. 'The Knox Coal Company killed him.'

'What?'

'Did you hear about that gas explosion at a Pennsylvania coal mine two days ago?'

'Yes, it was tragic. Nine, ten people died, I believe? I didn't know your father was a miner.'

'He's not – he wasn't. He's a mining engineer. Was.'

'Oh. I'm sorry, Tom.'

'Nine miners died, too. They pulled Pops' body out of the shaft last night. They said he was just checking out a structural problem at the wrong time. Ironic. I used to pester him all the time and tell him I didn't want him to go to work. He always used to tell me not to worry. He'd say, "I'm not a miner, Tommy. I hardly ever go down into the pit. I'm always coming home. I'm not going to get killed down there and leave you behind."'

'How's your mother doing? Maybe you should be with her now,' I said.

Tom's face contorted in pain. 'I don't even remember my mama. Pops told me she never got out of bed after I was born. She just got sicker and sicker and none of the doctors could help her. Grandma moved in after that. She helped raise me till I was seven years old and then she died, too.'

'No wonder you were so worried about losing your father when you were a kid.'

'I'm not a kid anymore. And I'm not a weeping woman. Can we get back to work now?'

'When are you leaving for the funeral?' I asked.

'Leaving for the funeral? Are you crazy? I can't get leave.'

'Sure, you can. We can go ask Charlie right now.'

'Charlie won't give me leave. There's a war going on, remember?'

'I'll make you a wager. If he doesn't let you go, I'll make you a home-cooked dinner.'

'And if he does, what will I have to do?'

I thought for a moment and smiled. 'You'll have to sit through a whole meeting of the Walking Molecules without making one negative comment about women. That is, if you think you're capable of that feat.'

He threw his hands up as if to ward me off. 'I don't always make derogatory remarks about women.'

'You make them so often, Tom, you aren't even aware you're doing it.'

'Ah, you women are all alike.'

'See.'

'Okay. You're on. Do I get to pick the menu?'

'Within reason – as long as it's something available at the market.'

'You've got a deal.'

Returning to the lab, I saw Greg glance in my direction with a raised eyebrow. I shrugged and grinned in response. Leave it to him to know something was up.

Tom and I were just feet away from Charlie's office when he blasted out of the room and shouted, 'Attention. May I have your attention, please?'

Half the room turned towards him – the others were oblivious. Greg stuck two fingers in his mouth and let out a shrill whistle. All eyes turned toward the sound.

Charlie cleared his throat and swallowed hard. His smooth, bookish face rippled with wrinkles between his eyebrows and around his mouth. 'Gentlemen. Libby. I regret to inform you that the president – our president – President Franklin Roosevelt has died.'

A tumult of voices raised in denial surged through the room. One loud voice declared, 'This is not funny, Charlie.'

'No. It is not. But, unfortunately it's true.'

'An assassin?' I asked.

'An internal one, Libby. Roosevelt died of a cerebral hemorrhage.'

'Are you sure? Maybe it's just Nazi propaganda,' a hopeful voice suggested.

'I wish it were,' Charlie said with a sigh. 'But he died today in the presence of his doctors in Warm Springs, Georgia.'

A sensation akin to panic pounded in my chest and my mouth felt crammed full of sawdust. How can this be true? We need him. The outcome of the war depends on him. Our work depends on him. I didn't want to think of the consequences so I switched to emotional concerns. 'Was the first lady with him? Any of his children?' I asked.

'I don't know.'

'Are you sure he wasn't poisoned?' Tom asked.

'I only know what I heard on the news, Tom. I seriously

doubt they would announce any cause of death if they were not certain they were right.'

'Right,' Tom said with scorn scratching through his voice. 'Like they always speak the truth. That's why all the Calutron girls know exactly what they're doing here. Right? We're family – isn't that what they always tell us. Well, families don't have secrets, at least, happy ones don't. Why don't we let everyone know that we're processing—'

'Tom, stop right there,' Charlie commanded. 'You are skirting very close to the edge. Just the words you uttered could get you removed from this project if I reported them.'

'And what, Charlie? Would it be a firing squad? Or would I be locked up for the duration of the war?'

'Tom . . .' Charlie began.

Laying a hand on Tom's balled fist, I squeezed it and said, 'Charlie, please overlook Tom's heightened emotions. He just learned that his own father has died and he needs leave to go to the funeral.'

Charlie's eyes narrowed as if he suspected me of improvising on the spot. 'Is this true, Tom?'

For a moment, Tom looked as if he were going to snap his cap, then he shook his head and looked at the floor. 'That emotional stuff is all wet. But it's true that Pops is dead, yes.'

Charlie stared at the two of us for a moment longer. 'Just write the dates down for me, Tom, it won't be a problem.' He spun on his heel, returned to his office and slammed the door.

I sighed knowing with certainty that later today or tomorrow, Charlie would excoriate me for not delivering that news in private. I wasn't looking forward to that discussion.

TWO

I didn't expect I'd get a thank you from Tom but the glare he threw in my direction was still a shock. He stomped across the lab with a piece of paper clutched in one hand. He pounded on Charlie's closed door with the other before shoving it open. I heard raised voices from the office but couldn't understand a word.

Moments later, the door slammed open so hard that it collided with the wall. Tom emerged and barreled across the lab and out of sight. Charlie stood on his threshold and looked around the room, shaking his head when I caught his eye. He went back inside but, at least, he left the door wide open.

I figured the best way to get back in Charlie's good graces was to do good work and lots of it. I retrieved the assignments I'd given to Tom and got busy taking care of his work as well as mine. I pushed myself and everyone in the lab on Friday and Saturday. It wasn't easy keeping them focused. Charlie kept popping out with news updates about our president's death, the funeral in Washington and his planned train ride to Hyde Park for burial. Whenever he dropped a tidbit, work devolved into conversation about his reports.

Another major diversion was that our vice president was now our new president – Harry Truman. Everyone had an opinion about him but no one had many facts. Some had even forgotten his name until he was sworn in. FDR certainly hadn't helped to make Truman a public figure.

When I finished up on Saturday, I was confident that I would be able to pack up and turn over another shipment to the courier on Monday. When I had first received the responsibility of that task, it had given me the heebie-jeebies. I had worried that the quality and quantity of the specimen would be criti-cized or that I would be given the third degree by the courier or another member of the military. After months of uneventful deliveries, it was now all rather boring and routine.

I tried to sleep in a bit later than usual on Sunday morning but my cat, G.G., only allowed me an extra half hour before he sat on my chest and wailed in my face. Breakfast time for the kitty. No rest for the weary.

I planned on a typical day off, curling up with a book in one hand, a coffee cup in the other and soft classical music playing on the radio. I'd finished the first section of *The Green Years* by A.J. Cronin and was anxious to see what the next part held in store for the poor Irish orphan shipped off to Scotland. Engrossed in the story, it took me a moment to realize a news broadcast had replaced the music. I set down my book and turned up the volume on the radio.

'Weimer, the birthplace of the German Republic in 1919, gives up without a shot being fired. The Yanks delivered an ultimatum to the Over-Mayor: "The American Army once again is marching triumphantly forward. Your city is surrounded and untenable. Surrender and you will be treated to the rules of the Geneva Convention."

'The Over-Mayor's response was succinct and unequivocal: "We want to surrender."

'In his limousine, the Over-Mayor drove to the edge of town where he met Captain Lawrence A. Degner who joined him in the vehicle. Together they led the American column into the city where people lined the streets waving and cheering.'

I closed my eyes in grief and despair – so close to victory and we've lost our leader. Will we lose our drive or change our strategy because FDR was gone?

I shook the negative thoughts away as the radio announcer continued. 'Subsequently, the Yanks overran the infamous Buchenwald prison camp in a nearby woods, three miles north-west of the city. They found 20,000 to 25,000 political prisoners there.

'American combat casualties since Pearl Harbor have reached 899,388. Secretary of War Stinson today reported the army dead and wounded at 802, 685, while the navy set its losses at 96,703.

'In further news from the US Department of War, a joint statement in conjunction with the State Department declared that the German actions uncovered are a shock to the civilized world. They charged Germany with "deliberate neglect, indifference and cruelty" in its treatment of American prisoners. Citing "deplorable" conditions, lack of food, adequate shelter and care, they added that "atrocities against American prisoners are documented by the pitiable conditions of liberated soldiers."

'The report concluded with a defining statement: "The

American nation will not forget them. It is our relentless
determination that the perpetrators of these heinous crimes
against American citizens and against civilization will be
brought to justice."'

I turned off the radio. I couldn't bear to listen any longer.
What will happen to us now? And what is wrong with me? It
was all good news and yet here I sit in agony. The lack of
certainty unsettled me. I felt myself torn in different directions.
Yes, I wanted the war to be over and the killing to end. But
would the unsophisticated Midwesterner Harry Truman be able
to wrap up the victory that Roosevelt and Churchill had crafted?
Or would he want to diverge from FDR's strategy and thus
prolong the war?

And what about the work I'd dedicated myself to for all
these years? Would it simply go to waste? Would the government simply say, 'Never mind. You can go home now.' I was
convinced that even if our goal was to build the most dreadful
bomb the world had ever seen, our work could be used for
good in peacetime. Would we be allowed to do that? Or
would the authorities shut as all down and deny that we ever
existed?

My reverie was cut short by a knock on the door. I wasn't
expecting anyone but unannounced visitors on a Sunday were
common. As I walked across the room to greet my unknown
guest, G.G. darted past my feet and hid in the bedroom. He
definitely was not a fan of strangers.

I opened the door and doubted I was really seeing who was
on the other side. She stood there in saddle shoes and a hand-
knitted blue sloppy joe sweater with a big grin on her face.
Her once long hair now ended at her shoulder in a Juliet style
where brushed-out pin curls framed her jawline in fluffiness.
Ruth – my country girl friend looking like movie star Norma
Shearer on her day off. It couldn't be Ruth, but it was.

'You gonna stand there staring like a Dumb Dora or are
you gonna invite me in?'

'Come in, come in, come in, Ruthie! I can't believe
it's you. What are you doing here?'

'Well, you see, you never answered my last letter.'

'It just got here yesterday!' I protested.

'See,' she said, 'the mail's just so slow, I decided to take matters into my own hands.'

'How did you get past security?' I asked, knowing that she had been ordered off the grounds in the not so distant past when she refused to believe the official line about the death of her sister.

'I was just joshing about the mail, Libby. I'm here on accounta I got my old job back.'

'You got your job back? You wanted it back? I thought you were glad to see the last of this place. Come in to the kitchen with me. I'll put on a pot of coffee.'

'Gee, your place hasn't changed much while I've been gone. Ceptin' you seem to have a bigger stack of books on the floor by the radio. Why don't you get one of those scientist boys to make you a proper bookcase?'

'I don't think any of them know how, Ruthie. They're not handy that way.'

'Really? Then who would want to marry one of them?'

I laughed at Ruth's practical assessment of husbands and said, 'You haven't answered my question about your reasons for coming back. I can't believe you're here – that you wanted to be here.'

'I can't think of any other place I'd rather be than right here with you – you're my best friend in the world.'

'But your mama? And your little brother?'

'Mama passed, Libby.'

'And you didn't tell me?' I said, finding it hard to believe even as the words crossed my lips.

'You're doing important war work, Libby. It's a lot like being on the front, ceptin' nobody is shooting at you. We hear all the time about keeping the spirits up of people like you. Can't be giving you bad news.'

'Horsefeathers, Ruthie! Friends tell friends everything.'

'Whew! I've got a lot to tell you. Sometimes, it's hard in a letter. None of the words seem right.'

'I suppose it is. Let's take our coffee into the living room and catch up.'

We sat side by side on the sofa, each with one leg curled up and our bodies turned toward each other. I remained quiet for a moment, waiting for Ruthie to begin. When she seemed content to do nothing more than sip on her cup and make pleasantries about how tasty it was, I interrupted. 'Spill it, Ruthie.'

'Okay, okay. Me and Ma worked out a nice routine, dividin' the housework and yardwork, taking turns mindin' my little brother Clyde. You wouldn't believe how much that boy has grown and he was gettin' old enough to take on some chores of his own. Not too long ago, he started gatherin' the eggs ev'ry mornin'.'

'Money was tight but Ma was still takin' in laundry to make some pin money and I was cleanin' house for the Carters and the Temples once a week. So we got by. Then my brother Hank came home from the war. He was so miserable, Libby. He felt worthless, useless and didn't see much reason for livin' – kept callin' himself a burden. It was pitiful.'

'You were going through all of this and you sent me cheery little letters?'

'I know, I know, Libby. I just didn't know how to say it. And besides, when I was writin' to you, I just forgot about all my problems for a while.'

'Sorry I interrupted, go on with your story.' I couldn't believe how blind I'd been to her hardships.

'The war was hard on Hank. All that killin' and dyin' and gunfire and smoke and stench and mud. Sometimes he'd wake up in the night, screamin' to beat the band. But the worst part was his arm. He still had it, but it was pretty useless. It just hung by his side like an empty sleeve. Some days he'd rage at it, some days he'd weep over it.

'But then Mary Sue started comin' round. She'd been stuck on Hank as long as I can remember. We worried that his tempers or his down-in-the-dumps times would run her off and Hank would be bluer than ever. That girl, though, she kept comin' back, day after day. One morning, we noticed Hank had started takin' care to look his best when it was time for her to visit. He started workin' round the house, too – he got Clyde to help him out when a second hand was needed and soon they were a good team.

'Then one day, Hank asked if Mary Sue could stay for

supper. When Ma said it was okay, Hank went outside and picked some zinnias and wildflowers and arranged them in a Mason jar on the dining room table. I had a fork halfway to my mouth when Hank stood up and announced that he and Mary Sue were engaged to be married. Ma pulled out a dusty bottle of Jack Daniels from the back of a cabinet and we toasted the couple more than once. And the next month, sure enough, they got hitched.

'Right after the wedding, Ma started gettin' sickly and Mary Sue stepped right in to nurse her while I took care of Ma's chores. I couldn't keep up with the ironing she'd been takin' in and I had to let that go. Ma got right upset. She kept insistin' that I just had to fill in for a short while until she was on her feet again. That never happened, of course.

'So, there we were. A man with a bum arm, a little boy who tried his best and now Mary Sue was with child. I started feelin' like one more mouth to feed. And, on top of that, seemed like I was intrudin' on the privacy of newlyweds.

'First I called Lieutenant Crenshaw and asked him if I would be allowed to come back. He didn't think it would be a problem. I talked it over with Hank and Mary Sue. Sure, they argued against it but I could tell it was a relief when I promised to send them some money every month if I got my job back. Next thing I knew, I got a letter from the administrative office telling me when I'd start my new job and thankin' me for helpin' the war effort. And here I am.'

'You should have called me to pick you up at the train station, Ruthie. After all, I still have your brother Hank's car.'

'I wanted to surprise you.'

'You sure did that.'

'I don't know what I'll do when the work here is done. I know it won't be long since the war's almost over . . .'

'Don't be hasty, Ruthie.'

'Hasty? Haven't you been listenin' to the news. We're closing in on Berlin thisaway,' she said swinging one fist from her side to her middle, 'and the Russkies are moving closer from thisaway.' She swung her other arm in to meet the first. 'And smash. They're done. The Nazis are in such bad shape we captured a soldier boy who was only eleven years old.'

'Yes. Everything does look like it's drawing to an end in Europe but we're still fighting in the Pacific. Mrs Childress up the street just learned that her brother was killed in a battle at Iwo Jima.'

'Aw, don't fret about that, Libby. Those Japs will surrender as soon as Europe falls.'

'I doubt it, Ruthie. We don't completely understand the Japanese people. Many of them were willing to climb into a cockpit and fly to Pearl Harbor knowing that they did not have enough fuel to return home. If they were that dedicated at the beginning of this conflict, how much more determined will they be when the end is near. An invasion would likely be street-to-street combat that could go on for years with more of our boys being wounded or dying – maybe even more than we've lost already.'

'You think they're that strong without the Nazis tying us up on another front?'

'Look at all of us, Ruthie. From coast to coast, Americans have sacrificed their men to the war, their women to the factories and their simple pleasures for the duration. How much more would we be willing to give if it was our nation being invaded?'

'Then we need to find a way to beat them without landing on their territory. But how?'

The answer was on the tip of my tongue. I knew what horror we labored to unleash on the innocent civilians of Japan but I could not speak of it. I turned away. I couldn't bear to look at her while I lied. 'I don't know, Ruthie. I simply don't know.'

THREE

Monday morning, as I set up my lab space to commence the final steps of shipment preparation, my thoughts were with Ruthie. I had missed her a lot while she was away but I compartmentalized that pain with all the other things I'd learned to do without during the war. I knew there was nothing I could do about any of it, therefore, any thought expended on any deprivations was a waste of time.

I wondered often about the nature of our relationship. On the surface, we seemed ill-matched to become friends. We had striking differences in education, cultural and social environments and expectations for the future. Yet, somehow, we felt like kindred souls. Contemplating that conundrum could keep my mind busy through eternity.

However, the thrill of being able to work with the new single-pan analytical balance scale, just created by a Swiss engineer, soon overshadowed any introspective questions. I had no idea how I ended up with one of the very few in the country but counted it a blessing. Its measurements were more accurate than the double-pan models we'd been using. That made me feel far more confident about my data as I prepared my shipment.

By the end of the day, the package was ready. I called and arranged for a military escort for a ride to the drop-off building tomorrow morning. It was close by and the package wasn't heavy; I could have easily walked it over. But the military had their rules and I tried to follow them whenever they weren't explicitly in my way.

I smiled as I climbed into the jeep. Tuesday morning was a lovely time for a drive. The woods were dotted with the white blossoms of dogwoods and the purplish-pink buds of the Judas trees. The scent of the air was intoxicating – enhanced by the fresh green growth and flowers of spring.

While we drove along, the soldier and I talked about the president and our sadness over his death. He was telling me a story about how, years ago, his grandfather had had lunch with the first lady when she came to talk to the Bonus marchers who had gathered in Washington, D.C. 'My granddad was playing a fiddle tune for her when—'

I jerked forward in my seat as the soldier slammed on his brakes. Up ahead we could see the building but smoke was curling out from the eaves and flames licked the inside of the windows.

'I got to get you out of here.'

'No,' I shouted. 'I have to make the delivery.'

Turning the jeep around, he said, 'Ma'am, there's something going on here that's not right. I'm charged with safeguarding your person.'

When he shoved the gear stick into reverse to complete the turn, I jumped out.

He lurched back, then forward and came to a stop. 'Get in,' he shouted, waving his arms in the air.

'No. I've got a job to do and I'm going to do it.'

'Ma'am,' he said, stepping out into the street, 'with all due respect, I am responsible for you. Please get back in the vehicle.'

I turned away from him and trudged uphill toward the burning building. He hurried to catch up, pleading with me to listen to him. When he touched my arm, I jerked away and shouted, 'Don't you touch me.'

He exhaled a noisy breath. 'Okay, okay. But I'm not leaving your side.'

'Fine.'

I reached the building, but saw no sign of the courier. I worried that he had already been inside when the fire erupted. I ran to the door but it was engulfed in flames. The intensity was growing with every passing moment. I heard the approaching clang of our new fire truck but I was too close to the billowing smoke of the burning structure to see more than a foot ahead of me. I stepped back away from the source and spotted the emergency vehicle approaching with a convoy of military jeeps and trucks trailing right behind.

I wasn't sure what to do. I'd been told to go to the rendez-vous point and if the courier was not there, I should go inside and wait for his arrival or for someone to arrive and present me with a new set of orders – but I certainly couldn't go inside. My soldier rushed to assist the firefighters – so much for always staying by my side. I felt quite vulnerable standing on the edge of the chaos holding the precious cargo in my hands.

My suspicious mind was building a case around the possi-bility that the fire was merely a ruse to isolate me and steal the crystals. I was thinking about driving off in the jeep, securing the package in the lab and returning for the soldier, when I heard my name shouted in a very familiar voice. The rigid posture and stony face of Lieutenant Colonel Crenshaw headed my way.

'Clark!' he said as he got near. 'What in the blue blazes are you doing standing out here in the open?'

'Sir?'

'When you are carrying valuable materials, you don't post yourself in an exposed position. What were you thinking?'

Crenshaw was such a fat head. 'Well, sir,' I said, 'I was thinking that since the place I was supposed to be right now was as hot as blue blazes, I ought not to go inside.'

He poked a finger in my face and said, 'This is a matter of national security. This is a grave situation. It could be an act of sabotage. I will not tolerate a flippant attitude from you.'

My jaw closed tight and I drew down my spontaneous, angry reaction. Through gritted teeth, I said, 'Sir, I feel the need to remind you that I am not part of the military. As such, I am not required to follow your commands even when I have willingly agreed to assist a military mission as I am doing now.'

'You people are becoming more of a problem every day.'

'What people are you referring to, sir. The civilians at Oak Ridge – or just the women?'

'Scientists,' he hissed. 'And not just here, at every installation. I've been briefed. I know what's going on. Some of you are having second thoughts about your work. We've got our eyes on you.'

'Tell me, Lieutenant Colonel, how can we possibly have second thoughts when no one has actually explained what exactly it is that we're doing. No one has informed us of the end result of our work. No one has deemed that we have a need to know.'

'I'm not naïve, Miss Clark. I know how you scientists are. You never accept anything you are told. You question it all. And when you don't get answers, you theorize until you reach a conclusion. None of you would survive in the army.'

'You see something wrong with seeking the truth?'

'Don't be such an idealist. Truth is often a casualty of war.'

'And you wonder why we do not accept what you tell us at face value?'

Crenshaw placed his hands on his hips and leaned his upper body into my space as he shouted, 'Why don't you tell me the truth about your little group of rebellious misfits? Tell me, right now, who are the people in your lab who are questioning your mission? Who is having doubts about continuing the work? Why don't you act like a patriot?'

'If I weren't, sir, I wouldn't be here,' I yelled back at him.

He stepped back and lowered his voice. 'You're avoiding my other questions and jeopardizing the safety of our mission in doing so.'

'Applesauce! We are jeopardizing nothing. In fact, you owe us all a debt of gratitude. Do you really think that you could have wrapped up the spy ring without our assistance? As a result, you now know the names of more members of our group. They weren't happy about being exposed to the military but knew that doing the right thing sometimes calls for sacrifice. And yet, you still are not satisfied. And you will not find your satisfaction from me.'

'So, there are some in your group who would work to sabotage our mission?'

My hands wanted to fly up in the air in exasperation but they were impeded by the package I was carrying, making me shake in exasperation. 'Just stop asking me, Crenshaw. I know of no one whom I would suspect of setting this fire. Which, by the way, you don't even know if anyone deliberately started – it could have been nothing more than an electrical short. What you should be concerned about is whether or not the courier died in that blaze.'

'If you didn't have the protection of General Gates . . .'

'What? What would you do?'

Crenshaw's jaw throbbed but he didn't say another word – not even a goodbye when I hopped into the jeep. I went back to the lab and secured the package until I received new delivery instructions.

FOUR

My life felt full of complicated relationships: Ruth, Crenshaw, my mother, and my off-again, on-again romantically-flavored bond with Teddy. For the last couple of years, I'd been blaming the war for this state of affairs. Lately, however, I've been trying to discern how much of the erratic nature of my interpersonal social interactions was generated by me, consciously or unconsciously.

Certainly, the war, our current work and concerns about our future careers did add stress to our lives. Others around me, though, seemed to keep their personal life on an even, steady keel in spite of it all. A line from Shakespeare kept running through my mind at the most inopportune times: 'The fault, dear Brutus, is not in the stars but in ourselves.' Even the bard was shaking my confidence in my sense of self-awareness.

After dinner Tuesday evening, I curled up with a cup of tea and a book with G.G. dozing and purring by my side. At ten, I scooped up the kitty and we both crawled into bed. I surprised myself on this chaotic day by falling asleep with ease. Blissful rest didn't last long. I shot straight up in bed without knowing what had awakened me. Then, I heard pounding on my front door. I glanced at the clock. Ten minutes after midnight. It had to be bad news.

G.G. darted under the bed as I slipped into my robe before rushing to answer the insistent knock. I looked at the window and saw a uniform. Whatever it is, it must be worse than I'd imagined. I swung open the door. The fist of the man pounding still hung in the air as he said, 'Miss Clark, you need to come with us.'

'Why, sergeant?' I asked noting that his straight ahead stare was focused at some point above my head.

'Ma'am, we are following orders. We were told to take you to the lab immediately but we were not told why.'

'Of course not. And even if you were you probably couldn't tell me.'

The sergeant had the decency to blush and bring his gaze down to my eyes as he responded, 'Yes, ma'am.'

'I can change into street clothes first, can't I?'

His blush brightened a bit more as if he just noticed my bedroom apparel. 'Yes, ma'am. Of course, ma'am,' he said while nodding.

Not knowing where this night-time expedition would lead, I opted for hiking clothes. I didn't want to end up in the woods somewhere in inappropriate attire. After dressing, I rushed to the door and stepped out onto the landing to another surprise. Soldiers at attention were lined up down the whole length of my stairs and seven military vehicles were parked in the street.

The sergeant led the way, escorting me to a jeep. We were in the middle vehicle of a midnight convoy. I suspected all this security and secrecy had something to do with my botched rendezvous with the courier. When I arrived at Y-12, soldiers lined the sidewalk to the entrance. The noise from the always-spinning Calutron sounded like a prehistoric beast trying to break free, disturbing the peace on an otherwise serene night. None of the soldiers followed me inside to where Lieutenant Colonel Crenshaw waited.

'Sorry for the inconvenience, Miss Clark. Please retrieve the package and we'll be on our way to the meeting point.'

'Where are we going, Crenshaw?'

'You have no need to know.'

Crenshaw trailed me as I walked back into my work area, ignoring my mumbles about the arrogant ways of the military. They are free to wake me in the middle of the night and cart me off but I don't have the right to know where I'm going. So typical.

Back outside, Crenshaw escorted me to a black sedan and opened the back door. I slid in one side and he on the other. The driver got behind the wheel and we watched as the soldiers, jogging en masse, split into small groups to board their assigned transports. After two jeeps and two trucks pulled away, we joined the formation, followed by another four vehicles.

Since I was skeptical that the fire had been set deliberately and doubted the suspicions of a dark conspiracy, these precautions felt a bit silly. Crenshaw, however, was on heightened alert, which he obviously felt was essential. The question I couldn't answer was if he knew more about the fire than I did or if his paranoid reaction was a hallmark of his character.

We plunged through the gate and into the countryside, making turns down one twisty road after another. Sometimes, it seemed as if we were passing the same spot more than once. However, the darkened farmhouses and barns barely visible on the hills and in the valleys, bore a relentless sameness in the murky light. It all but made it impossible for me to know with certainty whether we were traveling in circles or if it just seemed that way.

At last, we pulled up a dirt drive and stopped at a brightly lit red barn with a silvery tin roof. I reached for the door handle but Crenshaw grabbed and squeezed my arm. 'Not yet,' he ordered.

We sat in the car until a group of soldiers drill-marched into the building and another group lined up from the car to the barn door. The man closest to the sedan opened my door and offered a hand to help me out.

I followed Crenshaw down the path lined with men leading us into the barn's spacious interior, capped with high ceilings and filled with farm implements. The familiar earthy aroma of livestock and hay still filled the air but the dust on the tractor seat made it apparent that we weren't on a working farm. Standing in the shadows was a man wearing a dark suit and fedora, casually smoking a cigarette as if it was a normal night in a normal place.

'Miss Clark,' he said, 'I'll take that package off of your hands.'

'One moment,' Crenshaw barked. 'Let me see your identifying papers and your orders.'

He pulled a handful of documents out of his suit pocket and presented them to the lieutenant colonel. Crenshaw turned toward the nearest light, perused and returned them before he said, 'Carry on.'

I handed over the shipment unsettled by the shadows engulfing the nameless man's face and by the clandestine creepiness of the whole scene. I couldn't wait to get back to the familiar comfort of my own bed.

'This way, Miss Clark,' Crenshaw said as he led me back outside and into the car.

Again, we waited for the outside troops to hop into the assortment of vehicles. None of the men in the barn emerged. This time, two vehicles led us and two more brought up the rear.

We drove back in silence, taking a far more direct route and arriving back at my flat-top in less than half the time it took to arrive at our clandestine destination. As I stepped out of the car at the bottom of my stairs, the lieutenant colonel said, 'This expedition never happened, Miss Clark.'

I nodded.

'I need verbal confirmation, Miss Clark.'

'Yes, sir,' I said while giving a mock salute, hoping I successfully communicated my sarcastic intent. Those initial heebie-jeebies about this assignment had now returned with vengeance.

FIVE

Despite my middle of the night ramblings, I woke early Wednesday morning. I wanted to dawdle over my coffee and breakfast but I felt too unsettled and anxious. Once again, I arrived at work before anyone else was in the lab. I unlocked the door and in the dim light seeping in from the hallway, I thought I saw a movement inside. I thought it had to be my imagination but I turned towards it just the same. Two glittery orbs caught my attention and then they were gone. Was it nothing but a reflection or was it a pair of beady little eyes?

I switched on the light switch and saw a furry rump and a whip-like tail go over the edge of the top of a table, followed by a soft thud and scampering feet. A rat? I couldn't think of any other explanation. I shivered as I exited the room, slammed the door shut and relocked it.

I rushed to the building exit and informed the soldier on guard. He laughed. 'What, lady? You scared? You ain't ever seen a rat before?'

'You don't understand. Our lab conditions are a controlled environment. A rat can contaminate and compromise results. It can also damage the wiring that enables some of our equipment to work. It needs to be gone. Now.'

'Okay. I get it. You're scared.'

In anger, I sucked in a loud breath and exhaled harshly. 'Private, roll up your flaps. This is a serious matter. Contact your superior officer and tell him we have an urgent situation demanding an immediate solution.'

'Jeez! Don't flip your wig, lady. I'll get on the horn right now.' As he spoke, his hand moved toward his brow.

'Don't you dare salute me,' I snapped. The last thing I wanted right now was to have my act of sarcasm to Crenshaw thrown back in my face by another member of the military.

The response to the private's call was quick, abundant and quite gratifying. I feared that all the brass would be as dense as the private. Still, the situation was more complicated than it should have been. Apparently, rat eradication had its own department and the experts had been in and out of cafeterias, dormitories and other buildings without a problem. In this case, these men were being admitted into Y-12 without having security clearance to go there. Crenshaw personally showed up to remind them of their loyalty oath and the importance of secrecy before they were let into the lab.

Half an hour later, Crenshaw emerged with a reddened face and a furrowed brow. Poking a rude finger in my direction, he shouted, 'How could you work in there with all those rats and not notice a thing? Don't you pay any attention to your environment?'

'One rat, sir. That's all I said. Just one rat.'

'There's a lot more than that in there. They're crawling all over the place.'

'What?' One rat could happen. An unnoticed exploding population, on the other hand, was not in the realm of possibility.

'Yes. How could you overlook this for so long?'

'Sir, it is not possible that we have been infested with rodents for an extended period of time. Rat feces and hair would have shown up as anomalies in our testing results. We might not have known what they were in our initial analysis, but we would not have stopped until we identified them. However, if they are all over the place as you say, then I suspect that there is a recent and peculiar reason for it.'

'What? The big cheese rat led a group raid on the lab in the middle of the night?'

'You're mocking me, sir.'

'Why would I do that?' Crenshaw asked, his wide-eyed ridiculing expression on full display.

'I was very skeptical of your suspicions about sabotage at the fire on Monday but I am beginning to think that you were correct. And that this is another act designed to create problems for us.'

'So, you think someone broke in and dumped rats in the lab? Or do you think the rats set the fire and then moved over here? Really, Miss Clark? Ludicrous ideas. But I suppose to protect your pride you would have to believe it was something other than negligence by you and your staff – your blindness to what was going on all around you.'

Fortunately, at that moment, someone called Crenshaw back inside. If he'd stood in front of me another moment, I would have said something I might regret. As it was I shouted, 'Fathead' at his disappearing backside. He gave no indication that he had heard which was probably a good thing.

What would be the motivation for an act that seemed just as much prank as serious disruption of our work? Surely, no one could think that we'd throw up our hands and quit over this incident. Or even over a fire at the exchange point. The only logical reason was that someone or some group wanted to cause delays or undermine morale – or both. Wasn't it? Or am I too close to the situation to discern the motivation?

'Hey, Libby!'

'Teddy? They cleared out your lab, too?'

'They said they're checking for rat infestation. Why would they interrupt our work for that? Couldn't they do it overnight?'

I paused before answering. Aware of the many ears roaming about outside of the building, I had to be cautious. We weren't supposed to talk about what was happening in the lab with people outside of our own. Was the topic of vermin covered by that rule, too? 'It seems there is a problem in our space. I imagine checking the adjacent lab is just an added precaution.'

'I hope they're quick about it. I've got just—' he stopped to look down at his watch – 'forty-two minutes before I need to interact with my project or the whole sample will be wasted and I'll have to start again.'

'A lot of folks milling about right now, Teddy. Best we talk about this at the meeting tonight.'

I heard my name called again by another voice. Charlie, just emerging from the building, was coming my way. 'If you'll excuse us, Teddy.' Grabbing my elbow, Charlie steered me away from the others.

'I'm going to send everyone home and ask them to come in as early as possible tomorrow morning.'

'We're going to lose a whole day? Why?'

'There are dozens of rats in there, Libby. They're considering using an aerial poison to make sure they've gotten them all.'

'A poison gas? What kind? And what will it do to our equipment? Our samples?'

'Apparently, I don't have a need to know what they are thinking about using. Anyway, they haven't made a firm decision on that one way or another. The supervisor assured me that everything would be sealed up first and the lab would be sealed from the rest of the building. As I said, though, they're not sure if it is needed. The supervisor explained that it would only be necessary if they find any evidence of nesting and thus far they haven't, which is good news on a couple of fronts.'

'No nesting means no colonizing which means they have not been present for much time at all?' I asked.

'Exactly, as well as minimal damage and contamination,' Charlie said with a nod. 'But there's also bad news.'

'Of course, there is. It means they were introduced by human hand, right? Has Crenshaw been informed of that?'

Charlie laughed. 'The super said that Crenshaw is too busy decrying the idiocy of the lab personnel to listen right now. He said in an hour or two he should be certain of his conclusion. Then and only then, will he face down Crenshaw.'

'I can't say I blame him for that. So, if he'll be done in an hour or two, why can't we just wait him out and then get back to work.'

'Rats are very efficient masters of destruction,' Charlie said with a sigh. 'They've spotted damage to cabinets, walls and electrical wiring. Electricians and carpenters are coming in once the exterminators clear out. But if the death squad decides to fumigate, they'll need to clear the air in the labs first. In that case, the repair teams won't get in until tomorrow.'

Seeing Teddy and others head back through their lab entrance, I pointed it out to Charlie. 'Looks like they don't have a problem like we do. Any indications of similar situations anywhere else?'

'Not that I've heard about. But reportedly K-25 is working round the clock, seven days a week right now so it would be unlikely that anyone could pull it off over there.'

'Do you know what they're doing in K-25? What makes their work more pressing than ours?'

'That, I don't know. I know it's different but have no idea of how it differs. Well, let's spread out and spread the word before our guys start getting too impatient with waiting.'

Fifteen minutes later I looked around and saw no one from our lab still lingering outside the building except for me and Charlie. Charlie offered me a ride back home but I waved him off. I needed to think and walking always helped.

The fresh tang of spring in the air did little to ease my anxiety as I headed home. An indisputable and unsettling fact pushed its way into dominance in my thoughts. If the fire and the rats were both deliberate acts to stall our progress, then the person responsible had to be someone who worked with me. Someone I knew well. An individual working in my lab. But who?

We only had one new member working here. Stan had joined us a couple of weeks after Marvin's murder by members of the spy ring. We'd discussed bringing him into the Walking

Molecules. Consensus was that he'd be a valuable and enjoy-
able member of our little group, but paranoia had a firm grip
on some of our members making us decide to give it a little
more time before we extended an invitation. Tom had been
with us since the beginning and had just suffered a loss. That
did make him vulnerable to acting out of character, but he
was at his father's funeral in Pennsylvania and out of the
picture.

A couple of other men in our lab were strongly suspected
of being recruited to report back to the authorities about their
co-workers. They never questioned authority. It seemed as if
they would be the last to take any subversive action. Was it
possible for something to happen to one of them causing that
person to sour on the whole system?

Maybe. More likely, it was someone I trusted. A person no
one would suspect. It could be any one of us. The only person
I could vouch for with any certainty was myself. That was a
lonely place to dwell.

SIX

I saw a package nestled against my door. The experience
with the anonymous gift of mittens that had been left on
my doorstep before made me wary. I went up the steps
slowly, holding my breath, until I saw the return address. Aunt
Dorothy. I grabbed the box, hustled it inside, sat down on the
rug, cutting the parcel string, tossing it in the air. G.G. snatched
it before it hit the floor and scampered off to examine it in
privacy. I tore at the wrapping, praying there was coffee and
chocolate inside.

And there was. That and four new books I hadn't read: *A
Bell for Adano* by John Hersey, *The Razor's Edge* by Somerset
Maugham, *Earth and High Heaven* by Gwethalyn Graham
and the one I had requested, *Dragon Seed* by Pearl S. Buck.
I pulled out the letter that accompanied the goodies.

Dearest Libby,
I know you asked for just one of these volumes but
when I went to the bookstore, there was a sale. I couldn't
resist. I hope you enjoy them all.

I clutched the letter to my chest. How could I possibly not
love Aunt Dorothy? Just seeing her very recognizable handwriting always filled me with warmth and fondness. I pulled
her note away from my body and continued to read.

I traveled down to Richmond during my Easter break to
visit your mother at the Virginia State Penitentiary. What
a dismal, gloomy place! Before I even saw Annabelle, I
entertained serious doubts that she could survive twenty
years in that place. After she walked out, I knew she
wouldn't.

I lowered the letter in dismay. Most of the time, I am successful
in banishing my mother from my thoughts. I always resented
it when my conflicting emotions towards her were pushed to
the surface. Aunt Dorothy knew that. I had to trust that she
had a good reason for making me go to that troubling place.
I returned my attention to her correspondence.

Your mother is ill – very ill. Most prisoners gain weight
behind bars. Annabelle, on the other hand, has shriveled
up. She used to be thin and now she is gaunt. She appears
to be in very bad shape – almost as wretched as the
photos of people we've seen recently at the liberated Nazi
prison camps.
I had to press her to tell me what the problem was.
She said that she has a lump in her breast that grows
with each passing month. I asked her what the doctor
said and she told me she hadn't seen one. I offered to
facilitate a medical visit for her and she shook her head.
She said, 'I know I am going to die in here and the sooner
the better. Why prolong it? Why undergo disfiguring
surgery to delay the inevitable?'
I argued with her, thinking at first it was her vanity

speaking. But her commitment to no treatment went deeper than that. She believes her death will be a relief to many, including you and your brother. You probably are wondering why I am telling you all of this. It's not to convince you to make peace with your mother and bid her farewell before she dies. If that is what you want to do, that's fine. However, you are an adult and have no obligation nor do I have any expectation for you to do so.

Little Ernie is the source of my concern. In his eyes, his mother is a hero. She saved his life on the day she took his father's life. He wants to thank her and tell her he loves her. I don't think he'd forgive any of us if we did not give him the opportunity to tell her goodbye.

I know Annabelle has forbidden both of you from visiting her. Nonetheless, I am willing to face her displeasure and accompany little Ernie to the prison. I am going to send her a letter explaining why she needs to agree to see him. I am hoping you will encourage her to do that in your next letter.

Thank you, darling and so sorry to bother you with my concerns but I felt it was necessary. Enjoy the books and tasty treats. When you have a chance, drop a line to let me know the package arrived safely.

Love,

Aunt Dorothy

I remained seated on the floor while familial obligations and work expectations clashed in my thoughts. My mood turned dark until G.G., with string in mouth, circled around me and collapsed his fury little face on one of my feet. The welcome diversion made me laugh. I teased him with the string for a while, tossing it out and reeling it back towards me. He'd crouch with his chin nearly on the carpet and his haunches stuck up high in the air, wiggling in place. Once he'd built the suspense to an excruciating level, he pounced and jerked the string out of my hand.

After playtime, my spirits were lifted and I rose from the floor with the new stack of books in my arms. I looked around

the room and set them down on the tiny dining table. Maybe
Ruth was right. I did need a proper bookcase. But where would
I put one in this itsy bitsy place?

I listened to the news while I ate my dinner on the remaining
table space. The broadcast was filled with giddy reports about
the progress of the war in Europe. 'Dateline Paris. American
armies, which have already virtually bisected Germany, broke
into the prize cities of Leipzig and Magdeburg yesterday as
British tanks tore loose on a 22-mile sweep that carried them
within 25 miles of the great port of Hamburg.

'Dusseldorf, the last major city in the Ruhr still held by the
Germans, was entered by Doughboys who have now whittled
down the Ruhr pocket to 125 square miles from its original
3000 square miles.

'German Radio Commentator Max Krull said that "with
the enemy breakthrough from the West and another from the
East, and with wedges pointing from both directions towards
Berlin, the organic structure of the German front has ceased
to exist. The terms West Front and East Front have lost their
meaning."'

That good news along with a report on the state of the
German generals made me believe optimism might well be
warranted. Of the fourteen of the Third Reich's generals in
power before the beginning of the war: two were murdered
by the Gestapo; two were executed for a plot against Hitler;
one committed suicide after our success in the D-Day operation; one was an Allied prisoner; one was relieved of his
command; two others had lost their prominent positions in
1942 and 1943; one other general had not been heard of since
last year's purge, and an additional military leader was under
arrest and facing trial. The announcer concluded the piece by
crowing that there was only one of the generals still in
command on the western front. 'How the mighty have fallen.'

It was all good news but still the difficulties in the Pacific
Theater continued. It seemed to me that no matter how many
island-hopping victories we had, it would take an attack on
the Japanese mainland to end that conflict. Would we march
in and die in the streets of the Land of the Rising Sun
or would the work I was doing end up raining death and

destruction on soldiers and civilians alike? Or maybe the optimists were right. With the announcement that much of our European-based equipment was now being redeployed to the Pacific Theater, perhaps Japan would decide that surrender was the only way to save their nation. I certainly prayed for the latter but rated its probability as low. I dreaded facing the near future events and the possible role I played in making them come to fruition.

SEVEN

Ping-ponging thoughts ricocheted in my head as I walked to the regular Wednesday night meeting of the Walking Molecules at Joe's. The war, my work, the current chaotic situation in my family. I felt as if everything was demanding my attention and nothing could be resolved in an efficient and satisfactory manner. No matter what good resulted from any of it, a trail of negative consequences would be bound to follow in their wake.

I entered the back room noticing that I was the last to arrive. It was the same old gang, minus Tom who was at his father's funeral and Marvin whose body we'd found in the woods last year. I had advocated enlarging our circle with Charlie, the head of my lab, and Jessie, the K-25 worker who was instrumental in uncovering the espionage agents. In the chaos of the spy chase, the identities of more members of our group had been exposed to Crenshaw and the military – a fact that made none of us happy. That resulted in the growth of group paranoia that made many of us more insular and suspicious than we had been before. Both of my suggested recruits were rejected. On the other hand, they had forgiven Gary's lapse of judgement and allowed him to return after he'd spent a couple of months as an outcast

After I was seated with a weak Barbarossa beer in hand, Gregg asked, 'So what's everyone's theory about the rat invasion?'

'Hey, Teddy,' Rudy said as he stubbed out one cigarette and lit another. 'Was it you and your buddies in the Alpha lab trying to show us up?'

'Don't forget, Teddy is not the only man in the room from Alpha,' Dennis said.

'Yeah, that's right,' Gary said.

Teddy laughed. 'Nah. Dennis, Gary and I are far too busy to worry about you plodders getting overloaded by our efficiency in sending you more product than you can handle. I think it was a plot by the Calutron girls to get our workload so backed up that they could take a day off.'

'Personally, I think they were German rats,' Stephen joked.

'You didn't notice their slanted eyes – they're Jap rats. Definitely,' Dennis said.

'Seriously guys,' Gregg pleaded, 'does anyone have a sensible idea? I, for one, find it hard to believe that we were working in a heavily infested lab without knowing it. Did anyone see any rat droppings around? I know I didn't.'

'I can resolve that for you,' I said. 'But, of course, it needs to stay between us.'

'Okay – that goes without saying,' Gregg said, looking around the table and collecting nods from everyone.

'I wish Charlie were here with an update but this is what I know so far. Charlie spoke to the supervisor of the crew that came in to catch or kill the rats. Right before I left the Y-12 grounds, that man told Charlie that they had not found any signs of nesting which means the rats were new to the environment. Charlie was sticking around to see if that changed. But I haven't spoken to him since.'

'What exactly does that mean?' Teddy asked.

'It means someone placed them in there – probably last night, well after midnight. At 12.30 a.m., there were no indications of their presence in the lab.'

'How do you know that?' Teddy asked.

With Crenshaw's warning that 'this expedition never happened' thundering in my ears, I said, 'I was there but I am not at liberty to explain why.'

'Aw, c'mon, Libby,' Teddy complained, banging his mug down on the table.

'Why she was there does not have any relevance,' Gregg said. 'What does matter is that not like just anyone can get into the lab – there's all of us and the people we work with in the two labs. We are the suspects.'

'No, wait a minute,' Dennis objected, 'except for our supervisor, none of us working in Alpha have clearance to enter your work space which puts us in the clear. It has to be one of your people.'

Stephen stood, his white-as-a-worm face turning as red as an overripe strawberry. His agitated jerky movements sloshed beer on to the table and floor. 'Why would we put rats in our own lab?'

'Hold on, Stephen,' I interrupted. 'If the pest control supervisor's initial impression is correct that is exactly what Crenshaw will think when and if he learns that the rodents were a recent addition. Don't jump on, Dennis. He is just stating an obvious deduction. We've got to figure out who among us could be responsible or why none of us are. We need to be prepared for Crenshaw.'

'For example,' Gregg added, 'he could believe that someone from Alpha borrowed one of our IDs – with or without permission – and thus gained entrance to our lab.'

Dennis nodded. 'I can see that. I imagine that would make just one person above suspicion.'

'Who?' Stephen asked.

'Libby.'

'Why?'

'For the obvious reason,' Dennis answered. 'She's the only woman and she would be noticed by the guard on duty and remembered for that reason. But Libby, that makes your visit to the lab after hours last night relevant, with all due respect to Gregg's assertion to the contrary.'

Great. Another tightrope to walk. 'I was there but I was not alone. Someone was with me every moment.'

'Who, Libby?' Teddy said. 'I don't mean to be a stickler but that does matter under these circumstances.'

'I'm not at liberty—' I began.

'You've got to tell us,' Gregg said. 'I now agree with Teddy. It does matter because it makes you Crenshaw's main target.'

I rubbed my eyes. I hated being in this position. I felt cornered but I knew that I would be demanding answers if the situation was reversed. 'Crenshaw can't suspect me because he was the individual who accompanied me in the lab.'

'That puts you in an even worse position,' Teddy said.

'How do you reach that conclusion?' I asked.

'If Crenshaw knows you are not involved, he will pressure you more for information since he won't consider you a suspect.'

'I doubt that, Teddy,' I said. 'Remember I was present at the fire and I discovered the first rat, he probably looks at me as public enemy number one.'

Multiple voices asked the same question: 'What fire?'

I described Monday morning's incident but stopped short of telling them about the middle-of-the-night rendezvous. I didn't hesitate on that point not because I didn't trust them, but rather because I believed that the less they knew the better off they all would be if Crenshaw questioned them. I hoped I made the right judgement call but like so much in this place, I could not be comfortable with any assessment at any time.

'Secrecy,' Dennis said, 'creates an impenetrable murkiness for everything in close proximity to it. I can't wait for this war to end.'

Murmurs of agreement went around the table. I let it die down before speaking again. 'We need to assess all the people in both labs and look for any scientist who has turned against the ultimate goal of our work.'

'Easier said than done,' Rudy said with a hearty exhale of smoke. 'Since we aren't supposed to know what that goal is and we're strictly forbidden from discussing it, how do we manage that?'

'Besides,' Stephen added, 'wouldn't that be like spying on our peers. Isn't our objection to doing that a big part of why we formed this group in the first place?'

'Nobody said that we need to turn anyone in to the military or the administration,' I said. 'But if the fire and the rats are connected and we can identify who is responsible, then we can discourage that person from doing anything further. Make sure that he understands that Crenshaw is on his tail and that we know who he is.'

'How can we distinguish between someone who is ethically bothered by our work, from the person who is willing to take action against it. I think many of us are disturbed – or at least conflicted – about our ultimate goal. Essentially, we are helping to create something that we really hope will never be used,' Rudy said.

'Speak for yourself. If we had the gadget right now, I say we deploy it as close to Hitler as possible. And then do the same to the Japs,' Stephen snapped back.

'Stephen, that is an irresponsible attitude,' Dennis said. 'You are talking about the death of civilians as well as possible—'

The entrance of the waitress brought the conversation to a dead halt. 'More beer,' she asked with a big smile that quickly faded when she picked up on the tension in the room. 'Well, ya'll just holler if you need me.' She backed up a few steps, spun around and speed-walked out of the room.

'As I was saying,' Dennis continued, 'not only the immediate death of large numbers of innocents but the possibility of unknown long-term effects.'

'Innocents? There's not an innocent person in Germany or Japan. We ought to wipe them all off the face of the earth,' Stephen said.

In response, the room went silent. Stephen's face reddened. 'Don't tell me none of you agree with that?' His glance traveled around the group where most members stared down at the table top. I, on the other hand, kept my gaze riveted on his face. He kept his eyes focused on me as he shoved out his chair, rose and stomped out of the room.

I half expected him to barrel back and lambast us for a lack of patriotic fervor but two minutes passed before Teddy broke the silence. 'I hope there are cooler heads in Washington.'

'I can't say I trust the generals to choose the route of fewest casualties to our enemies,' Dennis said. 'But I did trust our president. When Roosevelt was holding those reins, and weighing the consequences, I was convinced he wouldn't use the gadget until all other options had been considered. I just hope our new President Truman will do the same.'

When Joe cleared his throat, everything turned quiet. He seldom spoke up in the group but when he did, we all knew he'd been digesting and analyzing from the start. 'I believe Stephen gave us another question to consider. I have never heard him talk quite like that before. Have any of you?'

He looked around at all of the shaking heads. 'What if he is trying to cover up his trail to brush away any suspicion? What if he set the fire and released the rats or is in cahoots with the person who did?'

It was an unsettling thought. As I looked over these men who I trusted with my life, I wondered if I really knew any of them. Were they all wearing masks to hide their true intentions?

Gregg stood and asked, 'Aren't we all getting a little ahead of ourselves? A fire in an unoccupied building and a short-term invasion of rats: does anyone here think it would be possible for these pranks to stop the project?'

'Just how do you know that building was unoccupied?' Rudy asked. He took a deep draw on his cigarette and exhaled a large cloud of smoke. 'Were you there when the fire started, Gregg?'

It felt as if all the oxygen had been sucked from my lungs. Gregg still stood, his jaw slack and his arms hanging uselessly at his sides. All around the table mouths opened as if to speak and then closed without uttering a sound.

'Really?' Rudy said, shaking his head. 'Let's not pussyfoot around here. The prime suspects are all here in this room. There's no sense in pretending otherwise. If we can't ask the blunt questions, how can we get answers?'

'I think we may be overlooking another possibility,' Dennis said. 'Something more sinister. What if the military was responsible? What if their goal was to destroy our trust in one another? To break us all apart?'

'If they are, they are doing a fine job,' Gregg admitted and adjourned the meeting.

Lost in a cloud over the unexpected turn of tonight's meeting, I did not realize that Teddy and Dennis were both following me until their voices rose in obvious disagreement. I stopped and both bumped into me.

I turned with arms akimbo as they spluttered apologies. 'What are you two arguing about?'

'I was just explaining to Dennis that I always walk you home after the meetings and there was no need for him to tag along,' Teddy explained while donning a look of total innocence.

'He wasn't exactly that polite. I told him that I wanted to talk to you privately and he refused to give me that opportunity,' Dennis said in his defense.

Another piece of evidence that men may be more trouble than they are worth. 'Teddy, first of all, I have told you repeatedly that I am a grown woman and I don't need to have an escort to walk home. I am actually capable of accomplishing that feat on my own. And Dennis, if you wanted to talk to me privately, why didn't you tell me instead of Teddy. He is not my keeper.'

They both stared down at the ground as if waiting for me to say more. I remained quiet for a minute hoping that one of them would speak up, concede, or something. When neither did, I said, 'Teddy, go home. Dennis, let's talk.'

Once Teddy had moved off reluctantly, I said, 'Okay, what concerned you about tonight?'

'Everything. I've never seen us at each other's throats like that. But that's not why I wanted to talk to you.'

'What then?'

'I wanted to know if you and Teddy were serious.'

I knew exactly what he meant but I didn't want to give him that satisfaction. 'Serious about what?'

'Each other?'

'Why does that matter to you?'

'Teddy makes it sound like you are everything but engaged.'

'Does he? And that is your business, because . . .?'

'I'm not saying it is. I simply wanted to know the lay of the land before . . .'

'Before what, Dennis? Aren't you engaged to a girl back home?'

'I was. Annie was very disappointed that I took this job instead of going on the front line and fighting for our country. I could never explain what we were doing and how important it was. So, I guess she decided I wasn't good enough for her. Last week, she married a soldier on leave. She didn't even have the courtesy to send me a "Dear John" letter. I had to hear it from my mom.'

'Sorry about that, Dennis, I really am. But what does that have to do with Teddy and me?'

'I just wanted to know before I made a fool of myself asking you out to a movie or dinner or something.'

I walked the last block saying nothing and could feel discomfort radiating off Dennis. When we reached the foot of my stairs, I turned to him. 'Dennis, I am not going to describe my feelings towards Teddy to you. Right now, I'm not even going to talk about my attitudes toward marriage. But I will say this: if you want to go out with me, ask me sometime. Just don't do it now. At this moment, I am irritated with you and with Teddy. You will not like my answer.'

I turned and mounted the steps. When I reached the door, he remained rooted to the spot. I shook my head and stepped inside.

I couldn't really blame them. I was raised in the same society they were: an environment where the ultimate goal for women was getting a husband and having children. They both seemed to logically understand that I was different, but emotionally they were still rooted in the past. In their hearts, I don't think they could comprehend that some women would rather be alone than be a pampered pet in a cage.

EIGHT

Thursday morning, I was eager to get back to work and make up for lost time. I was dismayed when I entered the lab. Charlie was waiting with a depressing message: 'Crenshaw will have a car here to pick you up in ten minutes.'

'I can't, Charlie. I have too much to do,' I objected.

'It's Crenshaw, Libby. You must go. Look on the bright side. If he wanted to arrest you, he wouldn't give you advance warning.'

'That is some comfort. I'll redistribute some work and hopefully that will help keep the backup under control.'

I was outside exactly ten minutes after speaking to Charlie but no one was there. I waited ten more minutes and then went back inside to inform him.

'Go back out. I'll call up to his office and find out what's happening.'

I sighed and went back to my position on the boardwalk.

Charlie joined me a couple of minutes later. 'They had to change all the tires first.'

'What? Why?'

'They said that all the tires on all the vehicles at Crenshaw's disposal "were in need of replacement."'

'And they just realized that this morning?'

'That's all they told me, Libby. If you find out anything more, let me know if you can. I suspect it was not normal maintenance.'

A few moments later, a jeep jerked to a halt in front of me and a private jumped out, stood at attention and started to raise his hand in a salute before dropping his arm. 'Miss Libby Clark?'

'Yes, private, I'm Libby Clark.'

'I'm here to escort you to Lieutenant Colonel Crenshaw's office, ma'am.'

Before he had the sentence finished, I was seated in the front passenger seat. He scrambled in beside me, his long legs banging into the steering wheel in the process.

'You changed the tires this morning?' I asked.

'Yes, ma'am. Even if you drive slow, you can bend up and ruin the rims when the tires are flat like that. You see—'

I raised a hand to interrupt. 'I understand how that works. Were all the tires flat?'

'Yes, ma'am, flatter than a stale pancake.'

'How did that happen?'

'Something sharp, ma'am, ripped right through the rubber.'

'Are you saying it was intentional?'

'If you ask me, it had to be.'

'And this vehicle wasn't the only one?'

'No. We had a dozen jeeps up there and every single one of them had four flat tires – too much of a coincidence to be accidental.'

'What does Crenshaw think happened?'

'For all I know, he thinks it's gremlins.'

'Gremlins?'

The private laughed. 'We G.I.'s blame gremlins for everything that goes wrong. But seriously, I can only assume Crenshaw sees it the way I do, but I sure can't tell what he's thinking and he sure wouldn't be sharing his thoughts with me.'

As we reached the administration building, the private swung the jeep into a U-turn to allow me to step directly onto the walk. It was definitely an improvement over the early days when I'd been lifted from the car onto safe ground.

Of course, I had to sit and wait once I arrived even though Crenshaw knew exactly when I'd be there. I was never sure if he did that to communicate that he was more important than I was or if his motivation was to ratchet up my anxiety before I sat down across from him. Whatever it was, it was annoying.

When I was finally summoned into his presence, he gestured to a chair, a straight-backed, armless wooden seat that made slouching to feign indifference impossible. He turned to his aide and said, 'Bring Miss Clark a cup of coffee from the fresh pot. A little cream but no sugar.'

I was amazed that he knew that. I couldn't recall when we'd had coffee together or if we ever had. If not, how did he know how I liked it? Once again, the man had unsettled me. I straightened my posture in response.

'Just bear with me for one more moment, Miss Clark,' he said. He looked over and signed two sheets of paper. The aide returned, set down my cup and retrieved the documents before going out of the door and closing it behind him.

'I have a few questions for you and the sooner and more fully you answer them, the quicker you can get back to work.'

I sat still and stared at him across his desk.

'Do you understand, Miss Clark?'

'Of course, I do.'

'Tell me everything you know about Gregg Abbott.'

'He is a chemist. He is dependable. I rely on him to fill in for me whenever I am forced to abandon my work as I was required to do this morning in order to meet with you.'

'And . . .?'

'What else do you want? The color of his hair or eyes, his weight or height?'

He closed his eyes and exhaled. 'You know very well what I mean. Is he disgruntled?'

'About what, sir? His accommodations? The food at the cafeteria?'

'Don't play the Dumb Dora with me, Miss Clark. Does he have doubts about the work he is doing here? Is he likely to act on those doubts with destructive actions?'

'Are you referring to your shredded tires, sir?'

'How did you know about that?'

I was not about to turn the private into a target. 'Logic, sir. Why else would all the tires need to be changed at the same time?'

He peered at me with a furrowed brow. 'Answer my question about Mr Abbott.'

'No, sir, I cannot imagine Mr Abbott destroying tires, smuggling rats or starting a fire.'

'Teddy Burke – what do you know about him?'

'He's a chemist. He does not work in my lab, he's in Alpha.'

'Is he disgruntled?'

'I cannot imagine Mr Burke destroying tires, smuggling rats or starting a fire.'

'Joe Barksdale?'

'He's a chemist. He works in my lab. And no, I cannot imagine Mr Barksdale destroying tires, smuggling rats or starting a fire.'

Crenshaw leaned back in his chair, his arms folded across his chest, his face looking as if he had just inhaled a very bad odor. 'Mr Morton?'

'Charlie? Are you kidding me? I call him Mr Stickler.

He's so devoted to following the rules, he should be in the
military.' Charlie wasn't quite that bad – not by a long shot
– but . . .

'You're a curious woman – always asking questions and
forming theories – so who do you think is responsible?'

'Gremlins, sir.'

He folded his hands in front of his mouth and stared hard
at me. I sat straighter and made sure I didn't squirm. 'You are
not acting as if you are in any hurry to get back to work.'

'You are not acting as if you have any respect for my work,'
I snapped back.

'You know, Miss Clark, after the fire, I was certain that a
scientist was responsible. But now, I look at the primitive
approach with the tires and rats and I think that perhaps it is
someone with less sophistication, less education.'

I felt some of the tension seep out of my body but kept
listening for any nuance in the words that followed.

'Perhaps it has nothing to do with the work here *per se*.
Perhaps, these are acts of petty revenge from someone who
feels as if they've been treated badly here.'

I wasn't sure where he was going but I knew he was toying
with me and my anxiety inched up to its original level.

'Perhaps it was someone who just returned here to work
after being away for a while. Perhaps someone like Miss Ruth
Nance.'

If possible, I was now coiled even tighter than when I'd
entered the room. I swallowed hard to hide my dismay.

'She did return here the day before the fire, didn't she?' he
asked. 'That's when it all started. Well . . .' He shrugged his
shoulders and splayed his hands

'Miss Nance is an honest, hard-working young woman. She
does not have a duplicitous bone in her body. She might tell
you off to your face but she would never go behind your back.
You need to drop that line of inquiry.'

'Or what, Miss Clark?'

I exhaled through clenched teeth making my lips rattle
against the enamel. 'You know I have no bargaining chip here,
lieutenant colonel. You know how valuable I have been in
previous investigations. You can have my support to find the

culprit or you can turn me away. However, I will not go away quietly if you unjustly come after someone who matters to me. I will find the truth despite you.'

'And if I get in the way, you'll call General Gates, right?'

'Despite the problems that you have created for me, I have not done that yet. But yes, if I felt it was essential, yes, I would.'

'Someday, Miss Clark, someday . . . You are dismissed.'

I remained seated, staring at the wall, refusing to acknowledge his command.

'Do I need to have you forcibly removed?'

I smiled. 'Thank you for your time, Lieutenant Colonel Crenshaw. And for the lovely cup of coffee. I really must be going now.' I stood and reached my hand across his desk.

Taken by surprise, he shook my hand but I could tell by the look on his face, he'd be fuming about this moment all day.

NINE

I received a lot of questioning looks when I returned to the lab. I ignored them and got to work.

Gregg sidled up to me a while later. 'What was all that about?'

'Crenshaw.'

'Charlie told me that much. What did he want?'

I was reluctant to discuss the morning's interrogation until I had the time to process it and draw a few conclusions. 'Gregg, I'm very busy right now. But when the day is over I would like to talk to you, Teddy and Joe. I don't want to go through the story multiple times and answer the same questions over and over.'

'Okay. I've got plenty to keep me busy until then. Are you all right?'

I nodded. 'A bit unsettled but I'm fine.'

'I imagine Crenshaw has that effect on a lot of people.'

*   *   *

Joe and Gregg were waiting for me on the walkway when I left the building at dusk. 'I sent word into Teddy,' Joe said. 'He'll be here in a minute.'

Feet shuffled and small talk started and died. I could tell both of them had questions to ask but were trying to keep them stuffed inside while we waited for the last member of our party. A long seven minutes later, Teddy emerged and hurried over to the group. They all started talking to me at once making it impossible for me to understand a word.

I held up a hand. 'Listen first, okay. Questions later.' I related everything I could remember as precisely as I could recall.

'Aside from the three of us and Charlie and your friend Ruth, did he mention anyone else?' Gregg asked.

'No and that surprised me. He was acting rather smug and I anticipated that meant he had something up his sleeve – like a name from our group that we were unaware that he knew.'

'He probably thought he'd put you off-balance by naming Ruth,' Teddy suggested.

'Maybe. Or maybe it was a warning. Maybe Ruthie is in the line of fire.'

'He can't really believe that on her first full day back she'd start causing trouble,' Teddy objected.

'He is a very suspicious man. Who knows what goes on in that paranoid mind of his?'

Joe cleared his throat and said, 'Don't overlook the possibility of psychological warfare.'

My eyebrows shot up to my hairline. 'What do you mean?'

'Maybe he's trying to isolate you or make you feel that way – suspicious of everyone. Or, as Dennis would say, he's following the example of a pack of coyotes who separate one from the herd in order to take him down.'

I didn't know what to say but Teddy filled in the gap. 'I suspect we all felt a bit that way after last night's meeting. I know I spent the evening wondering if I really knew any of you – if I really could trust you.'

'And did you reach any conclusions?' Gregg asked.

'Yeah, I'm not going to take any Tokyo Rose or Axis Sally

seriously even if he's in uniform with more bars and medals than I can count.'

I stopped by Ruth's dormitory on my way into work the next morning hoping that I remembered her new room number. My doubt caused me to hesitate for a moment before knocking.

I'm barely average height but the woman who opened the door made me feel like an Amazon. She looked as cute as a pixie with her short haircut and diminutive size. 'May I help you?' she asked.

'Is this Ruth Nance's room?'

'Why yes, it is,' she said with a smile. 'I'm Isabel Rosendale, her roommate. Ruth isn't here just yet. May I give her a message when I see her?'

'Has she left for work already?'

'I imagine she's at the cafeteria or will be there soon. She's working the overnight shift this week and usually goes by the cafeteria for breakfast before coming back.'

'Does she always work nights?'

Isabel cocked her head to the side and asked, 'Who did you say you are?'

'Oh, I'm sorry. I'm Libby Clark.'

'The lady scientist?'

'That's me.'

'Oh, come in. Come in. Ruth has told me so much about you. I'm Isabel Rosen— oops! Told you that already. Just call me Izzie.'

I stepped inside and waited while Izzie searched for writing materials. 'Ruthie has a fill-in position. She goes wherever she's needed most. Next week she'll be on day shift and we'll be able to go in together.' She handed me a stub of a pencil and a wrinkled piece of paper. 'Will this do?'

'It'll do fine. Has Ruth settled in well?'

'Ruth? You've got to be kidding. I thought I was going to have to show her around and introduce her to people. Instead, she's introducing me to girls I had never met. She knows everybody.'

'That sounds like Ruth,' I said with a chuckle.

I jotted down a quick note inviting Ruth to supper early

Sunday afternoon, folded it in half and propped it on her pillow.

'You know,' Izzie said, 'you can wait here for her if you want. I have to go to work but I'm sure it'll be okay.'

'I've got to get into work, too. But thanks. It was a pleasure to meet you, Izzie.'

'If you're like most people, I'll spare Ruth the tedium of having to answer one more time. I am almost four foot, eleven inches high. It's not much but I'm scrappy,' she said with a grin.

I walked out of the room amused by the image of tall, thin Ruth paired up with tiny, little Izzie. I imagined they must be joshed about that a lot.

On Friday, I made a lot of progress with testing and analysis giving me high hopes of being on top of everything by Saturday's end. My plans were dashed when a loud siren blare forced me to cover my ears.

Charlie rushed out of his office. 'Fire alarm! Evacuate the building. Don't push. Don't shove. Move in an orderly fashion through the doors and out to the street. Now! Don't dawdle.'

Instead of panicking, my lab group tested Charlie's patience by being overly polite to one another. 'After you,' was the most common phrase heard in between our supervisor's loud exhortations to hurry.

Outside, three groups of people gathered in the street. The largest one, by far, was the predominately female cluster of workers from the Calutron area. All the women were in overalls, wearing either short bobs or hairnets. Next was our much smaller group of scientists and then the gang from Alpha lab.

I explored the top and sides of the building searching for any signs of smoke or flames but saw none. And I couldn't smell anything burning. Even the Calutron girls grew silent when the clanging fire truck pulled up and firemen leaped to the ground and raced into the building.

Everyone spoke only in whispered tones for a while but, in time, the cacophony of a multitude of conversations filled the

air again. The noise grew more annoying to me minute by
minute as I fretted over the work that needed to be done
inside. I had committed to another shipment on Monday but
the longer I remained outside, the more doubts I had about
my ability to deliver on my promise.

One hour and twenty minutes into our exile, firefighters
emerged from every exit. The fire chief waved over Charlie and
a couple of other men in suits. Moments later, Charlie walked
back to our huddle, shaking his head. 'False alarm. You can all
go back to work now.'

We rushed around him babbling questions. Charlie just said,
'Inside. In the lab.'

When we were all there with a door closed, he said, 'I hate
to do this but here is what I need. Every one of you needs to
make a list of all the people you are certain were within your
range of vision at the time the alarm went off. No guessing.
No approximating. Just the unvarnished truth.'

'Why?' Gregg asked.

'Someone opened the fire alarm box and pulled the hook.
We want to talk to that person and find out why. The fire crew
found no sign of any fire. So either the person responsible
was mistaken or that individual intentionally disrupted the
work day. I repeat again: do not guess who was around you.
If you name someone that ends up being the culprit, it will
reflect badly on you and on our lab. Okay. Get busy. Get me
the list and then get back to work. Or if you'd like to confess
to setting off the alarm, come see me in my office – the door
is open.'

I wasn't paying attention to anyone when the loud clanging
had disrupted my task. I was focused on my work area and
nothing else. I had raised my head and looked around at the
first sound of the alarm, though. Who did I see in that moment?
I closed my eyes to visualize that scene, trying to recall each
face. As quickly as I could, I wrote down the people I knew
I saw and dropped the list onto Charlie's desk.

'Do you have any suspicions, Libby?'

I shook my head.

'Let me know if that changes. Are you going to be able to
send out a shipment Monday?'

Sometimes it seems like he reads my mind. 'I plan to work late tonight until I know I'm on schedule or until I drop.'

'Let me know if there's anything I can do.'

'I think I can manage it, Charlie. If I can't, you'll be the first to know.' I walked back to my space wondering if everything from the fire to the rats to the sliced tires and the evacuation of the building were all related or if I was manufacturing a plan out of a cascading series of simple coincidences.

TEN

I hummed in the kitchen as I fed G.G. and fixed my first cup of coffee. I had everything I needed for the supper I'd planned for Ruth. A gorgeous roasting hen sat in the refrigerator – all cleaned out and ready to pop in the oven. Potatoes rested in a basket under the sink and I had one last jar of home-canned green beans waiting in the pantry. I was especially pleased about the beans. I decided to make them in that southern style Ruthie liked – cooked long and hard with a piece of fatback in the pot for added flavor. Aunt Dorothy would not approve but Ruth would be delighted that I remembered and went to the trouble to prepare them just as she likes them.

I pulled out the piece of paper with a handwritten recipe for buttermilk biscuits. I'd never tried it before but sweet, white-haired Mrs Ferrell, who seemed to live in her apron, wrote it out in her spidery hand and had assured me that it was as easy as pie. When I told her that I'd never made pie either, she just laughed at me.

First, I needed to make a jelly roll for dessert. I didn't have directions for that in writing but I'd helped Aunt Dorothy's German cook and housekeeper do it so many times, I felt fairly confident that I could be successful. By the time I had finished whipping up the cake batter, my arm was sore from the mixing. I slid it into the oven, grabbed my second cup of coffee, sat down in the living room and cracked open *Dragon Seed* to read while it baked.

I had a hard time getting into the story since the urge to check on the progress of my creation made me jump up and run to the kitchen every few minutes. At last, I pulled the golden cake out of the oven and put the chicken inside to roast. I smeared blackberry jelly on the thin cake, rolled it up, sprinkled the top with a dusting of confectioner's sugar before wrapping it all in a piece of wax paper and putting it in the pantry. I smiled at it as I set it on the shelf. Getting all the ingredients and putting it all together without any help had been a challenge, but I did it. The similarities between following a recipe and conducting a lab procedure still surprised me every time I labored in the kitchen.

While the potatoes boiled on the stove, I mixed the biscuit batter, spooned it onto a cookie sheet and set it down by the stove. I had drained the potatoes and grabbed the masher when I looked out the window and saw Ruthie coming up the street. I pulled out the chicken, slid in the biscuits and ran out to meet her.

We worked side-by-side in the kitchen on the finishing touches, filled our plates and sat down at the little table after I set my pile of new books on the sofa. 'Biscuits! I can't believe you know how to make biscuits,' Ruthie said. A few minutes later, she added, 'Oh, these green beans are as good as Mama's!'

We both ate more than we should before carting the plates into the kitchen and starting the clean-up. Before we made much progress, we heard a knock on the door. I opened it to see Dennis standing there with a fistful of flowers. The western boots and cowboy hat made him appear taller than usual but what really amazed me was his suit. It was like something out of a Randolph Scott movie – embroidered curlicues running down from his shoulders accented with a lariat tie. I was speechless.

'Are you still irritated with me?' he asked.

'No, Dennis, I'm not one to hold a grudge.'

'Good. I stopped by to ask you if you might consider going out to dinner with me on Saturday night. Afterwards, we could walk over to see a movie, or maybe there's something else you'd like to do.'

I hesitated for a moment, wondering if I was making a big mistake. But, honestly, I was still miffed at Teddy and felt I needed to prove something to him. 'I'd be delighted, Dennis.'

I heard a gasp behind me. Looking back, I saw Ruthie peering out of the kitchen door. When she saw me, she ducked out of sight.

A grin split Dennis' face as he bobbed his head. 'I'll come by for you at seven Saturday night, then.'

'I have a better idea. I'll drive my car and come pick you up at the dorm.'

Dennis blanched, stammered and recovered in record time. 'Yes, ma'am. I'll see you then.' He thrust the flowers at me, spun around and executed a fast retreat as if he was worried I might change my mind.

When I returned to the kitchen, Ruthie batted at me with the kitchen towel. 'What do you think you're doin'? What kind of game are you playin'?'

'What?' I asked, feigning ignorance.

'What about Teddy?'

'Teddy doesn't own me.'

'That's not the point. Remember what you said in your letters? You said that Teddy understands. Teddy is supportive of your career in every way. You said that you were extremely fond of him. I thought that meant you couldn't bring yourself to say that you loved him but you did.'

'Teddy is acting a bit too possessive.'

'So, your answer is to risk losin' him and at the same time toy with this other guy's affections?'

'You think I'm toying with Dennis?'

'Yes, I do. I think you are pushin' Teddy away, too. What are you afraid of Libby?'

One of the things I always liked about Ruth was her forthrightness. At this moment, though, I felt the sting of it and wasn't sure it was such an endearing quality after all. Before I could summon even a flimsy response, we were interrupted again by a knock on the door.

Outside, a corporal stood, his posture rigid, his demeanor grim. 'I have orders to bring Ruth Nance in for questioning.'

I was trembling inside but I forced a steely tone into my voice. 'Who gave that order?'

'Miss Clark, I was specifically told not to share any information with you.'

'Sir, I am not in the military. Miss Nance is not in the military. Your orders have no weight here in my home.'

The corporal sighed. 'Ma'am, we do not want to use any force, however, we have been instructed that if you try to prevent us from carrying out the command then we should bring you in, too.'

I slammed the door in his face and heard the sound of his foot thumping on the door as he failed in his attempt to block its closing. I threw my body against it and dug in my heels. 'Ruthie, quick, drag the chair over. It should hold the door until the two of us can get the sofa in place. Then . . .'

I heard grumbling communications coming from outside as Ruth placed a hand on my forearm. Her dark brown eyes looked straight into mine. 'I'm goin' with them, Libby. And you're goin' to let me. I don't want you arrested, too. I need you free so that someone will know what happened to me.'

Her logic was inescapable but the idea of allowing them to take her without a struggle galled me. 'But, Ruthie, we can—'

'No, Libby, we can't. Step away from the door.'

Seeing the determination in her face, I yielded and stepped away and Ruth pulled it wide open. 'Well, gentlemen, I reckon we oughta get a move on.'

I watched her walk down the steps and climb into the jeep. She waved as they pulled away. I stood there for a long time after I could no longer see her. My conflicting emotions – admiration for my friend, frustration with my helplessness, and anger at Crenshaw who I knew must be behind this – left me devoid of constructive thought. Soon, my stubbornness reasserted itself. I grabbed a pencil and paper and created a plan of action. Then, I headed out the door.

ELEVEN

A different corporal sat at a desk by the door to Crenshaw's office. This one looked as if he spit-polished his face each morning. His tiny eyes and bushy eyebrows made him appear pig-headed and petty. 'The lieutenant colonel is not in his office.'

'When do you expect him?'

'Tomorrow morning at 0800.'

'Where can I find him this afternoon?'

'I am not at liberty to provide that information, ma'am.'

'I am a scientist working in Y-12 and—'

The corporal grinned. 'Of course, you are, ma'am.'

I slapped my badge on his desk. 'I am certain if you are manning this desk you have been briefed on the coding of the badges. Am I correct?'

'Yes, ma'am. I am. My apologies. What can I do for you?'

I was pleased to see his reddened complexion as I scooped up my identification, but it wasn't all I wanted. 'I need to speak with Lieutenant Colonel Crenshaw immediately because of a recent development.'

'Your name is Libby Clark – did I remember that right?' he asked as he pulled open the top middle drawer and extracted a piece of paper.

'Yes. I am Libby Clark.'

'I'm sorry, ma'am. But you are not on the lieutenant colonel's list of those who are entitled to know of his whereabouts in an emergency.'

'Obviously, his list is incomplete,' I said as I spun around and walked out into the hall. I didn't even know he had something like that. And if I had been aware, I had no delusions that he would include my name. The likely place to see him between now and tomorrow morning would be at his home. I doubted he was there right now but I was willing to wait.

I knocked on the door of his cemesto home and

Mrs Crenshaw opened it. 'Why, Miss Clark, what a pleasant surprise. I'm afraid, however, that my husband is out right now.'

'Do you expect him back soon?'

'Oh no, dear. I am not sure when he'll be back. When he left this afternoon, he told me not to keep supper for him tonight since he expected to be busy for quite some time. So I put the roast back in the refrigerator and my son and I are just going to have leftover stew. I'm sorry.'

'Do you know where I could find him?'

Mrs Crenshaw put her fingers up to her mouth and chuckled. 'You certainly aren't the wife of a soldier or scientist around here. They tell us nothing. He could be next door or two states away by now. I wouldn't have the slightest idea. I will tell him you dropped by when I see him.'

'Thank you, ma'am,' I said and returned to the street in front of the house. How do those women live that way? They were like ladies in waiting, hostage to the whims of the monarchy. Most of them seemed so happy. There were those women who sat home quietly drinking all day, but they were the exception. Most accepted their lives in captivity with total equanimity.

I looked around the neighborhood for a place where I could wait for Crenshaw's return home without being obvious. I spotted a tree house nestled in a large, leafy oak tree behind a home on the other side of the street. I saw no sign of life in the cemesto beside it. The boards nailed like steps into the side of the tree were narrow and more suited for child-sized feet than my own but I managed to hoist myself up and take refuge inside. The interior was deep enough that I could lean against the back wall and even my shoes remained in the shadows. Best of all, I had an excellent view of the front of Crenshaw's house.

At first, I wished I'd brought a book along but soon the sun lowered and I realized my reading time would have been very limited. The loss of warmth walked hand in hand with the decreasing light. The warm spring day turned into a chilly evening, making me now wish I'd brought a sweater.

I hadn't meant to fall asleep and didn't realize I had until I awoke with a start. For a moment, I did not know where I was but it all came together with the sight of Crenshaw strolling up the sidewalk in front of his home. 'Crenshaw,' I shouted as I flopped around and made my way down the tree.

'Miss Clark?' he asked, chin thrust forward, his eyes squinting in a vain attempt to penetrate the darkness.

'Yes, sir. Where is Ruth Nance?'

'Were you in that tree house?'

'Yes sir. Where is Ruthie?'

'How long have you been up there?'

'I don't know. A while. Where is Ruth Nance?'

'I don't know.'

'Sir, please show me enough respect to give me an honest answer.'

'That is an honest answer, Miss Clark,' he said, lifting his arm and turning the face of his watch into the porch light. 'It has been a half hour since I last saw her. I have no idea where she went.'

'What did you do to her?'

'I just asked her a few questions.'

'And then you just let her go?'

'Yes, Miss Clark, please relax. Unclench your fists. It is not becoming in any woman and particularly not a professional.' He turned and took two steps toward his front door.

I grabbed his arm. 'Is that the truth?'

He pinched one of my fingers to lift and remove my hand from the sleeve of his jacket. 'Yes, Miss Clark. You are acting unhinged. Now go away or I'll be forced to call for MP intervention.'

I stood staring at him for a moment, then I turned and fled into the night. I had to find Ruth.

I stopped first at the dormitory. Izzie opened the door before I had a chance to knock. 'Ruth thought you might come here looking for her. I didn't want her to go out again, all alone. But she said she had to go to your place and I had to stay here in case you showed up.'

'How is she, Izzie?'

'Shaking. Trembling. All over. She said if you weren't at home, she was waiting there until you came back.'

'Thanks, Izzie. I'll take care of her. She might want to spend the night with me.'

'Then, I'm coming with you,' she said reaching into her closet to grab a sweater. 'I won't sleep until I know she's OK.'

We arrived at my flat-top short of breath, relieved to see Ruthie sitting on the steps. 'Ruthie, why didn't you wait inside?' I asked.

'I reckoned I could get ambushed by those soldiers again if I did. This way, I'd see them acomin' and run off before they saw me.'

A simple, logical statement but it made me sad. Again, it seemed we were sacrificing our individual freedoms on the altar of national security. I prayed we could do a better job of balancing the two when the war was over. 'Let's go inside to talk. You, too, Izzie. I'll fix a pot of tea.'

The night's chill had permeated the thin walls of my home. After putting on water to boil, I started a coal fire in the stove. By the time we sat down with our cups, the room was quite cozy.

To answer the endless questions from Izzie and I, Ruth related her experience. 'We drove into the military housing area, then went a bit further. We stopped in front of a one-story building and went down into the basement. The hallways on the lower floor were really long – it seemed like it had to be bigger than what was up on ground level.

'They put me in a room with a table, a chair on either side and a desk lamp on top. One soldier pushed me down into a seat and told me to stay there. He said that he'd handcuff me if I didn't stay put. So, I did. It seemed like an awful long time before Crenshaw, a corporal and a woman showed up. Long enough that, by the time they got there, I needed to go really bad.

'They let that woman take me to a bathroom but she wouldn't answer any of my questions or talk to me at all. When we returned, the questionin' started. Crenshaw started out tellin' me that he knew I was responsible for all of the pranks. He said he'd go easy on me if I would tell him who else was involved.

'I told him I never pulled a prank on anybody since I was

ten years old. Then he asked me, "Where did you get the rats?" "Rats?" I said. "Can't stand those things. They get in the grain and make a mess of it." He said, "So, you brought them here from your farm." I asked him if he flipped his wig. I said that there was no way I'd be a'travelling on the train with a bunch of rats.

'Then he wanted to know how I got into the lab. He said he knew I borrowed your identification card, Libby, whenever I wanted to go somewhere I shouldn't. Imagine that.'

'Was he implying you did it with my consent?'

'Implyin'? He was out and out accusin'. And I gave him a piece of my mind. I told him that you were a good American and the best friend I had in the world. I said that I wouldn't use you like that. I told him that you solved my sister's murder when he just wanted ever'body to hush up. I said, "Maybe you put those rats in there just to make Miss Clark look bad." He didn't like that one little bit. That little vein on his forehead was throbbin' to beat the band.'

I knew it wasn't wise for her to sass the lieutenant colonel but still I had to smile. No one would ever call Ruth timid.

'Then, he started askin' me about where I was at a bunch of different times. I remembered most of them – I was at work on night shift or I was sleepin' or one time, I was in the administrative buildin' fillin' out paperwork. After that, I sat alone in that bare, boring room. After a bit, I got up and paced, then remembered the handcuffs and sat back down. Finally, a private came in and said I was free to go now. He offered to give me a ride but I told him "No thank you very much." I felt safer walkin' than ridin' with any of them.'

The three of us planned on getting together again next Sunday. Ruth accepted my offer to stay overnight. Izzie, though, turned down the offer to sleep on the sofa and went back to the dorm.

Before turning out the light, Ruth said, 'Libby, I think Crenshaw's done with me but it sounds like he's acomin' after you and maybe your scientist friends, too. Y'all need to be careful.'

TWELVE

Since Ruth was on day shift this week, we walked up to Y-12 together, parting only when we came to her entrance. She gave me a hug and whispered, 'Remember, girl, careful.'

I don't know how she did it. Changing from one shift to another each week to be where she was needed most. I know there were a lot of girls working swing shifts like that but I doubted that I could handle it without falling asleep on the job.

Charlie approached me a couple hours into the workday. 'Have you heard from Tom?'

'No. Should I have?'

'When he left for his father's funeral, he told me he'd be back to work today or he'd let me know that he'd been delayed and I haven't heard from him,' Charlie said.

'Maybe he is travelling back today.'

'Maybe. But he wasn't in the best shape when he left here and I'd feel better knowing he was okay. Do you have any way to contact him?'

'I think I can get a phone number for a family member this evening.'

'If you reach him, ask him to call me. I'd like to talk to him directly,' he said handing me a piece of paper. 'I gave him my home phone number before he left but in case he misplaced it, you can give it to him again.'

I walked across the room to Gregg's station. 'Did Tom write down an emergency contact on the list we circulated in our group?'

'I'm pretty sure everyone did. Was he supposed to be back today?'

'Yes. I was thinking, at the end of the day, I could go back with you to your dorm and you could run in and get it for me.'

'No problem. I also have a bunch of change I can give you to use in the pay phone.'

'Perfect, thanks!'

After lunch, I was in the middle of weighing new samples when Joe shouted my name. He stood at the door to the lab with sopping wet shoes and pant cuffs. 'The bathrooms are flooded. I went in the men's room and all the faucets were on. There's water rushing under the ladies' room door, could you . . .?'

'Yes, on my way,' I said as I rushed past him. The faucets were all wide open. I turned them off but still heard running water. I checked the first stall. The toilet was overflowing. The top was off the back of the tank and the rubber gasket that stopped the flow was on the floor. The rod that worked the mechanism was bent out of shape. Repair might be possible but I took the quickest route to a solution and turned off the water flow to the tank. I went down the line doing the same in all the stalls.

When I stepped out into the hall, the maintenance crew was already busy with the clean-up. Joe and I sloshed back to the lab and greeted a puzzled Charlie. 'What in the blue blazes is going on around here?'

We explained what we found down the hall and Charlie asked, 'Our prankster again?'

'It looks like it,' I said.

'Or,' Joe suggested, 'someone who wants us to think that.'

'I suspect we'll be seeing more of Crenshaw after this,' Charlie said.

'Yes, you will,' Crenshaw said as he walked up to the doorway. 'I'd like to speak with Miss Clark, please.' He latched on to my elbow and exerted a slight tug toward the exterior door.

'Sure,' Charlie said, 'come on in. No need to go outside. You can use my office.'

'I believe—' Crenshaw began.

'No problem at all,' Charlie said, as he put a hand in the small of my back and steered me in the other direction. 'You can close the door and have total privacy.'

Joe folded his arms across his chest. Gregg and Stephen joined him, mimicking his posture. Crenshaw looked at the three men and at the other staring faces around the room and apparently decided a low-key response was in his best interest.

'I believe I know the way. Thank you for your accommodation.'

Crenshaw latched onto my elbow again in a painful grip as he led me to Charlie's office. I glanced back over my shoulder to flash a grin at Charlie. He returned it with a wink.

Crenshaw sat in Charlie's chair on the opposite side of the desk and cast a disdainful glare at the cluttered desktop. I sat on the edge of the seat closest to the door, my back straight, hands folded in my lap.

'Relax, Clark. I'm not going to drag you out of here.'

That comment made me more agitated. 'What do you want from me, sir?'

'Just a little cooperation. So that you know, I have already checked out your suspicious Miss Nance, learned that she was at work today and never left her post without accompaniment. I won't be bothering her over this matter.'

I suppose he wanted me to say 'thank you,' but I wasn't about to give him that satisfaction.

'I have concluded that a member of this lab must be responsible for these pathetic acts of sabotage. Your supervisor assured me after the false fire alarm that everyone was accounted for. I don't think he lied to me but I suspect someone in this lab is covering for the culprit. I also strongly suspect that you know about everything and everyone in there. You might not have proof but you have a strong certainty about who is involved.'

I could deny his accusation and I'd be telling the truth but I knew he wouldn't believe me. I said nothing.

'You are one obstinate woman. Perhaps you confided your suspicions to someone. It could have been Miss Nance. Maybe I could convince her it would be in your best interests to divulge your secret.'

The burning in my chest almost made me explode. I knew, however, he wanted me to react in anger. He wanted me to lose control. I inhaled and exhaled with force but said not a word.

He slapped his hand down on a pile of paper on the desk, sending a few sheets flying. 'These are stupid, juvenile, amateur pranks – very unprofessional. I cannot believe you would protect a fellow scientist who is jeopardizing the freedom of his peers and the outcome of this war. These acts might be childish but they are also treasonous. You may win the battle, Miss Clark, but you will not win this war.' He stood, knocking the chair back into the wall and marched out of the office slamming the door behind him.

For a moment, I could not move. His wrath was as fierce as a conflagration. I prayed no one I knew was responsible for fueling his flames.

THIRTEEN

Gregg and I went together to the phone booth with Tom's emergency contact number for his Aunt Gertrude and a pocketful of change. Someone was on a call when we arrived but there wasn't anyone standing in line. Five minutes later, I was dialing the number.

The woman who answered confirmed that she was Tom O'Malley's Aunt Gertrude and asked, 'How is he? Is he hurt? Is he sick? Oh, please tell me he's not dead, too?' The last question sounded like a wail.

'Ma'am, I'm not calling because I have news about Tom. I was hoping to speak to him. We work together.'

'Why did you call me?'

I explained about the group's list and said, 'He left here last Tuesday to attend his father's funeral.'

Her silence felt as heavy as a free-falling boulder.

'Ma'am?' I prodded.

She hiccupped a sob. 'He did not arrive for his father's funeral. I simply thought he couldn't get away from work. I haven't seen him since he left here to go to that lab. He said he was in the war effort but I don't know where he was living. He said he couldn't tell me.'

'No, ma'am. None of us were allowed to tell our families.'

'I just don't think that's right. How can I even report him missing when I don't know where he was last seen?'

'Ma'am. I will promise you this: we will look for him. If we find him, I will personally contact you immediately. If I am unable, someone else from my group will. Even if we don't find him, one of us will contact you this coming weekend to let you know that much. I am so sorry.'

'I'm worried,' Aunt Gertrude said. 'I know he and his father, my brother, had words the last time they talked. Unpleasantness like that can take a toll on one's soul. I hope Tom hasn't done something rash. I hope he hasn't . . . oh, I can't bring myself to say it.'

After hanging up, I asked Gregg. 'If you were to commit suicide . . .?'

'She's worried that he took his own life?'

'Yes, I think that's what she meant. If you were to do that, how would you do it?'

'It's not something I've ever thought about, Libby.'

'Think about it now.'

'Well,' Tom said scratching his chin. 'I suppose it would be easy to get a rope and go out into the woods and hang myself. Or . . . or . . . better yet. I'd hike up to Dossett Tunnel, guzzle a bottle of Splo and lay down on the tracks. I can't believe I'm even talking about this.'

'Obviously, we are going to have to find time in daylight to search for him.'

'It'll have to wait until Sunday, then. Why don't we report him as missing? Then the police and military can do that work right away.'

'If Tom is still alive, he'd hate us for alerting the authorities about him. And, honestly, it's been nearly a week. If he's dead, letting the search wait a few days won't make any difference.'

'What if he's just injured and waiting to be rescued?'

'Wishful thinking, Gregg. There's no reason for him to be in the wilderness when he was supposed to be going into Knoxville and taking a train home. Do you think we can move our group meeting to Tuesday night instead of Wednesday to talk this all out?'

'I should be able to find most of the guys in the dorms and if I miss anyone, we can catch up with them at work tomorrow.'

'Just make sure you find someone in Alpha lab tonight or it could get tricky. I will have to tell Charlie in the morning, too.'

'Of course, he asked you to call. Just don't make any commitments to him until we've talked to the group. Persuade him to give us enough time to get together before he takes any action.'

I walked back home at a slow trudge. I wasn't any more active physically today but the emotional toll had sapped all my energy. When I reached my flat-top, I discovered a letter from my Aunt Dorothy. Just the sight of it forced me to think about my mother. I'd pushed her out of my mind all week and I felt guilty about doing that but sometimes I couldn't sleep if I didn't shove some of my worries to the back of the closet.

G.G. put on a scampering show as I entered the door. He raced around the living room, into the kitchen and back again. He didn't wag his tail like a dog but he always made it clear he was glad to see me. I scooped him up and nuzzled his chin. He bounded out of my arms and led me to his food dish. I refilled that bowl and set a saucer of milk down beside it, wondering if his desire for food fueled more of his excitement than any affection he might have for me.

I put on the tea kettle and opened the letter.

Dear Libby,

Thank you for your promptness in letting me know the package arrived. However, I was disappointed that you had nothing to say about your mother. I expected at least some acknowledgement of the situation even if you had no desire to see her before she dies.

I will be going down to the University of Virginia for a conference in early May and hope you will consider joining me there and accompanying me and your half-brother to the jail.

    With love, despite my disappointment,

    Aunt Dorothy

I had expected a rebuke of some sort but still reading the words stung me deeply. I knew she was right. When cancer is concerned, time is not on anyone's side. I needed to decide one way or the other. I needed to talk to someone. It couldn't be Ruthie – she thinks family is first no matter what. The only person I could think of who would understand was Teddy. He made it so hard by being so bossy. He knows that irritates me but somehow, he can't seem to help himself. If I'm honest with myself, I realize he doesn't mean it the way I perceive it, yet it bristles me every time. What did Aunt Dorothy always say? We are responsible for our own perceptions. And we can't change how another person acts but we can change how we react. I know she's right but living up to that philosophy is not as easy as it sounds.

I changed into my nightgown, fixed a cup of tea and a cheese sandwich and took them with me when I curled up in bed with *Dragon Seed*. G.G. jumped up beside me and tried to steal some cheese. I gave him a small piece but devoured the rest. With a full stomach and a warm furry body by my side, I fell asleep with the book in my lap and a half cup of tea turning cold on the nightstand.

FOURTEEN

Tuesday morning, I packed up another shipment of crystals and called for a soldier and jeep for my escort. The ride through the sunny late morning was quite pleasant but my driver was silent. No matter how hard I tried, I couldn't get him to engage in the most innocuous conversation. I suspected that was the result of an order from Crenshaw.

I delivered it to the new rendezvous point right by a guard

station with my imagination working overtime. I scanned the eaves of the building seeking any sign of smoke. I saw a puff in the air and nearly ran back to the jeep before a soldier smoking a cigarette came around the corner of the building. I opened the door and stood to the side of the opening, leaning against the wall for a moment before stepping inside. I saw threats everywhere. I had never been more relieved to turn over a package.

The rest of the afternoon, I couldn't drown out the negative thoughts of something or someone interfering with the courier before he reached his destination. I was glad when the workday ended before any calamity struck. Afterwards, I rustled up dinner for me and G.G. before heading to the Walking Molecules meeting. Half the group was there when I arrived, the rest followed shortly thereafter. Except for Tom. I had been hoping against hope that he'd surprise us all, show up and eliminate one serious worry.

Teddy sat down beside me and I told him that I wanted to talk to him about a personal matter after the meeting. He studied my face until I was uncomfortable.

'Will you?' I repeated.

'Is this about us?'

'No.'

'Well, please put that on your agenda. We really need to talk. I don't understand the signals I've been getting from you lately.'

To my great relief, I saw Gregg standing to get everyone's attention for the start of the meeting. 'Later, Teddy,' I said, pointing to the head of the table.

Gregg started the story about Tom and then turned it over to me to finish it up, just interrupting me once to find out if Charlie was willing to go along with our decision to wait before contacting the authorities.

'Yes, he is. He was not particularly comfortable with the delay. He did, however, point out that it would be easier for him to hold Tom's position open for his return if he didn't tell anyone that he had disappeared.'

After I reiterated my phone call with Tom's aunt, I fielded questions from the group. All were the same ones Gregg and

Charlie had already asked but I repeated my answers just the same, with Gregg nodding in agreement as I spoke.

Gary, though, grew more agitated with every word out of my mouth. 'Tom would not commit suicide. You can forget about that.'

'I don't know, Gary. Guilt and grief are a toxic combination. Who knows what any of us would do under similar circumstances,' Dennis said.

'I do know Tom wouldn't commit suicide. He told me it was a sign of weakness,' Gary insisted.

Silence filled the room until Gregg broke it with a pacifying statement. 'Nonetheless we still need to explore the unlikely or improbable for no other reason than to eliminate them.'

'Waste of time,' Gary said.

'If Tom has not shown up by Sunday, some of us will gather at Libby's house to check out the tunnel and the woods. Any disagreement here about not informing the authorities?'

'I agree with that,' Joe said. 'Crenshaw's visit to the lab yesterday was eerie. Someone is informing him about every move we make.'

'He came to your lab yesterday? Why?' Dennis asked.

'Libby, you talked to him,' Joe said. 'What did he want?'

'He wanted me to point the finger of blame for the fire, the rats, the fire alarm and the flooding of the bathrooms. He is certain the prankster is someone in my lab.'

'What did you tell him?' Gary blurted.

Before I could answer, Joe chuckled. 'Not what he wanted to hear. You should have seen the steam rolling out of his ears when he stomped out the door.'

Gregg cleared his throat and we all turned in his direction. 'It's hard to ask this question but someone has to do it. If someone in this room is playing these pranks, tell us about it. We're all bound to keep anything said within this room. We will not turn you in. We need to know why you are doing it. You need to help us understand.' Gregg looked from one person to another moving on when he got a negative response. 'I have to trust each one of you. I also ask if you find out anything that points to the identity of that person, bring it to this group. Right now, Crenshaw is on Libby's back. Sooner or later he's bound to exert pressure on more of us – maybe on everyone in both labs. We need to find answers and we need to bring this all to an end.'

'So. You want us all to be stoolies?' Gary asked with scorn dripping from every word.

'No, Gary,' Gregg said. 'Being a stoolie means turning that person into the authorities. I don't plan to do that. I just want the chance to convince the guilty party to stop on his own and save himself – and all of us – from a lot of trouble.'

When the meeting broke up, Teddy remained seated next to me and Dennis approached me from the other side. 'See you Saturday night,' Dennis said before leaving the room.

I nodded, hoping that Teddy had not heard what he said. I was not so lucky.

'Saturday night? What was that about?'

I shrugged my shoulders. 'Nothing much. Dennis and I are going to dinner and a movie together, that's all.'

'That's all? That's a date. What are you doing? Are you breaking up with me?'

'How could I possibly do that, Teddy? We don't have any kind of commitment.'

'Maybe you don't but I sure do. I thought I made that clear. I want to marry you when the war is over.'

'And I can stay shut at home dusting and making babies.'

'We've been over that. You know it. I've told you more than once that I'm okay with being married to a woman with a career. I am comfortable with your ambitions and I told you I would follow you wherever your work took you. What more do you want from me? What are you afraid of, Libby?'

I audibly sucked in my breath, then slowly exhaled. 'You are the second person to ask me that this week.'

'What was your answer the first time?'

'I didn't have a chance to answer. The MP's arrived and took her away.'

Teddy wrapped both his hands around mine and his eyes filled with warmth. 'I'm so sorry, Libby.' He looked down at the table then raised his head and grinned. 'Is that what happens to everyone who asks a question you don't want to answer? Am I next?'

I couldn't help but smile back. 'Stop it, Teddy.'

'Will you visit me behind bars?'

I swatted the side of his arm. 'I can't deny the fact that you and Ruth are right. I am afraid of something, but honestly, I can't put my finger on what it is that has me frightened.'

'I think maybe I understand it better than you. All around you are women who dropped everything to follow their scientist husbands to this outpost – women who accept broad generalities and don't question the specifics, women who know nothing about what their husbands do. You see their public faces and think they have sublimated their personalities to their husbands. But, seriously, Libby, you have no idea of how many of the male scientists have shared all their secrets with their wives. They will never tell you because they would never betray the confidences they received and jeopardize their husband's careers. The world is not a black and white place, Libby. There is gray everywhere.'

I sighed. 'I should have known that, shouldn't I? Now that you said it, it seems like an obvious possibility. It never crossed my mind.'

'I know I'm not alone. I know there are other men out there who value a woman's intelligence and perspective – men who would not make an important decision without first debating it with their spouses.'

'Don't forget that there are a lot of backward, domineering men out there.'

'I can never forget that – it is what drives me to be the best man I can be. But, listen, Libby, I understand your fear. And I am willing to give you time. I don't want to pressure you. However, it would make me feel a lot more secure in our relationship if you would commit to making it an exclusive one for as long as it lasts.'

The fear inside me struggled like a tempered child screaming and beating its foot against a barrier. I ignored those wails of outrage and said, 'Yes, Teddy. I would like that. But it's got to be after Saturday night. I've already accepted Dennis' invitation.'

'You've got to be honest with him, Libby, before you go to dinner. You don't want him spending his money on you and feeling as if you led him on.'

'You're right. I'll tell him we're going Dutch, then I'll explain why and let him change his mind about spending the evening with me if that's what he wants.'

'I can live with that. I will be feeling little tweaks of jealousy all night but I won't act on them. So, what was it you wanted to talk to me about?'

The waitress stepped into the room and startled when she saw it wasn't empty. 'I'm sorry. Didn't mean to interrupt.'

'No problem,' Teddy said. 'Do you need the room?'

'No, not at all. Do you want anything?'

Teddy looked at me and I shook my head. 'We're fine,' he said and then we were alone again.

'It's about my mother,' I said.

'Oh jeez. What now?'

I explained her fatal illness and my Aunt Dorothy's request. 'I feel torn in two different directions – so torn I haven't wanted to think about it at all.'

'I understand your ambivalence about your mother. I believe I would feel the same way in a similar situation. But remember what Dennis said about guilt and grief at the meeting tonight.'

I nodded, knowing exactly where he was going. I needed to hear it verbalized anyway.

'I don't want to see you facing that. I don't want you reflecting on your loss and being shredded by feelings of guilt. Just because guilt isn't warranted doesn't mean it will stay away. In fact, I think sometimes people feel guiltier over things they shouldn't than over what they should. I don't want you carrying that burden.'

'I guess the question is: will I feel guilty?'

'You said you have been struggling to forgive your mother for a long time?'

'Yes.'

'And you said that you felt you were close to doing so?'

'Yes.'

'What if the day she dies you realize that you have found the ability to forgive her?'

I closed my eyes and nodded my head. 'Thank you, Teddy. You've given me a lot to think about.'

'Let me know what you decide. No matter what it is, I'm here to support you – even if you don't take my advice.'

'You're saying you are free of the human impulse to say "I told you so."'

'When it comes to you, absolutely. Now, how about if I walk you home. Between your mother and the prankster, you might be so deep in thought you'll walk right past your house.'

A nasty thought tickled the back of my mind: he's saying you're incompetent. I decided to ignore it and took Teddy's hand.

FIFTEEN

When we reached my house, Teddy asked if he could listen to the news broadcast that was about to start on the radio. I agreed and while he tuned in the station, I went into the kitchen to make a pot of coffee. He turned the volume up enough that I had no problem hearing from the other room.

'Reds circle Berlin. Two thousand tanks smash Bavaria. Dateline Paris. The Associated Press reports that more than 2000 American and French tanks crashed through the outer defenses of Bavaria, nearing Berchtesgaden, Hitler's inviolate retreat. The Red Army encircled the ruins of a tottering Berlin. Fanatical Nazi defenders have fallen back to take a death stand in one corner of the city.

'In other news, American legislators and editors departed Paris today to visit German horror camps at General Dwight Eisenhower's request. In Manhattan, the War Emergency Court sentenced meat dealer Maurice Muller of Elmhurst to five days in jail and fined him $25 for violation of wholesale meat ceiling prices.'

Teddy clicked the radio off. 'Sounds like the end is very near in Germany but still scoundrels are trying to take advantage of the public.'

'The scoundrels will always be with us. I wonder what we

will hear about those camps. I'm not sure I want to know the details of the evil. Some of the photographs I've seen are sickening.'

'Soon, life will be normal again,' Teddy said.

'What a nice thought,' I said with a sigh. 'We've been at war so long, I don't think I'll know how to act during a time of peace.'

'We can figure it out together,' Teddy said as he planted a quick kiss on my lips. He made his exit before I could react.

The next day, I skipped lunch and went to the telegraph office and sent a message to my aunt. I made it short and to the point – no need to pay for any more words than necessary. 'Send date STOP I want to be there STOP.' In one way, I felt better after making that decision but in another I felt more anxious. There was nothing clear-cut when it came to my mother.

The morning had been prank-free and I hoped the status quo would hold up through the afternoon, too. I could use a boring but productive day without any drama.

The hours flew by and my pile of reports grew while the stack in my inbox shrunk. I raised my head to look around the room and saw that everyone but Gregg had already left for the day. 'Ready to call it a day?' I asked.

Gregg lifted one finger in the air, jotted down one note and said, 'Finished. Hey, you look a bit more relaxed today.'

'No pranks. No worries.'

'At least none here. If something happened elsewhere, I wouldn't be happy but it might take some of the pressure off you.'

'Maybe. But I have a feeling Crenshaw will find a way to blame me regardless or at least claim with undying certainty that I know who did it.'

We walked out of the building together and chatted about co-workers and wondered about Tom and where he might be now. 'Maybe he didn't want to face family and didn't want to face work and just ran away,' Gregg suggested.

'You think he went AWOL?'

'We're not military. I know sometimes it feels like we are but still, it's not technically possible for him to be AWOL.'

'But you know that's how it will be seen if he just took off.'

'Yeah, right. The militarization of the civilian population. Even after the war, it's going to change who we all were before it started. I hope we have an easier time overcoming the possible negative consequences than we've had defeating the enemy.'

'Nothing but good news out of Europe these days,' I said.

'True, I think you're right. I believe that the Nazis can measure their future in days now. So much for the Third Reich. The Japs, however, seem even more willing to die for the cause. They got this all started with suicide pilots bringing bombs to Pearl Harbor. Will they know when it's time to surrender?'

'That is definitely beyond our ability to predict. I do hope, though, that they give up on their cause before we deploy the gadget. I sense it will change our world and our place in it more than anything we've experienced so far.'

Over Gregg's objections, we said goodbye at the men's dormitory and I walked the rest of the way home on my own. I had to be honest with myself, although I was not offended when Gregg offered to accompany me back, I would have had a more negative reaction to Teddy and that wasn't fair. I really needed to work on that.

I'd barely gotten my dinner dishes cleaned when there was a knock on my door. A square-shouldered woman of about forty, wearing a hat, gloves and heels, stood on my doorstep. She appeared dressed for a church service or a formal tea. I could not imagine what a pretentious matron of our little society here behind the fence would want with me. She had to have come to the wrong house.

'May I help you?' I asked.

'Are you Miss Clark?'

'Yes,' I said as my brow furrowed by its own volition.

'Miss Libby Clark?'

'Yes, ma'am. And you are?'

'Libby Clark, the scientist?'

'Yes. I—'

'I'm sorry. I was expecting someone much older and more scholarly in appearance.'

'Like a spinster teacher?' I teased.

She had the sensitivity to blush. 'Please, can we start again? I'm Eleanor – Eleanor Stanley.' She stretched out her hand.

I shook it and asked, 'Would you like to come in?'

'Thank you, I would like to talk to you. I appreciate you overlooking the first impression I made.'

'No problem. Coffee? Tea?'

'I would love a cup of tea if it's not too much trouble.'

'No trouble at all.'

I put the kettle on to boil, added tea to the teapot and placed it, cups and saucers, spoons, a pitcher of milk and the sugar bowl on a tray. The kettle was whistling as I finished. I carried it and set it down on top of the table.

Sitting down, I said, 'While the tea steeps, why don't you tell me why you came to visit me.'

'Miss Clark, have you ever been to the hutments?'

'No, ma'am.'

'Do you realize how deplorable the conditions are there?'

'I have heard some unpleasant descriptions but never knew what was true or what was simply unfounded rumor.'

'The word "deplorable" is not hyperbole, I assure you. Some of our maids have told us about how they are treated simply because of the color of their skin. We were outraged and decided to take an excursion there.'

'Who are "we," Mrs Stanley?'

'Sorry, I should have started with that. Most of us are the wives of scientists. A few are the wives of engineers. We started getting together over coffee and coffee cake but when someone told us what her maid said about the hutments, we all started questioning the help and we were appalled.

'There are more than a thousand individuals living there. The men are segregated from the women – even married couples are separated. They live in flimsy, packing-box structures set flat on the muddy dirt and their windows are just holes in the wall – no glass, not even screens. Y-12 and K-25 are like concrete palaces for all your gadgets while these human beings are living in squalor right under our noses.'

'You've seen this?' I asked. I'd hoped everything I'd heard was an exaggeration, but she was dashing my denial of reality. I poured our tea and carried the cups over.

'Yes, I have. And do you know what happens to a woman who gets pregnant?'

'No.'

'They are removed from the reservation and left on the side of the road to wait for a bus. Doesn't matter if the woman is single or married – all that matters is that she's a colored person. It is awful.'

'I can't deny that but why did you come to see me?'

'We thought that a woman like you – one who has defied the odds to become a professional in a man's world – would be the type of woman who would support our cause to improve conditions in the colored community.'

'What do you think I could do?'

'You are in a unique position to gauge the attitude of the men here. Some of those in our group have husbands who do not approve of what we want to do. They say, "We're in the south, what do you expect?" and then trot out that old canard, "when in Rome, do as the Romans do." That does not sit well with us. This is federal property. Our husbands are doing work for the United States Government. Some of the other scientists are black or brown men. This ground we walk on does not belong to a backward southern state. To allow this to stand is an assault on the democracy our boys are fighting and dying for. We want change.'

'I just don't see how I could make a difference.'

'That is only because you haven't had time to think about it. We think you can, Miss Clark. We've heard stories about you. We are confident when you have time to absorb the information, you will know what you can do and you will do it.'

I was speechless. Just what had they heard?

'I won't take up any more of your time this evening. Just think about it. I'll check in with you again soon. Have a pleasant evening, Miss Clark,' she said as she rose and walked to the door.

I certainly had misjudged her. Before today, I couldn't
have suspected that any woman of her position would dare
visit the hutments and, even if one did, I would not have thought
she would be bothered enough to be determined to change the
living conditions. Maybe more women were like Eleanor
Roosevelt than I ever imagined. I knew she was right: the situation did need to be fixed but I felt overwhelmed. One more
problem up in the air. Another ball to juggle. One moment of
clumsiness and they would all crash down on my head.

SIXTEEN

I received the response from Aunt Dorothy at work on
Thursday. I would be joined by Ernie in Bedford. We'd
meet our aunt at the train station in Richmond on Tuesday
evening. We'd stay at a hotel that night and go to the women's
penitentiary in Goochland on Wednesday. Anxiety tightened
my chest. I breathed deep and pushed those thoughts away.
There would be plenty of time to worry about the meeting on
the train to Richmond.

I was already overwrought about the true confessions
moment I'd planned with Dennis. Teddy promised to let him
know that I wanted to talk to him after work today. As the
end of the shift approached, I ran alternative opening lines
through my head until I couldn't tell them apart.

Dennis stood outside talking to someone I didn't know when
I emerged. They wrapped up their conversation and the other
man left with a wave.

'Hi, Dennis,' I said and then my mind went blank. What
was I going to say?

'Hi, Libby. You wanted to see me?'

'Yes. About Saturday night . . .'

'You're not canceling, are you?'

Oh heavens! His face looked so sad. 'No. I mean not but . . .'

'Libby, if you don't want to spend time with me . . .'

'It's not that, Dennis. It's just, well, Teddy and I . . . well, since your visit and my agreement, Teddy and I have made a commitment to each other to not date others.'

'Oh . . .'

'But I told him about Saturday and how I needed to honor my word. So, if you still want to go out, I am willing. I'd like to spend time with you but I would only feel right if we went Dutch.'

Dennis let out a huge sigh. 'Well, I guess I should have acted sooner. I would like to spend time with you, too, Libby. But under the circumstances . . .'

'Sure. No problem. I didn't think you'd want to keep the date. Still friends?'

Dennis hung his head, took a deep breath and reached out a hand. 'Friends,' he said.

I grabbed his hand with both of mine. 'Definitely, Dennis.' When I released my grasp, he gave a feeble grin, turned and trudged up the sidewalk. I stood there for a few minutes feeling like a fathead.

In the lab, Friday and Saturday went by in a blur. I tried hard to focus on the work at hand but thoughts about how badly I'd treated Dennis kept invading and breaking my concentration. When I'd banished that topic for a while, worries about Tom and what we may or may not find on Sunday banged around in my skull. I was confused about my feelings – did I want to find him or not? Yes, it would be good to know what happened to him but if he was dead – if he committed suicide – I didn't want to find another body.

I agreed to have dinner with Teddy on Saturday but my distraction was a big obstacle to conversation. I pleaded a headache when we finished dining and he walked me home. I buried myself in *Dragon Seed* and escaped to a far-off land.

Before dawn, I'd gulped down two cups of coffee and filled G.G.'s food bowl to the brim. As I laced on my hiking boots, a knock on the door heralded the arrival of the whole group. They must have met up at the dormitories and walked over together. Our first stop was Dossett Tunnel.

The new growth of spring plants surrounding the entrance softened the harsh look of the area. The tangle of vines embracing the tunnel had sprouted new leaves but many were already charred by the heat of the coal smoke that blackened the rocks on the outside rim and all the interior surfaces. The mouth, however, still looked sinister and forbidding. Its darkness stretched on to a pinprick of light and reminded me of the tale of Jonah and the whale.

'To be sure he's not in there, we'll have to walk the whole length,' Dennis said.

'If a train comes, we could all die in there,' Gary said.

That guy was really a nuisance. In his eyes, there was always something wrong with everything. 'We can't very well go halfway in and call it a day,' I snapped.

'Could we divide up and half of us enter from the other end and meet in the middle?' Rudy suggested.

'As I understand it,' Teddy said, 'to get to the spot where the tunnel starts, you'd have to climb up a steep rock face. I doubt if we could do it without equipment.'

'I would guess,' Joe said, 'if I climbed up to the top of the tunnel exit here, I could see further up the tracks well before the beginning of the tunnel and be able to warn you to get out.'

'But how would we hear you when we're deep in the tunnel,' Dennis asked.

'I didn't exactly think of that but I came prepared for any emergency,' Joe said as he opened his knapsack.

I peered inside. It was chock full of cotton string and twine.

'First, I need to go up and see what kind of view I have,' Joe continued as he pulled out the balls to uncover small pulleys. 'Then, I can tie one end to someone's finger, run it through a couple of pulleys attached to trees so it doesn't get tangled. I see a train coming and all I'll have to do is tug.'

For a moment, we all stood around him with our mouths open but didn't utter a word. Then Dennis broke the silence. 'Joe, I am sure this idea looks remarkable on paper. I am certain Rube Goldberg would be proud. But honestly, it has too much potential for unforeseen error. I'm afraid if we relied

on this set-up, we would get lackadaisical or careless and if
something went wrong – splat! I think we'd have better chances
if we all went in with our flashlights blazing and our senses
on high alert.'

'I think Dennis is right,' Gregg said. 'I think you have a
good idea, Joe, but I don't think we could move forward with
it without a lot of testing to work out any problems. We'd be
here all day and I would like to cover more territory before
the sun sets.'

'I like Joe's idea better,' Gary said.

Of course he did. I bit my tongue.

Gregg took a vote and the decision was made but before
we could act on it, we heard a train coming. We moved out
of its path, covered our heads and I tried not to wince as
the cinders bounced off my arms.

'Perfect,' Dennis said. 'We should definitely have enough time
to make it down to the other end and back. But we need to move
fast.'

'I'll stay here and be the look-out,' Gary said.

'Yeah, Gary,' Dennis sneered. 'You do that.' He walked into
the tunnel grumbling about cowards.

This time, with everyone around me, the journey into the
darkness and coal stench seemed much quicker than my solo
walk into the gaping maw a couple of years earlier. Still,
I was getting very nervous by the time we reached the far end.
We found no sign of a body or even anything that appeared
to be blood, but honestly, the beams of our flashlights on the
dark soot of the ground and walls could not give us any
certainty of the latter. We turned around and half-ran, half-
walked back to the other side.

Just before we got there, Dennis shouted, 'Gary, quick! My
foot is stuck and I hear the train.'

Gary stood, with the light of the outdoors silhouetting his
shape, shuffled and stammered but didn't move forward an
inch.

Dennis walked out with no trouble and gave Gary a shove.
'A real friend in need, aren't you, Gary? Why did you even
come this morning?'

'I couldn't see in there. I didn't have a flashlight. I didn't . . .'

'We don't want to hear your gobbledygook, Gary. Just try to make yourself useful in the woods. Tom was supposedly your closest friend. Act like it.'

Gary opened his mouth to speak but Gregg, standing next to him, gave him the zip lips sign and Gary just sighed and trudged along with the pack. Hopefully, we wouldn't all be at each other's throats before the day was over.

SEVENTEEN

Rooted in the echoes of the past, discomfort was our constant companion as we searched the woods in the same pattern we'd implemented to find Marvin's body last year. When we reached the trail by the old hickory and saw the scout blaze mark faded but still present on its bark, we came to an abrupt halt. I don't know what was in the others' minds but imagined it was much like mine.

I dreaded going down that trail with all the strength of an embedded ancient superstition. That awful tree down that path and the gruesome image of Marvin's mutilated corpse was still seared on my retina. After a collective sigh, Gregg led the way with reluctance apparent in every hesitant step. I stopped the moment I knew that in another yard or two the tree would come into sight. I closed my eyes, inhaled deeply and then trudged on.

The scars on the trunk of the old tree stirred up bad memories but it didn't look any different from any other tree of its age. No former coworker hung from its limbs. Nothing but dried leaves at its base and branches reaching to the sky. No longer did the odor of death tear through our sinuses, but the smell of relief seemed to rise from all of us.

We backtracked to the original path with far more enthusiasm. Occasionally, someone shouted out Tom's name but our only response was the rustle of birds in the trees. It was even more difficult to spot the shack Frannie had used as a hideout at the time. The undergrowth had filled in making the trail barely passable.

The shack itself looked even more derelict. The vines that had covered one side now claimed the entire roof. The door once hanging from a single hinge was now propped up over the entry. Gregg and Teddy moved it out of the way and we peered inside.

The vines had worked their way through the wall and now streamed across the ceiling. In one corner, two blankets laid in a disheveled heap. They looked almost clean; they'd couldn't have been out here long. Who had taken shelter here? And did that person have anything to do with the disappearance of Tom.

'Could the person who is staying here have hurt Tom?' Dennis asked.

'I doubt it,' Joe said. 'Didn't we agree there was no reason for Tom to come out to the woods unless he planned to take his own life?'

Teddy grabbed a stick and poked at the blankets, then flipped them looking for anything that might identify the person who had left them there. Nothing was buried there except for a few crumbly brown leaves.

'I don't think there is anything to see here,' Dennis said. 'I think we've hit a dead end. If Tom planned on suicide, wouldn't it make sense to choose a spot that had some meaning for him – like right here or out at the tree? We could wander around here for days only to return and find Tom sitting at his lab station.'

'Why don't we just go back a different way and keep our eyes out. We probably won't discover anything but we can try,' Gregg suggested.

Five minutes later, Gregg's words seemed almost prophetic. Gary shouted, 'Hey! Hey!' and zoomed off the path and into a thicket. He returned clutching a rumpled hat in his scratched and bleeding hand. 'This is Tom's hat. I'm sure of it.' He held it out for inspection.

We all gathered round. To me, it appeared to be a very nondescript brown wool felt hat with a decorative ribbon and a battered brim – there had to be thousands just like it.

'What makes you think that it's Tom's hat? I've got one that's almost identical,' Rudy said.

'He wore it every time he went into town,' Gary said. 'When he returned to his room, he always brushed it before he put it up on the shelf in his closet. And look, it's got a leather sweatband inside and you can still see his initials.'

I had to squint to see what was scratched into the leather. But he was right. T.O. was etched into the interior band. 'Okay, so what in heaven's name is it doing out here?' I asked.

'He had to have been out here. He had to have been wearing it when he left the dormitory to go to the train station in Knoxville. He had to have come out here. He has to be here,' Gary insisted.

'Well, I don't know, Gary,' Joe said. 'He could have lost it on the way into town or once he was there. Some hobo could have picked it up and worn it out here before losing it.'

'We've got to keep searching. He's here. I'm sure of it,' Gary said, waving his arms in a dramatic fashion. 'I don't know why but this hat meant more to him than anything else he owned; he wouldn't have lost it. We just have to find him.'

I turned in a circle looking at the woods that seemed to stretch on forever. 'The army and police would search if we reported him missing – there's a lot more of them than us. Maybe it's time to file a report.'

'You know Tom wouldn't like that,' Gary objected.

'What else can we do, Gary?' Teddy said. 'This place is huge. We could search this wilderness every day for weeks, walk near him every day and still not find him.'

'Face it,' Joe said, 'he's either dead or he's in hiding and doesn't want to be found.'

'Why would he hide?' I asked.

Joe shrugged. 'He was really distressed about his dad. I imagine he felt guilty for being here and not at home. He could have just snapped under the stress.'

I no longer knew what to think. I wasn't even sure why we thought we might be able to find him out here. Unlike Marvin, he'd never been a boy scout and knew nothing about marking a trail. Because of that, did he come out here and get lost? Or did he get on the train and just keep riding? The last option sounded very appealing to me right now.

'I think my whole idea of coming out here to search wasn't a very good one at all,' I said.

'We all were with you on this, Libby. And I think we needed to do it,' Gregg said. 'I imagine that most of us were thinking about our last search in these woods. I had some vivid pictures going through my mind. We all had to know he wasn't tied to that tree. I know I couldn't have lived with myself if I hadn't checked it out.'

Heads nodded all around. It made me feel a bit better but it still felt like a wasted day. 'That leaves us with a decision to make. Do we report him missing? And what do I tell Charlie?'

'Charlie's going to want to report it,' Gregg said. 'He's wanted to do that from the beginning but agreed to give us a little time. When you tell him we found nothing but his hat, he's going to insist on it.'

'Unless Libby can convince him otherwise,' Joe said.

'Mondays are usually full steam ahead. I don't know if I can find time to talk to him or not. After that, you're going to have to manage on your own. I'm catching a train for Richmond Tuesday,' I said.

'Richmond? Whatever for?' Gregg asked.

I sighed. I really didn't want to get into this now. I didn't even know where to start.

'It's personal family stuff,' Teddy interjected. 'It's not a good time for her to talk about it.'

I gave Teddy's hand a quick squeeze and saw Dennis wince. Oh dear, what a problem I'd created.

'I'll talk to Charlie,' Gregg said. 'Maybe I can get him to hold off at least until you get back.'

'How will you convince him to do that?' I asked.

'I'll think of something,' Gregg said.

'Just be honest with him, Gregg,' I said. 'If you start making things up, you'll get all tangled up in the end.'

Worried that work-related concerns would leave me no time for anything personal on Monday, I enlisted a neighbor to make sure G.G. had food and water during my absence. She promised to play with him, too, as much as she could. Then, I packed my bag and set it by the door.

Sleep eluded me for quite a while. Where are you Tom O'Malley?

EIGHTEEN

As I suspected, Monday was chaotic. I had the regular urgency of not working on Sunday while the Calutron kept spinning around the clock. To complicate matters, Charlie spent most of the day in a series of meetings either here at Y-12 or down at the administrative building. He and I never had a chance to speak.

The next morning, the train ride from Knoxville to Bedford gave me more time than I wanted to think. I tried to enjoy the scenery – the trees were so green and the hills cluttered with wild flowers – but questions kept dashing through my mind. Who is pranking our lab? And why? Does Tom's disappearance have anything to do with those events? If so, what?

As soon as I pushed work out of my head, my mother's situation started haunting me. Can I tell her I forgive her? Do I even care that she's dying? I know I should but I don't feel it as intensely as I thought a normal daughter would. Will seeing her change that?

I banished thoughts of her and went straight to war worries. Was the war over in Italy now? Had the Red Army conquered Berlin or are they simply boasting? And the death camps? Oh, dear God in heaven, how could you allow them to exist at all? Those poor people looked like the walking dead with their vacant eyes, blank faces and stick-like limbs. How could humans do that to other humans? I couldn't do that to a dog that bit me.

The whole world seemed mad and I was contributing to the insanity with the work I was doing. Every day, it was less likely that the gadget would ever be used in Europe. Do the Japanese deserve that fate? At one time, after my cousin died at Pearl Harbor, I would have shouted an unqualified yes. But now, compared to the Third Reich, were the Japs really that bad? Do they have death camps like the Germans do? If so, why haven't we heard about them?

The clack of the train tracks drove my musings in a circle from work to mother to war and back to work again. It was such a relief when the train stopped in Bedford and I'd finally have company sitting in the seat beside me. My half-brother Ernie was just an ordinary kid who would probably drive me crazy by the time we were in Richmond. That's what kids do and the distraction from my endless loop of worries was more than welcome.

I looked out the window as we pulled up to the station. I spotted him right away standing next to Mrs Early. My, had he grown. He was almost as tall as her now. And he looked so handsome. He wore a navy-blue suit with a pinstriped shirt and a red tie. His golden-brown hair, combed to one side and slicked back on his head, reminded me of the pictures Mother had of my grandfather when he was young.

I waved out the window and Mrs Early spotted me first. She turned to Ernie and pointed. He jumped up and down and returned my wave. As soon as the conductor let down the steps, he bounded up them. Mrs Early followed him carrying his small valise.

'Howdy, Libby,' she said. 'He told me he wasn't a baby and didn't need me bringin' him on the train but if I hadn't, he'd be goin' without a change of clothes.'

'Thank you, Mrs Early.' I didn't know if she loved my brother but I could tell from her smile and the light in her eyes that she was very fond of him. I felt even more certain that I'd made the right choice allowing him to stay in Virginia with her family.

'How many times have I got to tell ya, Libby. You're a grown woman now, you should be calling me Justine. Well, I better mosey. The conductor's givin' the all aboard sign.' She kissed Ernie on the top of his head. He did the requisite boy squirm and then thought better of it and gave her a big hug. As soon as she stepped onto the platform, we started pulling away.

'I'm so excited, Libby,' Ernie said, bouncing in the seat.

'I can see that.'

'I get to take my first train ride. I get to see you. I get to
see Aunt Dorothy. And I get to see Mama. Is it true that she's
dying?'

'I haven't seen her, Ernie, but it sure sounds that way.'

'That's not right. It's just not right.'

'No, it isn't.'

'And she shouldn't be in prison. She was protecting me.
Mothers are supposed to protect their children. It's not right.'

'Ernie, it's not fair. Not at all. But when Mama did what
she did, she knew she would go to prison and that didn't matter
to her. You mattered. She knew the consequences and she did
it anyway.'

'She's a good mother,' Ernie said. He went on and on talking
about all the things she'd done for him. All the special times
they'd had together. I knew it contained some exaggeration
and sugar-coating of reality but I understood why and was
fine with it. Still, listening to him talk, it was hard for me to
believe we shared a mother. She'd never been there for me
and she'd never stood up for me. My Aunt Dorothy had rescued
me from a miserable, uneducated fate under my now deceased
stepfather's control.

I would say none of this to Ernie. Our mother was dying
and he'd finish growing up without her. He had a right to cling
to a glamorized version, if he wished. She may have failed
me, but in the end, she'd been there for him.

Ernie switched topics without notice. 'Everybody at the
school says the war is almost over and the Nazis are dead.
Does that mean you're coming back home soon?'

'You've heard about the war in the Pacific, haven't you?'

'Yes, but they'll quit when the Nazis do.'

'Not necessarily, Ernie. We may need to defeat them, too.
But I imagine that with all our energies focused there, we
should be able to wrap it up in not too much longer,' I said
as I made a wish that it were true.

'What about you? Are you coming home to live at the farm?'

'I don't really know what I will do after the war is over,
Ernie. I'm a scientist and I like my work. I just don't know
where that will take me. I wish I could answer your question
but, honestly, I don't know.'

'Are you going to get married? Are you going to have a family? And don't you think the farm is the best place to raise your kids?'

'Not every person gets married. And not everybody has children. I may do neither but right now, I don't know what the future holds for me.'

Ernie scowled and slumped into his seat. 'I thought when you're a grown-up, you can do whatever you want.'

'That would be nice, Ernie. Being a grown-up does mean that you have more choices, but it doesn't mean you always know which choice is best.'

'Oh. Can we go to the dining car?'

'Are you hungry?'

'A little. But really thirsty. But most of all, I just want to see it and I want to walk between the cars.'

He went up the aisle but when we reached the first vestibule between the cars, I realized the enormity of my responsibility. 'Wait, Ernie. Let me go first and do exactly what I do, OK?'

I went through the first door, telling him what I was doing every step of the way. He concentrated on following my example so intently, the tip of his tongue stuck out with the effort. I grabbed his hand to walk to the next door.

He shook his hand trying to break apart. 'I'm not a baby.'

'No,' I said, 'I am and I'm scared. Please.' Fortunately, he fell for my deception. We repeated our actions with Ernie getting more proficient and confident with each passage.

We reached the dining car and Ernie's mouth dropped open. For a while, he was speechless as we followed the uniformed waiter to our table. After taking a seat he said, 'This is like a real restaurant, just skinnier.'

'What did you expect to see, Ernie,' I said with a chuckle.

'I don't know but not this.'

'We're lucky to have a dining car on this train – not all of them do.'

'Why not?'

'A lot of the dining cars are feeding our soldiers right now.'

Ernie sighed. 'It seems like the war has been going on for all of my life.'

'Our nation hasn't been part of it as long as some other countries have. All over Europe, battles were being fought for years before Japan pushed us into the conflict.'

'Hitler and Hirohito should take Mama's place in prison. They deserve it more.'

'You're right, Ernie. Unfortunately, there's not much we can do to change Mama's situation.'

Half an hour after we returned to our seats, we pulled into Richmond with Ernie's face smashed against the glass hoping to get a glimpse of Aunt Dorothy. He waved and bounced in the seat when he caught sight of her.

Ernie fidgeted in the aisle while we waited for the conductor to open the door and put the steps down. He rushed straight to Aunt Dorothy and asked, 'Did you bring me a new book?'

'Ernie, greet your Aunt Dorothy properly, young man.'

He looked at me with put-upon eyes, turned back to her and said, 'Hello, Aunt Dorothy, how are you? Did you bring a book?'

Dorothy shrugged. 'At least he's interested in books. Yes, Ernie, I brought you a brand new one,' she said as she handed him *Stuart Little*.

'It's about a mouse? That's the cat's meow!'

'I'm glad you approve, Ernie,' Dorothy said.

'Ernie, what do you say?' I asked.

He wriggled and said, 'Well, she knows—'

'Ernie, be polite.'

'Thank you, Aunt Dorothy.'

At the hotel, Ernie and I shared a room. Because he was excited about seeing Mama and I was twisting in emotional turmoil, I didn't think either one of us would ever get to sleep. Sometime though, in the middle of our bed-to-bed conversation, we both drifted off. The last thing I remembered about our give-and-take was Ernie's question, 'Are you sad about visiting Mama?'

In the morning, I wondered if I had answered him before I fell asleep.

NINETEEN

The lobby of the Hotel John Marshall was in total chaos when we came down that morning. Rollicking laughter, exuberant kissing and a buzz of constant chatter. It was as if we had stepped into a New Year's Eve party at the stroke of midnight. I finally got a giggling woman to stand still for a moment to answer my question.

'Berlin surrendered! An unconditional surrender! They say Hitler is probably dead and we won the war!' She swooped off before I could find out anything further.

As we drove out to Goochland, people celebrated in the streets in every small town we passed. I wondered if the recent developments might cause any problems at the prison. Aunt Dorothy assured me that the visitation would not be a problem. A friend of a friend had contacted Supervisor Elizabeth Kates and arrangements had been made in advance. 'The supervisor knew where we were staying last night and promised to call if there was any reason for our plans to be disrupted.'

I was chilled by the sign at the entrance: The State Industrial Farm for Women. It conjured up images of sweating women pulling plows, glaze-eyed ladies mindlessly dropping one unidentifiable chunk of metal into another, robotic females standing in endless lines with numbers instead of names – all without the benefit of freedom of movement that we take for granted. Much to my surprise, though, there were no signs of fences or other obstructions around the property. The brick building that loomed ahead looked nicer than I expected. My aunt told me that was because it was relatively new. Inmates had occupied it for only six years. 'The building at the penitentiary that used to house women was a crumbling abomination.'

There were construction sites around the grounds as the facility expanded to accommodate the growing population of prisoners. Still, stepping inside was a depressing experience. The halls were dreary and the air smelled of body odor, mildew and dirty socks. We gathered around a table in a visitation room and Mama was brought in to meet us.

The shock of seeing her nearly knocked me out of the chair. Ernie whimpered at the sight of her. She had always been thin but now cancer had ravished her, diminishing her arms to twigs. She reminded me more of the prisoners found in the Nazi death camps than the woman I'd known. Her hair looked brittle and lacked any shine even though it appeared to be clean.

Her steps scraped across the concrete floor as she shuffled, barely picking up her feet as she moved. Her prison dress hung from her shoulders like a limp pillowcase. She gave us a haunted smile through watery, pain-filled eyes. When I hugged her, I felt nothing but bones and feared I would break her in two. But she held me tight and long. My aunt and I allowed Ernie to claim all of Mama's attention at first. He babbled away as freely and easily as if they were sitting together at the kitchen table. Every couple of minutes, he reached out to touch her as if he needed the physical contact to be sure she was real.

After a while, Aunt Dorothy asked Ernie to come with her to give me and Mama time to talk. He objected loudly but she quieted him with the reminder that he could return and see her for a bit longer after she and I finished.

Mama and I sat quietly for a moment before she reached her arms across the table, and much to my surprise, my hands stretched out and clasped hers. Awareness washed over me as I looked at her ravaged beauty and the dark circles of death smudging her eyes. The woman before me had never envisioned being anything but a wife and a mother. When my father and brother had died in the fire, it was as if her self-identity perished in the flames with them. No wonder she latched on to the first man who came along – not out of love or affection – but out of fear and a desire to step back into the past where she felt safe and loved. As weak and self-centered as she was, she'd made my father happy and then she'd sacrificed herself to save her son in the only way she knew how. I'd been far too hard on her.

'Mama, I've decided I can accept your apology. I want to accept it. None of us have any right to demand perfection from anyone. And I was doing that to you. Can you forgive me for taking so long?' I asked.

'Nothing to forgive, Libby. I was a very poor mother to you. I owe your aunt a huge debt of gratitude for rescuing you from our horrible home environment. If the situation were reversed, I don't know how I would react so I certainly can't criticize you for needing time. I am very grateful you came to see me. I wanted to see you before I die.'

'What does the prison medical staff say about your condition?' I asked.

'They're surprised I'm still alive. I feel God kept me alive for this moment – to see you and Ernie again. Your visit has given me so much peace.'

'I'm sorry it took so long for me to give you that.'

She reached up one hand and laid it on my cheek bringing back a rush of emotional memories, resurrecting the feelings I had for her back when my father was still alive. Tears filled my eyes and puddled down my face. 'It looks like the war is coming to an end,' she said. 'Do you know what you'll do when it's over?'

'No. I don't. I honestly think that what I am working on now will have useful peace-time applications and I'd like to be part of that. I don't know, though, if that work will continue where I am or if I'll need to follow it elsewhere.'

'Will you be all on your own or is there someone special in your life?'

I told her about Teddy and my mishmash of emotions about him and my future. She listened intently. When I finished, she said, 'Libby, trust your instincts. Learn from your fear but don't follow it. Marrying your father was the best decision I ever made, but when he died I was so frightened. I allowed fear to make all the choices and by doing so, I ruined part of your life as well as my own.'

I gave her a final hug and she whispered in my ear, 'I love you. I will always love you. And I am so very proud of you I could burst.'

* * *

I had been operating under the assumption that I would return to work on Thursday but when I mentioned it, Aunt Dorothy suggested I look at my return ticket. In a rush to get out of town, I'd neglected to notice that I was scheduled to catch a train on Saturday. I objected to staying that long, insisting I needed to get back to the lab.

Aunt Dorothy argued that although I could exchange the ticket, it would not be fair to her or Ernie. 'Today was your mother's day, tomorrow is Ernie's and Friday is for me. Your country has demanded a lot of you the last couple of years. The least it can do is allow you a small amount of family time.'

Aunt Dorothy's stern expression and Ernie's big, begging eyes convinced me to stay two more days in Richmond, despite the niggling feelings of guilt that were always close to the surface.

The next day's activities were ruled by Ernie's enthusiasms. On the top of his list was a ride on the trolley – he didn't care where, he just wanted to go. He also wanted to pick up a present for Mrs Early and go to a movie. The movie caused the biggest debate. We looked over the current listings provided by the front desk. Aunt Dorothy and I were united in our belief that *The Lost Weekend* and Hitchcock's *Spellbound* were inappropriate for his age.

I suggested, 'Why not the Agatha Christie movie?'

'*And Then There Were None*?' Aunt Dorothy asked.

'Yes,' I said with a nod.

'That's a mystery like the Hardy Boys, isn't it? I want to go to that one, please,' Ernie pleaded.

Aunt Dorothy pulled on my arm, moving me away from Ernie. She whispered, 'What's wrong with you, Libby? Do you realize how many people are murdered in that movie?'

'His mother committed murder, it's not is if this movie will rob him of his innocence,' I hissed back.

'But it could be traumatic for that very same reason.'

'I doubt it but if it makes you uneasy, I'm fine with that. I can see it later. What do you suggest?'

'*A Tree Grows in Brooklyn* – it's playing at the Loew's Theatre. You liked the book, didn't you? You'll like the movie, too.'

All day, Ernie's excitement was contagious. Both Aunt

Dorothy and I grinned at his antics on the trolley and his head-back, mouth-open expression as he stared at the elaborate embellishments on the exterior of the theatre.

On Friday, Aunt Dorothy called the shots. First stop was the Virginia Museum of Fine Arts – not exactly an exciting prospect for a young boy but Ernie was on his best behavior even when we dawdled in front of a favorite painting. Our final stop that day was Miller and Rhoads. Ernie fell in love with a gold cross with a pearl at the intersection of the two bars but didn't have enough money to buy the pendant. Aunt Dorothy and I made up the difference. He was so proud walking out of the store. 'I heard Mrs Early admiring the plain gold cross her neighbor got for her birthday. I could tell she really wanted one and this one's even prettier.'

'Is it Mrs Early's birthday?' I asked.

'No,' he said, shaking his head. 'But she told me I could call her Mom and I said I couldn't – at least not while my mom was still alive. I don't know if I hurt her feelings. I might have. I wanted to show her how much she mattered to me.'

Saturday morning, Ernie and I boarded the train traveling to Bedford and Oak Ridge. Ernie checked three times to make sure he had Mrs Early's necklace safely packed away and then he curled up and fell asleep, exhausted from the excitement of the past few days. I stared out at the scenery hearing my mother's final words repeating again and again. I'm not sure how the mother I once saw as a pathetic weakling had managed to fortify me with so much strength. I didn't know then how much I would need that over the next days.

TWENTY

I didn't expect to see anyone that evening except for Teddy but when we pulled in to the station, however, I spotted Teddy, Ruthie, Gregg, Dennis and Joe on the platform. I waved to them and they jumped up and down and wrapped each other in hugs. Did they think I was never coming back?

Instead of opening the door when the train stopped, the conductor stood at the front of the car and asked for everyone's attention. 'We have a problem on the tracks ahead. Repairs are needed. If this is not your final stop, you still must disembark and find a place to stay for the evening. We are hoping to resume the trip by morning. Be here by 8 a.m. and you'll be informed if there is a reason for any additional delay.'

Passengers threw questions at the conductor but he passed through to the next car without answering a single one. Disembarking was far more chaotic than I'd ever seen. Finally, I set foot on the platform and my friends bustled me inside the terminal.

When we came to a standstill in a circle, I asked, 'What is going on?'

'The Germans surrendered,' Dennis said.

'Yes. I'd heard. But that doesn't explain why you all are here.'

'We wanted to make sure you arrived safely,' Teddy said.

'We didn't know what we'd do if you didn't but we would have thought of something,' Gregg said.

I turned to Ruth. 'Simple question, Ruthie: why are you here?'

'We heard about a train wreck but we didn't know where. We knew it was close by but nothing more.'

'Actually,' Joe said, 'we do know a little more . . .'

'Joe, that's just a rumor. We don't know if it's true,' Dennis objected.

I shook my head. 'What is the rumor?'

'People died in the accident,' Joe said. We were worried about you.'

Spreading my arms wide open, I said, 'As you see, I am alive. And uninjured.'

'Did you see any sign of disruption on or near the tracks?' Dennis asked.

'Not a thing. Judging by the conductor's announcement that no one on the train would be traveling any further today, it must be on the tracks up ahead.'

'Then it must have been a train traveling eastward. Yours was the only westward-bound locomotive this evening,' Joe suggested.

'Could it have been the train carrying raw materials to us?' I asked.

As if it were a planned choreograph, our bodies all twisted outward, scanning the crowd. I saw no one who seemed to be paying any attention to our conversation. Still, I knew we shouldn't be talking about such things here in a public space.

We went to the parking lot where we worked out the best configuration for getting everyone into the car. Dennis, having the longest legs, was appointed the driver. I sat on the passenger's side on Teddy's lap. Ruth got into the middle of the back seat with Joe and Gregg crammed in on either side. I looked back and judged from the grin on her face that Ruth was enjoying the tight quarters.

On the drive back to Oak Ridge, we decided to fan out and talk to as many people as we could to dig up anything more about the train accident and then meet together at my flat-top on Sunday morning. My suggestion of 8 a.m. evoked a negative response until I said I'd have breakfast ready. After dropping the men off at the dorm, I stopped by the grocery store and loaded up on eggs, sausage and bread for the next day. Then I made door-to-door inquiries of all the nearby houses. No one in my neighborhood had any new information to offer that didn't sound like wild speculation. The most outrageous stories were that the train was coming from Washington D.C. loaded with senators and every one of them perished in the crash; that the train was filled with German P.O.Ws who were now spreading through the countryside committing acts of destruction; and that scores of injured men who had survived the fighting in Europe had been killed on their way home to their families. Not one of those tales had the ring of truth to it.

The next morning, over breakfast, my first concern was Tom but no one had heard from him or anything about his whereabouts. Then, we shared the rumors we had gathered about the accident on the tracks. The only universal fact that we had learned from neighbors and friends was not anything different from what we suspected the night before: there had been a train wreck and some people had died. Joe, Gregg and I were tasked with talking to Charlie the moment he arrived at work on Monday morning to find out if he knew anything more.

Everyone carried their dirty dishes into the kitchen. Gregg tuned in the news broadcast on the radio, hoping the wreck would be reported there. Teddy and I remained in the kitchen; Teddy washed, I dried. While we worked we listened to the latest news.

In the European Theater, Saturday's events filled the report with good news. The Czech resistance fighters had launched the Prague uprising while the Soviets moved in from the other direction with their Prague Offensive. The German troops in the Netherlands had officially surrendered and Denmark was set free from Nazi domination by the Allies.

The next story was bittersweet – the liberation of the Mauthausen concentration camp. Freedom for the enslaved prisoners was wonderful news but the nausea-inducing details of the conditions suffered by the men, women and children incarcerated there were revolting. Led by an armored car, a US Army team from the 41st Reconnaissance Squadron of the US 11th Armored Division had passed through the gates of the death camp and disarmed the Nazi police. All around them, the prisoners with emaciated faces and stick bodies cheered with as much energy as they could muster.

In the Pacific Theater, the news was discouraging. The Japs continued their successful kamikaze attacks around Okinawa. From Oregon were reports of the first enemy-inflicted casualties on the mainland: Pastor Archie Mitchell, his pregnant wife Elsie and five children had been playing with a large paper balloon in the woods. What appeared to be an innocent toy was actually a deadly weapon: a Japanese Fire Bomb. When it exploded, all their lives were lost.

Teddy and I joined the others in the living room where we exchanged worried glances with each other. My concerns were reflected in their faces, a collective dread of unforeseen consequences that could descend on the world at any time.

'It might be happening right now,' Dennis said.

'Then why are we still processing product for the gadget?'
Gregg asked.

'Simple,' Joe said, 'the military doesn't want anyone to
know the timing and they certainly do not trust any of us.'

All we could do now was work and wait.

TWENTY-ONE

In the morning, we all went to our respective workstations
waiting for Charlie to enter his office. When he did, we
converged on his doorway where he waved us all inside.

'Charlie,' I said, 'what is going on? Was there really a train
accident and what happened?'

Charlie looked from one of us to the other. 'Close the door.'

Gregg pushed it shut.

Charlie continued, 'I am not supposed to discuss any of
this . . .'

'The truth needs to get out, Charlie,' Gregg said. 'The rumors
are ranging from hysterical to preposterous.'

Charlie raised his hands. 'I said that I'm not supposed to
tell anyone. But if you'll agree to keep it within your group,
I will tell you what I know. But it's not much. The train was
serving double duty as troop transport and cargo shipment of
raw materials for our facility. As it approached the bridge, the
engine brakes screamed, alarming the men in the caboose.
When the train stopped with a jolt, the men in the back ran
to the front to discover that the engine hung sideways over
the abyss. The next couple of cars fell on their sides providing
some dead weight to hold the locomotive in place for the
moment but it was not stable.

'One man from the back of the train crawled on the sides
of the downed cars and yelled into the engine car but got no
response from the three men in there. The crew feared that the
weight of the engine would pull the whole train into the abyss.
They had two choices, they could try to evacuate the train, but
knew that at some point the loss of weight in the back cars

would cause it to cascade over the edge before everyone could escape – and when it fell, it could easily sweep many of those beside the locomotive into the abyss. No matter how they looked at it, lives would be lost. Since they did not know if the three men in the engine car were still alive, they opted to uncouple it from the train.

'The crew decided that to be absolutely safe they needed to sacrifice the first two cargo trains as well and uncoupled it there. They saved the troops and most of the cargo but if anyone remained alive up front, they would not have survived the fall. We still don't know if they died in the original crash or after the plummet down into the gorge.'

Possibilities ran higgledy-piggledy through my thoughts. 'What happened to the bridge? Do you think it was intentional? Was it an act of sabotage?'

'I have no idea, Libby.'

'Do you think we'll ever know?' Joe asked.

'You mean do I think whatever the truth is, the military will bury it?' Charlie asked.

'Yes.'

'It wouldn't surprise me.'

The rest of the morning, I startled at every small noise and jumped at every movement in my vicinity. I didn't know why the train accident had set me on edge like it did. Maybe it was a delayed emotional reaction to seeing my mother. Or perhaps, the surrender of Germany made me apprehensive about the reaction from Japan. At any rate, I was as jumpy as my kitty cat but I wasn't enjoying it the way he did.

When I went to the cafeteria for lunch, I saw two M.Ps leading Joe into a jeep and driving off towards the military area of the reservation. I rushed back inside and told Charlie.

'I'll call around and see what I can learn,' he said. 'I have that right since he is one of my scientists but that doesn't mean I'll get any answers. Go eat. I'll do the best I can.'

I spotted Gregg in the cafeteria and talked to him about Joe. 'I just don't understand. Do they think he had something to do with the accident on the bridge?'

'It could be something totally unrelated. It could be because of one of the pranks.'

'It's possible they think it's all connected.'

'But wouldn't that be bizarre?' Gregg said. 'People were killed on the tracks. No one was hurt here in the lab. How could they have anything to do with one another?'

'I wonder if Crenshaw picked up Joe, hoping he could be rattled easier than me. Maybe they think he would reveal the names of everyone in our group.'

'I don't think he would. But why in heaven's name does Crenshaw even care?'

'He hates not knowing. He thinks everyone should obey him. And it infuriates him when there is something being hidden. He expects to be omniscient and resents when he is not.'

'Are we sure that Crenshaw hasn't locked up Tom somewhere?'

My stomach twisted and my appetite fled. 'No. We can't be. We can't be sure of anything.'

I went straight to Charlie's office when I returned to the lab. He didn't have good news.

'I've been assured that no one picked up Joe,' he said.

'But I saw it with my own eyes.'

'I know. I believe you. But no one will admit it.'

'I think you need to report Tom as a missing person now. Who knows? He could be locked up somewhere, too.'

'I've irritated the military enough for one day. At the end of the day, I'll go down to the police station and see if I can get anywhere there. And, yes, I'll ask about Joe, too.' He pulled on his suit jacket and his felt hat. 'Wish me luck.'

Luck was his only hope. The authorities always appeared willing to hide the truth behind the veil of patriotic duty and the war effort.

I was in worse shape that afternoon than I had been in the morning. I broke a piece of glassware and dropped a sample on the way to the scale. I mumbled at myself as I prepared another one to weigh.

I walked out of the building with Gregg at day's end. We

froze and stared at the street. A line of jeeps filled with M.Ps sat parked with their engines running. Two uniformed men walked in our direction. 'I think we need to go back inside,' I said.

We turned and took a step. A voice boomed out, 'Abbott. Mr Abbott.'

Gregg turned around and so did I.

A sergeant stepped in front of him. 'Mr Gregg Abbott?'

'Yes.'

'I need you to come with me.'

'Why?'

'Because I've been ordered to pick you up.'

'Why?'

The sergeant stared at him and sneered, 'I didn't ask. Are you going to come with me voluntarily or do we need to take you by force? Either way works for me.'

Gregg took two steps forward and two soldiers bracketed him for the walk to their transportation.

'Where are you taking him?' I shouted.

Although all the civilians in front of Y-12 were staring at me, not one member of the military acknowledged my existence. I repeated my question but nothing changed. I ran after the sergeant and pounded on his back with my fist.

He spun around. 'I could take you in for that.'

'Fine. Do it.'

'Go home, little girl. This is none of your business.'

Now I wasn't just worried, I was seething. Before I could respond, though, commotion at the far end of the building drew my attention away. Dennis and Teddy were both being escorted to jeeps by military police.

I ran in that direction but before I could get there, the two vehicles took off. Teddy spotted me, smiled and waved. I turned to go back inside, intending to update Charlie but I saw him emerge from the building with an MP on either side. I sensed that Crenshaw was behind these arrests and could only blame myself for not finding a way to allay his suspicions.

I hurried up to Charlie and used both fists to pound on the man holding his right elbow. 'Lady, I don't know what you think you are doing but you'd better stop right now.'

'No! Let him go.'

'Libby,' Charlie said. 'Don't do this. I need you here. You need to keep the lab running. Stay here. Do your job. Please.'

The pleading look in his eyes hit me harder than his words. My hands dropped to my sides and I slumped in defeat. I felt so helpless and useless. Then I thought of Ruth and rushed to the dormitory to make sure she'd made it home from work.

TWENTY-TWO

I arrived at Ruth's room out of breath from my speedy walk from Y-12. I bent over with my hands on my knees to catch my breath before knocking. I was straightening up when the door flew open.

'Good heavens, Libby!' Izzie said. 'What is wrong?'

'Ruthie, is she here? Is she okay?'

'Sure she is. Come on in.'

'Libby, what has you in such a state? Were you worried about me?' Ruth asked.

Izzie put an arm around my waist and said, 'C'mon, let's get you over to the bed where you can sit down and finish catching your breath.'

They sat down on either side of me and tears welled up in my eyes. Their kindness melted my anger and exposed my underlying distress. I struggled to keep my voice steady as I described the events at the lab. 'And then, I thought about you, Ruthie. I was so scared that you'd been hauled off again. And it's all my fault. If you weren't my friend, Crenshaw wouldn't have bothered you.'

'Oh, pshaw! You don't know that. It could be he was fixin' to question anybody who just arrived here. If that's what he was doin', you had nothin' to do with it.'

'Maybe you shouldn't be seen with me for a while.'

'Izzie, what do you think?' Ruth asked. 'Has she snapped

her cap? I guess that means I'll have to be spendin' as much
time with her as possible now, doesn't it?'

'Sure enough, Ruthie,' Izzie replied. 'Maybe we should stay
with her in shifts so she's never alone.'

'Okay, okay,' I said. 'I get the message. But still I will
worry about you, Ruthie.'

'Not as much as I'll be frettin' about you,' Ruth said.

I declined their invitation to join them for dinner. I wanted to
confront Crenshaw and see what he would tell me. I hopped
on a bus to his neighborhood. This time, I went straight to his
front door.

'Miss Clark, what an unpleasant surprise,' Crenshaw said
by way of greeting.

'Where are they? Why were they picked up? What is
happening?'

'You think I know everything? You think I'm responsible
for everything?'

Crenshaw exhaled harshly. 'All right, who are you claiming
was picked up?'

'Not claiming,' I said trying to keep the anger out of my
voice, 'witnessing. I saw it with my own eyes. MPs grabbed
Joe Barksdale, Dennis Jance, Gregg Abbott, Teddy Burke and
Charlie Morton.'

'When was this?'

My jaw clenched tight making it difficult to speak. 'Barksdale
at lunch. The rest after work.'

'It sounds as if Barksdale must have told someone something
that pointed to the others.'

'I imagine you want me to believe that.'

'I assume all of these men are part of your little group of
malcontents.'

I knew he wanted me to erupt over that description but I
forced myself to present a calm façade. 'No, sir. Not all of
them.'

'Really? Interesting. Well, it's been nice chatting with you.
My wife is putting dinner on the table and I don't want it to
get cold and upset her,' he said as he turned back to step into
his home.

I grabbed his forearm and forced him to face me. As he did, he shook off my hand. 'I'd advise you to keep your hands off of me, Clark. You don't want to push me too far.' He spun around, entered his house and slammed the door in my face.

I lifted my fists to pound on his door but decided it was not a good idea. Next stop, the Military Police office. I doubted my luck there would be any better but I had to try.

I walked up to the front counter and said, 'I am here to see Joe Barksdale, Gregg Abbott, Charles Morton, Theodore Burke and Dennis Jance.'

'Why do you think they are here?'

'Because I saw MPs take them away.'

He turned and rustled through papers on his desk. 'Sorry, ma'am, I can neither confirm or deny that allegation.'

'Don't you keep records of the people the MPs pick up? Or are they just allowed to go out and round up anyone they want on a whim?'

His expression turned thunderous. 'We do nothing on a whim. I suggest you move along.'

'I need to know where my co-workers are.'

'I need you to leave. Now.' He reached under the lip of the counter and in moments four MPs marched into the front office and stood shoulder-to-shoulder at attention behind him.

'Now, ma'am.'

I have never come so close to spouting a string of street profanity in my life. I stared at them while I mustered up as much dignity as I could, then turned and left the building.

What now, I wondered as I walked back to my flat-top. I could try to contact General Graves although I had serious doubts that he would interfere. By now, he probably doesn't remember my name. Perhaps in the morning, they would all be back at their stations with little harm done. I didn't really believe that but it was the best hope I had. I clung to it as tightly as if it were a solitary piece of wreckage in a storm-tossed sea.

TWENTY-THREE

My disappointment was palpable when I arrived at the lab and the lights were still off. Charlie was usually here by this time. At my station, I looked up whenever I heard footsteps. Each time, my hopes rose only to be dashed when it wasn't Charlie, Joe or Gregg in the doorway.

I felt powerless to do anything about the missing men. However, I knew I could keep the lab running smoothly in Charlie's absence. I entered his office to check on the inbox. First, I tackled the purchase order requests. I signed three and delivered them to the appropriate individuals. Then I approved two more that needed to go to the administrative building via the interoffice mail. One remained that I had doubts Charlie would approve. I set it aside.

He had numerous memos stacked in a pile. I reviewed and divided them into groups based on their urgency. I set most of them aside but two required immediate attention. One of those needed data I'd collected at Charlie's request. I retrieved the documentation from my station.

When I returned to Charlie's office, the phone was ringing. I lifted the receiver. 'Good morning, Charlie Morton's office.'

'Could I speak to Mr Morton, please?'

'He's not in the office at the moment.'

'Where is he? When will he be back?'

Oh dear. Is this someone who could help me? Or is this a trick? 'I'm sorry. I do not have that information.'

'Don't have it or don't want to tell me?'

'I do not know where he is or when he will return.'

'Who is this?'

I bit off the urge to turn his question back on him. 'Libby Clark, sir.'

'Miss Clark, Charlie speaks very highly of you. I find it hard to believe he didn't inform you where he was going or when he expected to return.'

'His departure was unusual,' I said.

'Let me be frank, Miss Clark. My name is Dr Barrett. There is a rumor floating around that he was picked up yesterday evening by the Military Police. I want to find out if there is any truth to that.'

After a momentary pause to consider my options, I decided to answer his question. 'It is the absolute truth. I saw the MPs escorting him away. They also picked up three other scientists – two from our lab and two from Alpha.'

'When was this?'

'One chemist at lunchtime. Two as they exited the building. They went inside to retrieve Charlie.'

'I don't know why the White House doesn't understand that scientists and the military are a volatile combination. This is ridiculous. Is this a result of the train incident?'

'I don't know. I don't have any details about what happened in the train accident.'

'It wasn't an accident.'

'It wasn't? Are you saying it was sabotage?'

'When are you breaking for lunch?' he asked.

I looked at my watch. 'I can be ready to leave in an hour.'

'Good. I'll park out front and wait for you. I'll stand beside the car holding a teddy bear to make identification easy.'

'A teddy bear?'

'Yes,' he said with a chuckle. 'My daughter left it in the car the other day, I might as well put it to good use. See you in an hour.'

The call was over so quickly that I didn't realize he'd left my question unanswered until I set down the receiver. Does he think sabotage was involved? Does he know it? Is he responsible? Or did Dr Barrett just lay a trap for me that he is about to slam shut?

I stepped out of the office and into the lab. Other than me, the only member of our group remaining at work today was Stephen. 'Stephen, can you break for a minute?'

'Just a second,' he said and walked across the room.

I led him into the office and shut the door. I explained about our missing members and Charlie as well as the phone call from Dr Barrett and my concerns about my meeting with him.

'So, if I am not here tomorrow morning, I need you to talk to Gary and Rudy.'

'Maybe this lunch is just that – lunch.'

'Maybe so, Stephen. I just want to be sure in case it's not.'

'You're probably making a mountain out of a molehill. But, yeah, I'll do that. Nobody knows where they all are?'

'I'm sure someone does but they're not telling me. Maybe Dr Barrett can get some answers. I also plan to go talk to Mrs Morton – maybe she's been told something.'

'Sometimes this place is scarier than a Lon Chaney movie,' said Stephen. He walked back to his lab bench, shaking his head.

I left the lab with hope in my heart and fear in my craw. I prayed Dr Barrett had only the best intentions.

TWENTY-FOUR

Dr Barrett was easy to spot. He really didn't need the teddy bear. He was standing next to a teal-colored Plymouth – not the kind of car you'd see around that often. From the small patch of gray at his temples to his impeccable posture, he radiated the stereotypical good looks of an urbane professor whose female students wanted to swoon when he entered the classroom. He opened the car door for me and we were off. He didn't speak about our telephone conversation until we were past the gates.

'Miss Clark, you asked about the train incident. Let me tell you what I know, but whatever you do, do not reveal me as your source. Can you do that?'

'Certainly, Dr Barrett.'

'It was not an accident. Someone damaged a section of the bridge. It wasn't a particularly big explosion as those things go, but the end results could have been worse if the train had approached from the other direction. As it was, the engine compartment went over the edge and killed three crew members. Everyone is still surprised that the rest of the train didn't follow. The oddest complexity was the posted signs along the tracks.

'Someone created handmade signs warning that the bridge was out – six of them leading up to the bridge on both sides. Right now, they don't know if the sign maker and the demolisher are the same person or persons or if one person was trying to defuse the situation.'

'Either way, it doesn't make a lot of sense. If a person wanted to cause an accident, why would he leave a warning? If it were a different person who made the signs, why wouldn't he contact the authorities?'

'Exactly. It isn't at all logical. If a scientist were responsible, you'd expect a more rational plan. However, I think the military suspects your fellow chemists of involvement and that's why they were picked up.'

'Was there something on the train of importance?'

'Yes. More raw material for the work at hand. They are determined to find out if the culprit knew that shipment was coming in at that time or if the coincidence was unrelated. That could be the question that they hoped to get answered by your co-workers.'

'But, I have no idea when a shipment is due to arrive. I only know when the refined material is going out. I really don't know how anyone in my lab would have that information.'

'As a manager, I suspect Charlie would know the shipment schedule.'

'Can you sit there and tell me that you think Charlie is capable of blowing up a bridge?'

'No, Miss Clark. Not the Charlie I know. But the military operates from an entirely different viewpoint than you or me. And we don't know if that's what they suspect or if they think he wittingly or unwittingly divulged that information to another party. If he did, I doubt you'll see Charlie again.'

'Charlie is not careless with information,' I said.

'I've never known him to be. Still, he was involved in your last escapade and was shot in the process.'

I bristled at his characterization. 'It wasn't an escapade. It was a mission in the service of our country.'

'Don't lash out at me, Miss Clark. I am only telling you how it is perceived by Crenshaw and the top management in administration. I understand, though, that you possess some information that they want. They could have rounded those men up to bypass you and find it elsewhere. What is it that you know?'

I folded my hands in my lap and stared down at them.

'Miss Clark?'

'You are better at making me feel guilty than my mother has ever been.'

'You think that's what I'm doing here?'

I kept staring at my hands.

'I want to help you – well, I don't really know you. It's not you – it's Charlie. I want to help him. I don't want him disappearing into some military installation somewhere for the duration of the war whether it's a month away or years away,' Barrett said.

'Dr Barrett, I am not free to answer your questions.'

'Are you doubting my motives?'

I closed my eyes. Then, I turned and faced him. 'Yes, sir, I do.'

Barrett sighed. 'We're just a block from the restaurant. Let's go have some lunch and continue this conversation on the way back.'

I sat across the table from him and contemplated using the powder room excuse to bolt out of the place and catch a bus back home. After the waitress took our orders, though, Dr Barrett launched into funny anecdotes about his daughter and the culture shock his wife experienced upon arriving in Oak Ridge. He was an excellent storyteller and proved to be very entertaining company. Still, I dreaded the ride back.

When we pulled out of the parking space, Dr Barrett said, 'I understand why you are not inclined to trust me but, honestly, I want to help.'

Why is it when people use the word 'honestly' I tend to doubt their credibility? Same for those who say 'believe me.' Both set my teeth on edge and make me doubt every word I hear. Dr Barrett was no exception. I start with accepting a person's words at face value but when they feel the need to qualify statements that way, I always have doubts. 'I need all the help I can get, Dr Barrett, but I've learned the hard way to be skeptical.'

'It's not surprising when you see your supervisor and co-workers taken away but . . .'

'Listen. I have asked multiple sources for the location of all those men but everywhere I go, I get denials. If you can find out who ordered them to be picked up and where they are right now, it would go a long way to allowing me to lower my skepticism.'

'I'll see what I can do,' he said, then switched the conversation to a discussion of the progress of the war.

After we entered the gates, I said, 'Could you drop me off at Charlie's home? I want to talk to Mrs Morton.'

'I'm not certain that is a good idea.'

'Well, I am and if you won't drop me off there, I'll still be going. I don't know if she's been informed about Charlie's whereabouts or not. If she has been, maybe she'll tell me. If she hasn't, she's probably worried sick about him staying out all night.'

A few minutes later, he pulled up outside of the Morton's cemesto house. 'Good luck, Miss Clark. If I can find anything out, I will let you know.'

'Thanks, Dr Barrett, and thank you for the lunch.' I walked up to the front door and it popped open before I could knock.

'Hello, Mrs Mor—'

'Libby Clark, right?'

'Yes, ma'am. I—'

'Where is Charlie?'

'I—'

'He never came home last night. Have you been working overnight?'

'I was hoping you'd know where I could find him.'

'Oh, dear. Come in. Come in. Follow me to the kitchen. I'll make some coffee. You don't know where he is?'

'No, ma'am.'

'He just disappeared?' she asked as she scooped coffee into the percolator on the stove.

'Not exactly.'

'What do you mean by that?'

I explained what I saw the day before as the worry wrinkles etched deep into her face.

'You haven't seen him since?'

'No, ma'am. Not Charlie. Not any of them.'

'Have you made inquiries?'

'Yes, I have. Everyone denies any knowledge of what happened.'

She poured two cups and set them down on the kitchen table with two teaspoons, the creamer and the sugar bowl.

As we stirred our coffee, I asked, 'Do you know Dr Barrett?'

'Rodney Barrett? Yes. Charlie and Rodney were in undergraduate school together. After Rodney got his doctorate, they renewed their relationship when they started working together. As a result, we were friends with Rodney and his wife Christina. Why do you ask?'

'He asked me to lunch today. He wanted to know if the rumors were true about Charlie being picked up. He said he wanted to help.'

'Really? Humpf,' she said with a sneer on her face.

'You doubt his intentions?'

'I probably should say nothing. Charlie likes him. He says my judgment of Rodney is too harsh.'

'But?'

'I just don't trust him. He told Charlie that he'd help him get a paper published. It was published all right but with Rodney's name on it. He claimed it was a secretarial error. I heard rumors about him taking advantage of others. I don't think he ever helps anyone unless he thinks there is something in it for him.'

'Interesting. He made me a bit uneasy, too.'

'Stay that way. Maybe I'm wrong but there's something about him . . .' she said staring into her empty coffee cup. 'Do you want another?'

'No, I'd better get back to work.'

'I'll go up to the administration offices this afternoon and demand an answer about Charlie's whereabouts.'

'I hope you get one.'

'You think they'll stonewall me?'

'They might. But it is worth a try. Would you let me know if you learn anything?'

'Of course. Come see me when you get off work. And stay for dinner. If I don't get an answer, I'll want to talk to you about what to do next.'

TWENTY-FIVE

As I entered the building the next morning, a flutter of hope beat against my ribcage. But, sadly, not one of the missing were back in the lab.

I checked for any new arrivals in Charlie's inbox. There were a few items but nothing that was urgent or pressing. I leaned back in the chair pondering whether I should take a chance that I would be remembered and contact General Groves. Before I could decide, Stephen rapped on the door-frame and walked into the room.

'You need to gather everyone together and tell them what is going on,' he said.

'But I don't know what is going on, Stephen.'

'Then tell them that. They need someone to acknowledge the upheaval in the lab and to know that someone is doing something more than sweeping it all under the rug. A couple of chemists think we're being shut down.'

'Okay,' I said with a sigh. 'Gather them up and I'll fully explain my ignorance.'

'Libby, please.'

'Don't worry, Stephen. Short of lying, I'll do everything I can to calm their anxieties.'

Within two minutes the staff had crammed into the space making it feel claustrophobic. 'I don't know much yet but I will tell you what I do know. As most of you are aware, Charlie, Gregg and Joe from our lab and Teddy and Dennis from Alpha lab were picked up yesterday by the military police. At this moment, I do not know why or who ordered it. I have spoken to Lieutenant Colonel Crenshaw and the

military police and they deny any knowledge. I am certain
someone – or everyone – is lying. Because of the timing, I
feel confident that it is connected to the incident out at the
bridge. I have no proof of that but I will not stop seeking
answers until our supervisor and our co-workers return.'

The questions rolled by like a river: 'Are we being shut
down?' 'Will all of us be sent home?' 'Are you sure they are
still here in Oak Ridge?' 'Will the MPs come for us next?'

'I do not think they are closing us down. I doubt if the
people in this room are scheduled to be sent home since none
of you were picked up yesterday. I don't know if that will
change. And, no, I am not sure if our co-workers are here in
Oak Ridge but I think they are.'

'Is that what happened to Tom – did they pick him up
first?'

'That's a possibility. I just don't know. But I will tell you
when I know more.'

'What can we do to help?'

'For now, please, just get back to work – and work harder
than before. We all need to apply ourselves to fill in the staffing
gaps. Thank you and feel free to come to me with any private
concerns you may have.'

I cleared out Charlie's inbox and went to my workstation.
It seemed as if everyone took my last words seriously because
no one even looked up as I moved through the room. All
assignments and samples given to Gregg and Joe yesterday
no longer sat in impotent piles by their areas. The other
chemists had picked up the slack. I imagined all of us would
be working late tonight.

When I finally left for the day, I spotted Gary pacing the
walkway running by Y-12. He perked up with my arrival and
rushed to my side. 'I think I saw Tom this morning.'

'Really? Where?'

'I got up early and went for a walk. I was going past the
chapel when I spotted a thatch of red hair walking away
from me. From the back, he looked like Tom. I called out
to him and he started running. I tried to catch up but I lost
him. For the life of me, I don't know how. It was as if he
disappeared.'

'Is this the first time something like this has happened?'

'Yeah. I've had other times I thought I saw him, but it always turned out to be someone else.'

'Maybe it wasn't Tom . . .'

'Well, why did he run when I hollered? That was when I was sure it was him.'

'You may be right. He has to be somewhere, why not here? Let me know if you see him again.' I tried hard to put myself in Tom's shoes – to imagine that I was filled with grief and anger – and then figure out what I might do if I were that overwrought. But imagining that and living it were two different things. I could not conceive of any reason for Tom to miss his father's funeral and not return to work without informing someone. Maybe that was because there was no logical reason. Perhaps Tom had had a nervous breakdown. I never knew anyone who experienced that and I didn't really know if it was a realistic notion. Maybe Tom simply needed to be alone. I did not know him well enough – and I didn't think anyone here did – to determine if this possibility was likely.

I needed to get the remnants of our group together and try to hash it all out between us. But right now, I needed food and sleep more than anything else.

I trudged up the steps to my flat-top. My feet felt like grounded anchors tangled in sunken debris. It was an effort to get to the door. Before I opened it, I saw a folded piece of paper partially pushed across the threshold. I picked it up and carried it inside.

G.G. demanded my immediate attention and I knew from experience, he would not relent until I filled his food bowl. I dropped the paper on the table, took care of the cat and put on a kettle for tea. Then I unfolded the paper and read: 'I need to talk to you but I'm afraid. I made a big mistake and I don't think I can ever make it right. Tom.'

I stepped out on the landing and looked all around my home. I walked the perimeter, looking for any sign that Tom was nearby. I saw no one moving and few houses with lights still lit. Back inside, I wrote on his note: 'Yes. When and where? I will come alone.' I grabbed an empty canning jar and set the paper with the container on top of the front porch. I could only hope he would return and find it.

Where are you Tom O'Malley and just what are you thinking?

TWENTY-SIX

The next morning, I checked the stair landing. The jar was still there but the note was missing. I hoped Tom had picked it up but wondered why he hadn't left a response. One of the problems with living in a world where secrets were a way of life was that you were never sure if what you thought was true, really was. On the way to work, suspicion took hold. Was the note really from Tom? Or was someone trying to trick me or use me for an unknown purpose?

I tried not to question everything and everyone I encountered but I only had to listen to myself using code words for uranium and calling the end result of the project 'the gadget' and know that even I could no longer be trusted to be straightforward about anything – a dismaying development that I hoped was not a permanent erosion of my character.

Walking into the lab, I once again hoped to see at least one of the missing men. As unlikely as that possibility was, the sense of disappointment I felt was keen. I knew the morale in the lab now rested solely on my shoulders. I did my best to hide my anxiety and impending sense of doom. Everyone asked if I knew anything more than I did the day before. I didn't dare mention the note at my door. I shook my head and said, 'No.'

The internal mail from administration and other managers mingled with piles of equipment catalogs on Charlie's desk. I sorted through it all, answering whatever I could and placed the remainder in Charlie's inbox. Then, I matched requisition requests with materials available in the catalogs and placed the orders.

Finally, I got going at my workstation. The men still took

yesterday's charge to work harder seriously. They accomplished far more than I thought possible. I had a mountain of samples and reports to verify and confirm. When I got to the bottom of the stack, I realized I'd worked through lunch. I stood and stretched, becoming aware of how hungry I was. I looked down at the table and saw a sandwich wrapped in wax paper. It was like manna from heaven.

I grabbed it, held it in the air and asked, 'Who does this belong to?'

'It's all yours, Libby,' Stephen said. 'We brought it back from the cafeteria for you. I hope you like egg salad.'

'Love it! Thank you, Stephen.' I looked around the room and everyone was grinning. 'Thank you, everyone.' Any doubts about my ability to manage a lab dissolved. The group was working together and looking out for each other. Now, if we could only bring the missing back. It was time for another visit to Crenshaw.

Leaving work, I went straight to Crenshaw's home. His teenage son answered my knock and he seemed to have outgrown his perpetual surliness. He invited me inside and offered me a seat in the living room like I was a long-lost family friend.

Mrs Crenshaw entered the room wearing a frilly apron. 'The lieutenant colonel will be here shortly – he's making sure the yard boy is doing everything right. Would you like a cup of coffee while you wait?'

'No, thank you, ma'am.'

'Would you like to stay for supper?'

I really didn't want to sit at the same table with Crenshaw and I'm sure he felt the same way about me. 'No, thank you. I am supposed to meet someone for dinner tonight after I talk to your husband.'

'If you change your mind, let me know. We have plenty of fried chicken and all I'll have to do is set an extra place.'

At the mention of fried chicken, my mouth watered, tempting my resolve to waver. I swallowed down my primitive urges and said, 'Thank you, ma'am.'

She bustled back into the kitchen where I could hear her

whispering and a gruffer voice responding. Moments later, Crenshaw appeared. 'What now, Miss Clark?'

'As I am sure you are aware, my lab is still missing its supervisor and some of the other chemists we need to do our work for the war effort. We are working as hard as we can but it is a struggle to keep our heads above water without their help.'

'I know it is,' he said with a sigh as he slumped down into a chair adjacent to me.

'Then why have you not let them go?'

'It's out of my hands.'

I stood up and looked down at him. 'Sir, this whole place is under your control so that is not possible.'

'Sit down, Clark. I'm not as omnipotent as you think.'

'I find that hard to believe, sir,' I said as I settled back into the sofa, ready to leap up again.

'My plan was simple. Keep them overnight and try to scare some information out of them – like the names of your band of troublemakers or some information they might be hiding about the recent incidents.'

'Why them? And why aren't they back? Are they still here behind the fence?'

'I think so but I don't know.'

'You think so?' I said, reflexively bouncing to my feet again.

'As I said, they are in someone else's hands now. Please sit back down and don't raise your voice – you'll upset my wife.'

'Sit down? Really? I will lower my voice for the sake of your family but please don't assume that my fury is abated. These men who you've snatched up and carried off are the same ones who helped you identify a murderer and bust a spy ring. And you are just letting them be deprived of liberty? Where is your honor, sir?'

'I think you had far more to do with those past situations than anyone else . . .'

'But—'

He raised a hand. 'I know. I know. You're going to say you couldn't have done it without them. Spare me the theatrics and modesty. And please, for heaven's sake, sit.'

I slowly eased back down but kept my eyes on his face. I wanted to pummel him with my fists but, unfortunately, my upbringing stood in my way.

'I am willing to explain the sequence of events if you will keep your voice down, your emotions under control and relax for a minute.'

I nodded my head and swallowed hard. I knew I couldn't be relaxed but I was determined to fake it for the moment.

'I was not alone when I questioned your co-workers. There was an agent in the room with me. He didn't speak but leaned against the wall in the back of the room.'

'An agent? What agency?'

'I do not know which one but I suspect it's one of those nameless groups that have sprung up during this war. May I continue?'

I nodded again wondering how much patience I could muster.

'When I spoke to your supervisor Charles Morton, I first gave him a piece of paper and asked him to write down the names of all the people who were assigned to his lab. I picked it up when he finished. The agent walked up behind me and read it over my shoulder. I then went down the list one by one asking him if each person I named was in the lab that afternoon.

'I asked him about Joseph Barksdale and he said that he had never returned from lunch. We knew that, of course, since that's when we picked him up. There were no surprises until I inquired about Thomas O'Malley. It was at this point that he blinked his eyes a few times, looked down at the table and said, "No."

'I asked, "Do you know why he was absent?" and he said that Tom went to his father's funeral. When I asked when he was due back, he said, "Monday." I sensed something odd about his demeanor and asked, "Which Monday?" He sighed deeply and looked away. I pushed him for an answer and he said, "Last."

'I said, "Last Monday?" and he nodded. After that exchange the agent took custody of the whole group. He intends to keep them all until one of them reveals Thomas

O'Malley's location. I suspect the only way I could have any influence on their release would be if you would tell me where he is.'

'I don't know. They don't know. None of us know. We've been trying to figure it out. We called his aunt. We can't find him. You can't hold onto them for information they do not possess.'

'Has anyone heard from him?'

I leveled my chin, widened my eyes and stared directly into his. 'No, sir. No one has heard from him.' The image of the note on my porch burned at the back of my retinas. I struggled to keep any emotion off my face and maintain steady breathing.

Crenshaw was the first to look away. He pondered the floor while he shook his head. When he looked up, he folded his arms on his knees and leaned forward in the chair. 'I need total honesty from you if I am going to interfere. Swear to me that not one of those men knows the whereabouts of Thomas O'Malley.'

I gazed into his eyes, raised my right hand and said, 'I swear on my father's memory that none of those men knows anything about the whereabouts of Thomas O'Malley.' At least that wasn't a lie.

For a moment, Crenshaw's eyes roved my face, studying my expression, then he leaned back and steepled his hands. 'First thing in the morning, I'll see what I can do.'

'Why not now?'

'Don't try my patience or make me reconsider, Miss Clark. Now, if you don't mind, my wife has supper waiting and I want to join my family at the table.'

We both stood and he said, 'I can't make any promises. But I will try.'

'Thank you, sir,' I replied. I wasn't completely sure he would keep his word but it was time to let it all go and hope for the best.

TWENTY-SEVEN

I opened my door on Friday morning, ready to go to work when I spotted a curled-up piece of paper inside the once empty Mason jar. I snatched it off the porch and went back inside. Pouring another cup of coffee that was still warm, I sat on the sofa, pulled out the note and read it.

'Meet me at the shack tonight at 9 p.m. Tom. P.S. You may bring one person who will wait outside. ANYTHING else and I will be gone.'

I stared at the paper looking for answers to the questions galloping through my head. What has Tom done? What does he fear? What if the note was not from Tom but merely a trick? Who would do that? The person who had abducted Tom? That could be anyone. Another spy. Crenshaw. Someone in the administration. A bitter local. A criminal. Who? The note gave no hint of answers. Still, I could not ignore it. I had to take the risk. If Tom was in trouble, I had to respond.

I walked to work with the weight of worry making each step a chore. Turning off my street to the main road, I heard running footsteps pounding the walk behind me. I broke into a run for a few steps and then thought better of it. I needed to know who it was before I tried to retreat. I hid behind shrubbery until I heard the person race past my hiding place. I stood and saw Ruth's back moving away from me. 'Ruthie?'

She spun around and shouted, 'Libby!'

She backtracked and ducked behind the bushes. 'This man . . . I thought . . . he was . . .' she said, gasping for air.

'Catch your breath first, Ruthie.'

She bent forward and leaned her palms on her knees, breathing deeply. 'Okay. Got it. This man asked me out to dinner and to the dance last night.'

'That's nice,' I said wondering why she felt it was important.

'That's what I thought. He was handsome and acted like a gentleman. I was beginnin' to like him a lot. By the time dinner was over, I knew I wanted him to ask me out again. We were havin' a great time at the dance – he even spiked our punch with a flask he had in his pocket. When "Sentimental Journey" started playin', he swooped me into his arms and I just about swooned.

'That's when he whispered in my ear, "I like you a lot, Ruthie." I smiled and I said nothin' but I tingled all over. He whispered again, "I have to warn you, Ruthie. You need to stop seein' that lady scientist Libby Clark. She'll get you into a heap of trouble." Well, right then, I wanted to slap him in the face. But I thought, maybe he'll explain why so I can tell you. So I stopped, right there on the dance floor, and said, "Why?" He looked all around the room and said, "Let's take this conversation outside."

'I gotta tell ya, Libby, after he done said what he said, I was afraid to go out there with him. But I did it. I just made sure we stayed close to the buildin' and in the light from the windows. Then he told me that he knew that you and your scientist friends were behind the derailin' of the train. He said he believed that you were the ringleader. He said that one of the scientists told them that it was your plan to keep the raw material from getting to the reservation. He said you made sure you were out of town when it happened. That's not true, is it, Libby?'

'No. I had nothing to do with it. Maybe someone said that but it isn't true. I don't know what he's talking about. Did he say anything else?'

'He asked me a bunch of questions about you. He asked who was in your group of scientist friends and I said I don't know. I did know some of your friends in the lab but I ain't about to tell him. He wanted to know what you told me about the pranks in the lab and the train accident. I said "Nothin'," and that was the truth. Then he said that you were in a heap of trouble and if I saw you again, I'd be arrested, too. He said maybe I was only an accomplice after the fact but I still could be charged with aidin' or abettin' or obstruction or somethin' like that. He said that I better come clean or I'd be in the cell next to you. He scared me but I just told him that he was wrong – as wrong as he could be. I said Libby Clark is a patriotic American doin' her bit to help the war effort and he was all wet.'

'Thank you for standing up for me, Ruthie,' I said, smiling at my friend. 'But don't worry about him. He's just trying to frighten you. He was trying to trick you into saying something that they could use against me.'

'They asked about some guy named Tom. I told him I've known lots of Toms in my life and I don't know who he is talking about. Do you?'

'Yes, Ruthie. Tom works in my lab – or I guess I should say that he used to work in my lab – we haven't seen him since he left here to go to his father's funeral nearly two weeks ago.'

'Well, somebody loses their daddy needs some time.'

I didn't contradict her or tell her about my planned rendezvous with Tom. If she were picked up again, that know-ledge could only make her life more difficult. I changed the subject. 'Did you ever get back to the dance floor?'

'Yup. After I slapped him but I didn't dance with him again.'

'Why did you slap him?'

'Libby, he told me you were an evil force aligned with the Axis powers. He said that you duped me and were settin' me up to take a fall. He said you didn't care for me and were just usin' me. So, of course I slapped him.'

'What did he do?'

'He stood against the wall watching me with other men for a while, then he was gone. Good riddance to him.'

'Thank you, Ruthie. I am so sorry I put you through all of this. Maybe I should stay away from you for a while.'

'Don't you dare,' she said with a grin and slipped her arm into mine as we walked off to Y-12 together.

TWENTY-EIGHT

I hurried to wrap my work up as the lunch hour approached. I rushed outside and waited on the walk for Rudy to come out of the other lab in the building. I'd considered going alone to see Tom but decided that if it were only a trick, I needed a witness. I thought about asking Gary to accompany me but I thought that he would annoy me too often to be bearable. My first three choices were all still locked away. Rudy was the only acceptable possibility that remained.

When Rudy spotted me, he stopped so suddenly that the man behind him ran right into his back and nearly knocked him over. Rudy regained his balance and looked in every direction with squinted eyes. He approached slowly, scanning the perimeter.

'Are you afraid of me, Rudy?' I asked.

'Are they coming for me now?' he asked and kept his eyes on the horizon, jerking from side to side.

'Rudy, it's just me. If anybody is coming for you, I don't know. I don't even know if they're coming for me. Rudy, look at me.'

He shook his head. 'You aren't here to warn me?'

'No, Rudy. I'm here to ask you to help me.'

'Oh man, Libby, I don't think so. I don't want to get involved in a prison break scheme.'

'What are you talking about? A prison break scheme? You think I'm plotting to break the guys out of military custody?'

'Well, I've been thinking about it but it just seemed like such a long shot and I was sure I would fail and they would lock me up and never let me out and I just—'

'Rudy, Rudy,' I said putting my hands on his arms. 'Calm down. I'm not going to ask you to do anything illegal. I just need to take a walk in the woods and I don't want to do it alone.'

'At a time like this, you can think about taking a walk in the woods?'

'Rudy, look at me,' I said, bouncing an index finger on the tip of my nose. 'Focus. Keep your eyes on my face. And corral your imagination and listen. Okay?'

Rudy took a deep breath, exhaled and said, 'Okay.'

'Rudy, I came to you instead of Gary because I was afraid that he'd flip his cap if I asked him and you are acting every bit as crazy as I thought he might.'

'Libby, I'm sorry. Everything that's been going on has me as nervous as a hen surrounded by roosters. Tell me about this walk. If I can help you, I will.'

'It's about Tom.'

'You've heard from Tom? Is he okay? Where is he?'

'I don't know exactly where he is and I think he's alive. I found a note on my doorstep saying he made a mistake and he needs to talk to me. I left a note for him. And he responded telling me to meet him at 9 o'clock tonight at the shack where Frannie Snowden was hiding.'

'Oh, geez! I can't say I really want to revisit that nightmare. But I would like to see Tom.'

'That's the problem, Rudy. He gave specific instructions that only I could come into the shack. Also, I am worried that it wasn't really Tom who sent the note and it's a trap of some kind. In that case, I need a witness with me – someone who can escape with the truth if the worst happens.'

'I certainly can't let you go out there alone and I don't feel like I am the best option for protecting you. Unfortunately, the guys that would be better at it are locked up somewhere. I'll do my best.'

'Rudy, heroics aren't necessary. If matters do get ugly, I don't want you coming to my rescue. I want you to run away and inform others about what happened.'

'I thought we got rid of all those spies last year. You think we missed some of them?' Rudy asked.

'I suspect there are more espionage agents on the reservation, but in this case, the people that might want to trick me could be army or administration. Only, I do think it most likely it is Tom. I would think that anyone else wouldn't suggest that I bring someone else with me.'

'Unless this is another attempt by Crenshaw to find out who is in the group.'

I sighed. 'That is a possibility. You don't have to go with me, Rudy.'

'Are you kidding? Of course I'm going with you. I don't care if I'm exposed. He knows most of the names of the group by now anyway. C'mon, let's go get some lunch.'

After lunch, I went through the priorities on Charlie's desk and then returned to my lab station. It's good that I had a monumental stack of work piled up beside me. Without it, I'd probably dwell on the evening to come and grow more agitated counting down the hours until I went into the woods. I grew so focused on the task at hand that all the sounds around me faded away.

I heard 'Libby' right by my ear and jumped up off my stool. I blinked twice. My neck bent forward as I peered at the person standing next to me. I couldn't believe my eyes. Gregg. Hollowed eyes. Sunken cheeks. Slumped shoulders. Even his hair looked exhausted. But it was Gregg.

I threw my arms around him. 'Gregg, when did you get back? Are you okay? What about the others?'

'I don't know about all the others but Teddy and Dennis were dropped off with me. Teddy is waiting for you outside before he goes into his lab.'

I took both of his hands in mine and stared into his eyes. 'You won't go anywhere, right? You'll stay right here until I get back?'

'No, Libby, I won't go anywhere. Hurry, don't keep Teddy waiting.'

Racing outside, I again had that moment of disbelief when I spotted Teddy. He ran towards me and we collided into each other hard. If we hadn't clutched each other in the immediate aftermath, we would have both gone down. Teddy looked even worse than Gregg. I was surprised he was even able to move.

'Why did you come here? You look like you need a good, long sleep. You should have gone to your rooms.'

'I had to see you, Libby.'

'What did they do to you? Did they even feed you? Are you injured?'

'I'm tired. I'm hungry and I'm thirsty. But we want to get the group together at Joe's tonight at 8.'

'We really need to make it earlier,' I said.

'Why? What's going on?'

I explained about the rendezvous in the woods.

'Libby, you're taking Rudy? He's like Marshmallow Man. You gotta be kidding.'

'That's about what he said but what other choice did I have? If I took Gary, he might chicken out and leave me alone in the middle of nowhere.'

'That's true. We're back now. We'll all go.'

'Tom said only one person. Let's talk about it at Joe's. Can we meet at 7?'

'Sure. You tell Gregg and Gary.'

'I will. I hate to leave but I need to get back if I have any hope of finishing up before 7 tonight.'

'Wait,' Teddy said, and kissed me as if the end of the world was nigh.

TWENTY-NINE

I took care of the necessary communications and then threw myself into my work keeping an eye on the clock on the far wall. I finally reached the point where I could leave work without guilt at 6.45. I straightened up the disorder and scurried over to Joe's.

I stepped into the back room and every man at the table rose to their feet, raised their beer mugs high and shouted, 'To Libby!'

'Thank you but although I may have pried Gregg, Dennis and Teddy out of Crenshaw's claws, we still have Joe and Charlie behind bars.'

'You forgot, Tom,' Gary objected.

'Not at all. He never was locked up. I'll have more on that in a bit, but first I want to hear about our prisoners' experiences. Gentlemen . . .'

Gregg spoke first. 'We weren't in a jail cell, well, at least I wasn't. I never saw any of the others from shortly after our arrival until it was time to leave. The room was damp. We walked down a flight of stairs to get there. If it wasn't an actual basement, it was somewhere underground. There were no windows at all – just four concrete block walls painted a nauseating shade of green.

'I was directed to a stout wooden table under a very bright light fixture. Outside the cone of brightness, the rest of the place was gloomy and unsettling. I was ordered to sit on a hard, wooden chair behind the table. I sat there for what felt like hours before Crenshaw entered the room. With him was a chubby, balding man wearing a suit and tie. Crenshaw sat down opposite me and the man leaned against the wall, peering at me over the rim of his wire-rimmed glasses. I'll try to relate the interrogation word for word.' Tom's eyes drifted upward and glazed over as he recalled his experience.

Crenshaw asked, 'Where did you get the rats?'

'Rats? I haven't even seen a rat since my trip to Chicago where I was interviewed for this job.'

Inside, I was squirming but I dared not let it show and I struggled not to look away as Crenshaw stared into my eyes for far too long. Finally, he spoke again, 'When did Miss Clark tell you where she delivered the packages?'

'I was unaware of the location of Miss Clark's rendezvous point until after the fire.'

'What did you expect to accomplish by setting the fire at the rendezvous point?'

'Since I did not set that fire, I do not know how to answer your question,' I said.

'If you didn't then who did?'

'I wasn't there. I do not know.'

'What did you use to puncture the tires of my fleet of jeeps?'

'I have never intentionally punctured a tire in my life.'

'*Do you expect me to believe that you accidentally punctured four tires on seven jeeps?*'

'*No, sir.*'

'*You're admitting it was intentional?*'

'*No. The only time I accidentally punctured a tire, it was on my own car. I ran over a nail-studded board in the road. I should have missed it but I didn't.*'

'*How did you puncture the tires of my jeeps?*'

'*I did not.*'

Crenshaw stared at me, willing me to change my answers to what he wanted to hear. I returned his glare but said nothing. When he spoke again, he said, 'You have to admit that flooding the bathroom in Y-12 was a very juvenile act.'

'*Of course it is.*'

'*And you are a professional scientist. How did you even think of doing something so incredibly immature.*'

'*I didn't, sir.*'

Crenshaw started from the top, going through the same questions and I repeated my answers. When he reached the end, he began again. He was on the questions about the tires, when the man in the suit stepped up beside Crenshaw and slammed his fist down on the table. I startled and nearly fell out of the chair.

'*Let's get to the point,*' *the man said.* '*We know you took out the bridge. We just want to know who helped you and where you obtained the explosives.*'

I had thought Crenshaw's eyes were cold but when I looked into that man's eyes, they were as blue and chilly as an iceberg. No sign of human emotion, no sign of life, just dead, cold orbs. They stunned me speechless.

'*Mr Abbott,*' *Crenshaw said, drawing my attention back to him.* '*Where did you—*'

The man raised an open palm, pushing it aggressively into Crenshaw's face making him stop mid-sentence. The man glared at me for a few minutes before he asked, '*Who are you working for? The Germans? The Japs? The Soviets?*'

I was shocked by the question – he was accusing me of treason. I stammered when I answered. '*I work for Kodak on behalf of the United States of America to help us win the war.'*

He stood with both palms resting on the surface of the table. He leaned toward me so close that I could feel his angry spittle on my face as he shouted. 'Do you think I'm stupid?' Then, he pushed away from the table and walked over to the door.

Crenshaw asked, 'Do you need anything, Mr Abbott?'

Before I could ask for something to eat or drink, the chubby man turned back to the table and said, 'He gets nothing until he tells the truth about killing those men in the locomotive.'

I was left alone again for hours. When Crenshaw returned to the room, he was alone. 'Mr Abbott,' he said, 'that man has no patience. Stop being stoic. He won't care if you die of thirst. Let's just start with the names of the people in your little group of troublemakers.'

I asked, 'Who is that man?'

'He is a government agent.'

'Which agency?'

'All I was told was that it was a secret government agency. I was told I did not need to know anything more.'

'Do you even know the man's name?'

'I do not. I have filed complaints but I doubt if anything will come of that. I am doing my best to have all of you released. It would help my efforts if you would give me the names of the others involved in your group.'

'You know none of us will give you names – none of us will betray our friends.'

'You may believe that now but there are things that man could do that would make me give up my mother. You need to reconsider.'

I turned my head away from him and refused to say another word. He left then but the sessions with Crenshaw and the man in the suit or Crenshaw by himself continued with long pauses in between. I'd nap with my head resting on the table every chance I got.

The next morning, the man came in with a soldier. The soldier set two battery-charging cables and something that looked a lot like a car battery except that an electrical cord was attached to it. He plugged it into a wall socket and pulled a pair of pliers out of his pocket and set them down next to the battery-like thing. Then, he left me alone with the unknown agent.

Without saying a word, the man clamped the cables to the device and raised up the two ends making them touch and send off sparks. He set those down and picked up the pliers with his right hand and squeezed them down on the tips of his nails on each of the fingers of the other hand as if figuring out the best way to grab them and jerk them out. The unspoken threat made my ears ring.

He set down the pliers, rested his forearms on the table and leaned forward. 'Now is the time to talk. Before it is too late.' Then he went through a litany of accusation-laden questions. My mouth and throat were so dry, I didn't think I could talk even if I wanted to but I didn't even try. At that point, I figured I was about to be tortured beyond the lack of food and water. I prayed I could hold up to it. I didn't know any answers to his questions about the pranks in the lab or the damage to the railroad bridge. I was afraid, though, that I might betray you all.

After he left, I was alone until this morning. A soldier walked in carrying a tray with a big glass of water, a cup of coffee and a plate of scrambled eggs and toast. I grabbed the water glass first but just as the wet hit my lips, I wondered if this was a trick, if I was being drugged or poisoned. I set it back down and looked away from the table. It was the most difficult thing I've ever done – the smell was so tempting.

The soldier said, 'What's the problem? Are you on a hunger strike or something?' I didn't reply. Out of the corner of my eye, I could see his furrowed brow and puzzled facial expression.

For a few minutes, neither one of us moved or spoke. Then he said, 'Wait a minute. Are you afraid of poison or some kind of truth drug?' He sat down in the chair across from me. 'You are, aren't you?'

'The thought crossed my mind.'

The soldier laughed. 'Well, it's not.' We stared at each other across the table while my mouth watered. 'You scientists are afraid of your own shadows, aren't you? All right, watch this.'

He grabbed my fork and stabbed a piece of scrambled egg, took a bite of the toast, a sip from the coffee cup and a gulp of water. 'There!' he said throwing his arms wide. 'And I'm still alive.'

I hesitated for only a second before grabbing the water and guzzling it down. He grabbed the cup and pulled it away from my mouth. 'Slow down,' he said, 'you're going to make yourself sick. I'm not leaving until you eat every bite and swallow every drop but take your time.' The soldier folded his arms and rested his elbows on the surface of the table.

Sometimes my hunger and thirst got the best of me but each time it did, he reached up, grabbed my arm and made me slow down. When I finished, he cleared up the dishes and left the room. In less than five minutes, Crenshaw opened the door and stuck in his head. 'You're free to go, Mr Abbott.'

'Really?'

'Make it quick, Abbott, before I change my mind.'

I was out of that door in a flash not even noticing the wobble in my knees until I was out in the hallway and had to push against the wall for support.

When Gregg finished his story, he looked around the room and asked, 'Dennis, Teddy was it like that for you?'

Teddy said, 'It was pretty much the same for me except when that food and water came in, I didn't hesitate. If something was wrong with it, I wouldn't have come out of there alive.'

Dennis added, 'Mostly the same for me except that butterball agent acted a bit differently with me. If he came in by himself, he always made sure to flash his shoulder holster at me and make sure I saw the gun under his suit jacket.'

'Sounds like he was intimidated by your size, Dennis, which brings me to tonight. I think you're a better choice for escorting Libby out in the woods. I wouldn't intimidate anyone,' Rudy said.

Dennis, Teddy and Gregg fired off questions one over top of the other making it impossible for me to understand any of them. I raised up both my hands as if to fend them off. When they quieted, I explained about our mission for the night.

'I'm sorry, but I don't think you should go, Libby,' Teddy said.

'Teddy, are you pulling that "this-is-a-job-for-a-man" nonsense on me again?'

Teddy squirmed and stammered. 'No, no, no, absolutely not. Not what I meant. I was just, um . . .' His eyes jerked back and forth, making it clear to me that he was thinking up a reason on the spot.

'What I was . . . uh . . . thinking was that maybe two of us should go out there and negotiate with whoever is out there. If it's Tom and he's snapped his cap, maybe he'd try to take you hostage. He's less likely to try that on one of us, particularly not with Dennis. He and I could go and find out what he wants. If it's not him, well, I guess it doesn't matter but we don't know.'

'I can see through you like a new pane of glass, Teddy Mullins. We can talk about that later. For now, the decision is made. I am going. So, who's going with me?'

Everyone except for Rudy and Gary said, 'I'll do it.'

I sighed.

Rudy said, 'Logically, it should be Dennis. His size is the best deterrence against something untoward.'

That started a cacophony of objections that only ended when Gregg stood up and tapped a spoon on his beer mug. 'Libby, I hope you won't give me a hard time about this but we need safeguards. I am proposing that everyone who just volunteered accompany you as far as the fork in the trail. Then, just you and Dennis will go the rest of the way to the shack. If something goes wrong, we'll be close enough to have a chance of intervening.'

'If you're going to do that,' Rudy said, 'then I'm going, too.'

Gary said, 'I'll be at the dorm ready to report back if none of you return.'

'Of course you will, Gary,' Dennis said with a sneer.

'Okay,' I said, 'that should work. I need to change into my hiking boots and grab a sweater. You all do what you need to do and we'll meet at the chapel at 8.30, which means, I've got to hurry. See you soon. And don't tell anyone.'

THIRTY

As I walked back to my flat-top, the last afterglow of the sun disappeared behind the mountains. A soft light from the moon and a myriad of stars washed over my path. A clear sky foretold dropping temperatures. I didn't need a jacket now but I might before the night was over.

I had a glimpse of my kitty G.G. perched on the back of the sofa. He threw himself to the floor caterwauling as he circled my legs. I went to the kitchen, put food in the bowl and heated up the morning's leftover coffee. I turned on the radio, found a news report and went into my bedroom to change into woods-worthy clothing and boots.

Dressed and ready, I grabbed my warmed-over cup and sat on the living room chair to listen to the news at the top of the hour. The wrap-up of the war in Europe continued without a hitch. Prague, the last major city in the continent, was liberated at last. The Pacific front, however, still slogged along with more of our men dying and no end in sight. News from that side of the world continued to be depressing.

I stepped outside, over G.G.'s loud objections and peered down the street hoping to spot my colleagues converging on my house. I had expected them to straggle in one at a time, instead they arrived en masse like a ragtag army of resistance fighters ready to do battle. Stephen and Rudy led the pack and appeared to be the only two with the energy to take on the task at hand. The others looked haggard as they plodded up the road.

When they gathered around me, I said, 'Gregg, Teddy, Dennis – are you sure you are up to it? You probably need to be in your beds getting a good night's sleep.'

'We couldn't sleep knowing you are out there in the woods,' Teddy said.

No surprise that Teddy would feel that way but what about

the other two? 'Gregg, Dennis – after all you've been through, no one will blame you for sitting out this one.'

Gregg and Dennis both straightened up their spines making their slouch disappear. 'Just try and stop us, Libby. We're ready to go.'

The air had cooled with the setting of the sun but the vivid colors of the sunset promised a quick warm-up and possibly warmer than usual temperatures for spring tomorrow. The first part of our hike was easy going but then we reached the edge of the wood, the light from the night sky was obscured by the canopy of foliage. I smelled the fertile scent of mosses and fungi sprouting in rotten leaves. The new undergrowth was intimidating, surrounding us and snapping back over our path once we'd passed. A blackberry branch slapped against my face drawing tiny pinpricks of blood across my cheekbone.

As the infamous fork in the road appeared in the beam of our flashlights, sharp gasps of breath echoed in our midst. I didn't dare close my eyes for even a second because I knew the visions of Marvin's body tied to that tree not too far up the right-hand fork would flood my mind again. I could tell from the expressions on their faces that the men were experiencing the same sense of dread.

Dennis and I traveled up the left fork. The further we went, the thicker the branches and brambles crowded in around us. We reached the clearing – a clearing in name only as weeds had already infiltrated the space up to the door since we'd come here a short while ago. I called out to Tom.

'Dennis, stay right where you are. Libby, you can come up to the door.'

'That's Tom all right,' I said to Dennis.

'It may still be a trap. Keep your eyes open and don't hesitate to call me.'

I walked the rest of the way up to the door alone. 'I'm just outside, Tom.'

The detached door pushed up a bit giving me enough space to move inside in a crouch. He pulled the door shut behind me and struck a match to light a kerosene lantern. His up-lit face appeared as ghoulish as any in a horror film.

'Have a seat,' he said.

I lowered myself onto an old apple crate, hoping I would not rise filled with splinters. 'Okay, Tom, here I am. Tell me why you are here, why you never attended your father's funeral.'

'I did get on the train to go home, but I met a man.'

'Who?'

'It doesn't matter. We met in the club car and he asked me if I worked and lived behind the fence. I asked him, "What makes you think that?" And he said, "Lucky guess. You don't look like a local and you don't talk like a local."

'That made sense to me so I dropped it and we started talking about the war and FDR's death. He said his brother-in-law worked in the White House and he'd learned a lot about our new president over the years and didn't trust Truman one bit. He said he was a rube. He said that FDR kept him in the dark about a lot of things and that meant he could be easily manipulated by the Pentagon. He said that Truman wouldn't think twice about using the secret bomb on a bunch of slant-eyed Japs just to prove he was as strong as Roosevelt.

'I asked, "What secret bomb?" He just laughed and said, "Go ahead, play dumb. You won't fool me. The level of security around that place doesn't just speak of weapons development, it screams it from the mountaintops. And, I know, you can't confirm. Doesn't matter. Someone needs to slow you all down until the soldiers defeat the Japs. If you are not impeded, inno-cent men, women and children will die for the sins of their over-reaching emperor."

'After he got off the train, I thought about everything he said. I decided he was right, our work needed to be delayed before it was too late. One stop before my hometown, I disem-barked and exchanged my return ticket for an earlier train back to Knoxville.'

'And then the fire?' I asked.

'Yes.'

'How did you know that was the rendezvous spot? How did you know you wouldn't kill me?'

'I was careful, Libby. I followed you a long time ago simply out of curiosity and I never forgot it. I had no idea that I'd ever have any use for that information but that's how it is in this place. You never know what incidental thing will be a vital key to something you need to do.'

'And the rats? How? Where did you get them?'

'All the barns around here. It was easy. Easier than I thought it would be. I followed the cats. When a cat had one cornered, I pounced. Got scratched by a few angry cats and bit by a couple of rats but almost always I held on to my prize. I was nervous about getting into the building that night. I piled the crates filled with rats on a cart and rolled them in past a sleepy guard. I told him it was experimental equipment that had just arrived on a late train. He knew better than to ask any questions about the work we do.'

'And you kept going?'

'I admit that I was enraged when I punctured those tires. Through the first couple of vehicles, my anger escalated with each stab, then my fury started to drain a little bit every time I raised my arm. I finished the last jeep just for the sake of completing what I started. The next day, my hand ached and I couldn't lift my arm more than a few inches. Flooding the bathrooms was kind of goofy but it was less strenuous and it did serve its purpose. It caused a delay. Every minute lost was one that might save lives.'

'Tell me about the bridge, Tom.'

He bent over with his face in his hands. His shoulders heaved but he made not a sound. When he raised his head, tears glistened on his eyelashes. 'No one was supposed to die, Libby. I thought I was so careful. I'd stop the incoming supplies but no one would be hurt. I don't know what I did wrong. Maybe I underestimated the speed of the train. Maybe I over-estimated the ability of the engineer to react. Maybe my math was all wrong. I don't know. But you have to believe me: I did not intend to kill anyone. You do believe me, don't you?'

I kneeled in the dirt beside Tom and put an arm around his waist. 'Yes, Tom. I believe you. Tell me what happened.'

'I attached the explosives to the west end of the bridge.'

'Where did you get the explosives?' I asked.

'I can't tell you that. I can't put the blame on someone else. I tricked him and got what I needed.'

'Okay, Tom, and what happened next?'

'I put signs up on both sides of the tracks. I thought I placed them so that the train would have plenty of time to stop. When I finished that I set off the explosion. Honestly, I was shocked. I had no idea that it would do that much damage. I looked at it and still couldn't believe that a whole section of bridge had fallen. I thought I heard a train in the distance. I ran in that direction. I wanted to wave them down just in case they didn't see the signs.

'Then I heard the terrible squeal of the brakes. I smelled something burnt and metallic. And it didn't stop in time. The engine hung over the abyss. I didn't know what to do. The rest of the train started to inch toward the hole. I saw a couple of men running on the roof of the cars. One of them scrambled down to the first overturned car. He released the connector. He started climbing back up but wasn't fast enough. He sentenced himself to death to save the lives of the soldiers crammed into a couple of passenger cars down the line.

'I simply wanted to die. That man's sacrifice haunted me. I can't live with myself any longer but every time I think about taking my own life to escape the guilt, I realize that I'm too much of a coward. I'm frightened of hell and I know that is where I'm going.'

'Intent is the worst part of any crime,' I said. 'Your soul is not tainted with evil intent.'

'It doesn't matter, Libby. I killed those men as surely as if I pointed a gun at their heads and pulled the trigger.'

Tom threw his face in his hands again and this time he sobbed loudly then raised his head and wailed. I sat there numb and filled with an infusion of his pain. How could he go on living with that agony?

When he grew quiet again, I asked, 'What are your plans now, Tom?'

'I haven't had the courage to do anything but hide. I knew if I told someone then I would be forced to do something.'

'But what, Tom?'

'I haven't decided yet but know now that I have to take action. I either turn myself in or I flee – maybe to Mexico where I can drink mescal all day until it kills me. At least, I'd die with a numbed conscience.'

'What do you want me to do now?'

'Give me a day, Libby. One day. I'll either be long gone or you'll find me sitting in your house waiting for your return from work. I'll play with your kitty until you get there. Might be my last chance ever to stroke a cat and sit in a real house.'

THIRTY-ONE

When I emerged from the shack, Dennis said, 'Will he see me?'

I shook my head. 'Not now.'

'When?'

'Let's go meet the others. I really don't want to repeat myself more than necessary.'

We started walking back to the fork. Dennis said, 'Give the broad parameters then, without detail. Just brief me on the basics.'

'Tom is responsible for the pranks and the train wreck.'

'That can't be true. Are you sure?'

I stopped and looked at him. 'I just talked to Tom. What do you think?'

'Tom believes he did it but that does not mean that he did.'

Resuming our walk, I said, 'What are you getting at, Dennis?'

'Maybe he's covering for someone. That someone took advantage of his grief and manipulated him into a confession. Libby, this is not the Tom we know.'

'You're right about that. He didn't make a chauvinist comment once.'

'You know I don't mean that. You know—'

'Dennis, please, we're only a couple of minutes away from the others. We can hash this out together. We probably ought to talk with Gary, too.'

'That chicken. He's got a yellow streak up his back and it colors everything he says and does.'

'Maybe he's not chicken. Maybe he just has a strong self-preservation streak.'

'Same thing in the long run, isn't it?'

'Nonetheless, he probably knows Tom better than any of us.'

'I'll concede that,' he said and we walked in compatible silence to where the others waited.

Rather than setting off down to civilization, we decided to stand where we were and flipped off our flashlights to preserve batteries for our trek back down the hill. I conveyed the conversation I had with Tom trying to recapture the essence if not the actual words of what we had said to each other.

Gregg was the first to speak. 'What if he's just the fall guy and feels an obligation to shoulder someone else's blame?'

'All I can say,' I said, 'is that he seemed open and honest. He seemed shattered by the consequences of his actions. I think, for now, we need to accept what he said at face value. I expect that whatever decision he makes in the next twenty-four hours will provide clues to the truth of his confession.'

'What do you mean by that, Libby?'

'Tell me if you think I'm wrong – any one of you. I believe that if Tom is covering for someone else, he will run away as fast as he can. If he did, I suspect that Tom's guilt will drive him to turn himself into the authorities and accept the punishment as what he deserves. Does anyone disagree with giving Tom a day or with my assessment of Tom's motivations in his choice?' I asked.

Heads shook all around me. 'What worries me,' Rudy said, 'is what might happen to him before the twenty-four hours are up.' He turned and stretched his arm towards the path that led to the tree where Marvin died.

Teddy winced and said, 'Let's not revisit that possibility until we're out of these woods or we will get paranoid about every scurrying animal sound we hear.'

'Let's move out,' Gregg said. 'This spot is rubbing us all raw.'

'We could further this discussion back at the reservation,' Rudy suggested.

'I know I would benefit with having a little time to digest this information on my own first. Maybe we could get together for an early breakfast at the cafeteria in the morning,' I said.

'I think Libby is right,' Gregg said. 'Any disagreement with that plan?'

No one responded but Dennis asked, 'When? About 7?'

'Any objections?' Gregg asked. 'Hearing none, we'll all meet for breakfast at 7 a.m. in the cafeteria.' He turned to look at the back of the line. 'Did you all hear that?'

'Yes, Gregg. Seven a.m. at the cafeteria.'

Back at home, I scooped up G.G. and sat on the sofa with my legs folded up under me. I held him tight and stroked his ears while he purred and kneaded my arm. I tried to think up reasons why I shouldn't accept Tom's statements at face value and could find none that held up past a few seconds of reasoning. I then turned over another question: who would Tom be willing to protect at the cost of his own life or freedom? At one time, I would have said Gary, but not any longer. Lately, Tom had made it perfectly clear that Gary's slavish devotion to him was flattering at first but it had become too annoying.

I felt that in the right circumstances, Tom might protect me to his own detriment but I knew I wasn't involved. The only other person that I thought Tom would want to help that much was Charlie. Nonetheless, I couldn't imagine Charlie, who obeyed the rules with a reverence akin to religious devotion, would have done any of the deeds that Tom claimed he had done. Charlie only considered ever bending a rule if he felt pushed into a corner.

No matter how much I tried to map out alternative theories, I always circled back to the simple and forthright conclusion: Tom had done everything that he said.

THIRTY-TWO

The first thing Saturday morning, I raced to my front door to see if there was another note under the Mason jar. Nothing. Not one little scrap of paper. Feeling keen disappointment, I attempted to undermine the emotion with the reminder that I had just seen Tom the night before and therefore had no logical reason to expect any communication this early in the day.

G.G.'s wails of hunger and exasperation at my neglect of his needs grew louder as I stood and stared at the jar. With a sigh, I stepped inside, closed the door and went into the kitchen. I filled the kitty's bowl and he rewarded me with grousing growls as he chewed.

I gulped down a cup of coffee and hurried to the cafeteria. I arrived at ten minutes before seven and spotted Gregg back in a corner all alone. 'You got here early,' I said as I sat down across from him.

'I woke up two hours ago and couldn't get back to sleep. I tossed and turned for an hour or so, then gave up, dressed and came here. The smell of the bacon and sausages have made me regret not getting in line before I sat down. But I saw an empty, isolated table and felt it was my responsibility to requisition it.'

'Go, get in line. I'll keep the table secure while you get something to eat.'

'No, Libby, you go first.'

'Gregg Abbott, stop playing the gentleman. I've had a cup of coffee already and you've not had a thing. Go,' I said pointing to the short line queuing up near the food.

'If you're sure, I am really famished. Just don't tell my mother. She'll think I'm a barbarian.'

By ten after seven, the whole gang, including Gary, had arrived and taken a seat with plates and cups full. 'Where do we start, Gregg?'

'As I see it we have two problems and a world of possible actions. Problem number one: Joe and Charlie are still in custody. Number two: what can we do to ensure Tom's safety before and after he turns himself in.'

'There is one other possibility,' Dennis offered. 'What will we do if Tom decides not to surrender to authorities? If he does, supporting him seems automatic, in my mind at least. But if he doesn't, what are our options?'

'Agenda item number three,' Gregg said. 'Let's tackle them one at a time. Joe and Charlie: what do we need to do to get them released?'

'There's not much any of us can do,' Gary whined.

'Not true, Gary,' Teddy said. 'I doubt that the three of us would have been released if Libby hadn't badgered Crenshaw. Maybe she should go see him again.'

'I think we should give Crenshaw a little more time,' I said.

'Brown-nosing the commanding officer again?' Gary said with a sneer.

Hands slapped on the table as Teddy and Dennis barked, 'Shut up, Gary.'

I didn't think any further acknowledgement of Gary's remark was necessary. I plowed ahead. 'Crenshaw kept his commitment to me and because of that Gregg, Dennis and Teddy were able to join us for breakfast this morning. For that reason, at least for now, I think we need to trust that he will continue his efforts until Joe and Charlie have returned, too.'

'Makes sense,' Gregg said. 'A show of hands of those in agreement.'

Everyone raised a hand except for Gary who sat with his arms folded across his chest and pouty lips on his face. I regretted ever advocating for his return to the group after his last boondoggle.

'Moving on, what can we do to protect Tom, now and when he goes to Crenshaw?'

'As for now, I don't see any option but to wait and hope. We don't know where he is. Sure, we could go hunting for him but if we don't show up for work, it will draw more attention to the problem,' Dennis said.

'I think Dennis is right about that,' Teddy said. 'And then, after he turns himself in, he'll be in military hands and we'll never know if he's here or if they take him elsewhere.'

'We can negotiate his surrender,' I suggested.

A grin spread across the faces of Teddy and Dennis. I could tell they got the gist of what I was proposing. Furrowed brows told me the others didn't have a clue.

'Let's say he comes to my flat-top tonight. He can sleep in my spare bed and . . .'

Pale-as-a-worm Stephen pushed away from the table and turned the color of a fire hydrant. 'We cannot endorse that plan. We cannot allow that to happen.'

'Excuse me, Mr Albright,' I said.

'Just what do you mean?' Teddy added.

'I'm sure it's obvious to everyone but you, Teddy. You are blind when it comes to Libby. She is not a married woman. She cannot have a man under her roof all night long. It would reflect badly on all of us if we condoned her childish suggestion.'

Now, I lurched to my feet. 'Stephen, you are not my parent. You are not my minister. You are not responsible for the state of my mortal soul. You would never say that about a man in this room. How dare you presume to do so to me?'

'Yeah, you want to take this outside?' Teddy asked as he, too, stood up.

Gregg raised both his hands in a placating gesture. 'Let's all lower our voices and resume our seats and discuss the matter like the professionals we claim to be.'

I returned to the chair. Teddy followed my lead. Stephen scanned the faces around the table and lurched back into his seat. 'It is not acceptable.'

'Let us listen to the rest of Libby's plan before we pass judgment on any piece of it.'

Stephen grumbled but remained seated.

'Libby, you have the floor,' Gregg said.

I exhaled my outrage and began again. 'Tom spends the night in my spare bed – not in *my* bed, in a separate bed. I go to Crenshaw's house Sunday morning with one other person, preferably someone who can keep his emotions at bay and be a forceful and logical co-negotiator.'

Teddy leaned forward and looked ready to volunteer. I looked straight at him and continued, 'Someone who will not feel a need to rush to my defense if Crenshaw attacks or belittles me.' Teddy slouched back.

'I think I can handle that,' Dennis said. 'My size should help. I'm taller than Crenshaw and I could counteract any physical intimidation moves he might make to undermine you, Libby.'

'Good point, Dennis,' I said, nodding my head.

'What are the points of negotiation? What are our demands?' Dennis asked.

'I would want assurances that Tom would stay here for the duration of the war, that he would receive three decent meals a day, and that he would be allowed visitors every day. I am willing to accept a less frequent visiting schedule but not less than three times a week.'

Dennis said, 'I think you need room to move on the first two points as well to get Crenshaw's cooperation. I'd suggest asking for him to continue working in the lab for the duration of the war and to insist on meals from the officers' mess as well as snacks and coffee on demand.'

'He'll never go for that,' Gregg said.

'Of course not,' Dennis said with a grin. 'But if we start there and end up where we want to be, we will have appeared to have made significant concessions.'

'I like the way you think, Dennis,' I said. 'You've got the job.'

'Okay. All in favor of Libby's plan, raise your hand.'

Stephen, his face still effused with color objected. 'I can't believe you would even consider this.'

'But we are,' Gregg said. 'Raise your hands if you are in favor. The ayes have it.'

Even Gary lifted an arm into the air but Stephen remained locked in his moral outrage. 'I want to note my objection on the record. I refuse to be part of any scheme that taints the honor of a woman, whether she is in favor or not.'

'We keep no records, Stephen. We just keep our mouths shut about what goes on in this room. Is that clear?' Gregg asked.

Stephen stood with his fists on his hips. 'I can't believe you are now questioning my ethical fiber. I am going back to my room and good riddance to you all.' His steps slowed as he neared the door as if waiting for objections. Then he thrust it open and stomped out, leaving the door ajar behind him. Dennis leaned back in his chair and swatted it closed.

'Now, the toughest question of all. What do we do if Tom doesn't surrender to the authorities?' Gregg asked.

'Do we really have to deal with that now?' Rudy asked. 'It might never come to that.'

'Rudy's right. Let's cross that bridge when we know we have to, not before,' Dennis said.

'Sounds good to me, too,' Gregg said. 'Anyone object? Okay, let's finish our breakfast and get to work.'

We walked to the labs as a group and came to a screeching halt just in front of the first entrance. We watched as a jeep pulled up with an unexpected passenger.

THIRTY-THREE

Joe jumped out and ran over to us with a grin on his face and fatigue in his eyes. After a moment filled with back slaps and overlapping questions, Joe said, 'Looks like I wasn't the first to be released. Is Charlie back?'

'You don't know,' Gregg said. 'We were hoping you could tell us.'

'I didn't see him once while I was there. I only knew that he'd been picked up because of the games they played with me. They named everyone they had in custody and said that someone had implicated me in the bridge explosion.'

'Will we ever see Charlie again?' I moaned, not expecting any response.

'Listen, Libby,' Joe said, 'I was the first one picked up – at first I thought I was the only one. Last night, they did something I hadn't expected – they let me speak to my sister on the telephone.'

'I am surprised that they allowed you to call her,' I said.

'It wasn't exactly like that. At the time, I thought that it was either a desperate desire to break me and get information before they had to release me for some reason. Or they were never going to let me go at all. But back to my sister: she was aware that I was in custody and was told that I was protecting someone and I wouldn't be released until I stopped being stubborn. In typical big sister fashion, she delivered a fiery tongue-lashing. When she finally gave me the opportunity, I told her that I had no idea of the person involved. Then she said, "I think you need to quit your job and come home. We don't even know where you are, have no idea of what you're doing and no clue why you would be involved in this nefarious attack.'"

'And yet, here you are,' Dennis said.

'I made it clear that I couldn't tell them what I didn't know and I wouldn't be quitting before the war was over and maybe not even then. She didn't take it well. She's always been a bit bossy,' Joe said with a chuckle.

'Why don't you go to the dorm and get some sleep. You look dead on your feet,' I said.

'Are you kidding me? I wouldn't sleep anyway. Give me a few assignments and I'll get busy.'

As we all worked away at our respective stations, I kept an eye on Joe. If he looked ready to tumble off his lab bench, I'd order him to go get some rest. But I knew that I would share his attitude in the same circumstances – the shortest road to recovery from a bad experience was keeping busy at all costs.

By the end of the day, I had done everything necessary for delivering another shipment Monday morning. I straightened up my space in preparation to leave for the day.

I looked up when I heard a familiar voice saying, 'Looks like you can operate just fine without me.'

Charlie! We all converged around him and repeated the same disjointed welcome we'd given Joe that morning. Charlie raised his hands in the air and said, 'Enough of the babble. I want to hear all that you have to say but one at a time. And I want to sit behind my desk again. At times, I really doubted I'd ever make it back here ever again.'

We crowded into his tight space with the overflow poking heads in through the doorway. Charlie sat in his chair, patted his desk top and grinned. 'Never realized how much I loved this place. Okay. None of you need to feel any obligation to stay here. I want to hear about what is going on in the lab, though, and anything else that impacts your lives. Judging by the pristine shape of my inbox, Libby has been doing a great job of juggling my work in my absence, so I'd like to start with her.'

I pointed to the left side of his desk and said, 'That is a list of all your inter-office communications and my responses.

Underneath it is a list of the purchase orders I signed and other requisitions I made on your behalf. Everyone still remaining in the lab worked intently to cover the responsibilities of those who were absent.'

'I expected nothing less. Was anyone else here hauled off besides Joe and Gregg?'

'Two men from the Alpha lab were taken into custody but you were the last one from our group.'

'I see Joe and Gregg are back, what about the Alpha lab folks?'

'They're back, too,' I said. 'At least they were all here this morning.'

'Joe, Gregg, I will want to compare your experiences to mine, but first I have a couple more questions for Libby. Are you ready to deliver another shipment?'

'Yes sir.'

'What about Tom? Have you heard anything about his whereabouts?'

'Not exactly,' I said.

'Do you think he was picked up, too?'

'Not unless it's happened in the last 24 hours,' I said.

'You've seen him then?'

I nodded and explained the current situation as well as our plans to negotiate his surrender to the authorities.

Charlie scowled. 'You're playing with fire, Libby.'

'I know there's a risk, sir. But isn't that true of everything we do in his place?'

'Valid point. Anything else you need to tell me about, Libby?'

'Nothing that comes to mind right now, Charlie. I'm sure though that the others do.'

I leaned against the wall thinking about the night ahead as Joe, Gregg and Charlie exchanged information about the events experienced under guard. All were remarkably similar. The big difference was that Crenshaw and the nameless man held Charlie responsible for any actions committed by personnel under his command.

'I told them each time, that in my lab, we don't operate under a rigid military structure. Of course, Crenshaw always countered with: that's why you've had all these problems. I knew he was wrong but who can argue with a high-ranking military man and hope to score any points.'

An hour later we straggled out of the building to find Dennis, Gary and Teddy waiting for us. None of the gaggle broke off for their dorm rooms when we passed the buildings. Every one of them, including Charlie, followed me like ducklings straight to my flat-top. We stopped at the foot of the stairs.

'I've got to go in alone. If Tom is there and he sees a mob, he might panic.'

Murmurs slid through the group but no one openly objected. I opened the door and called Tom's name but got no response. I scooped up my kitty and shouted out the door at my motley crew.

They tromped up the stairs and sat on my furniture or the floor. I went into the kitchen and put on the coffee. Dennis said, 'He's not here. What now?'

'It's not quite 8.30,' I said. 'I left Tom at about 10 o'clock last night. His time isn't up yet.'

Multiple discussions started around the room making my little house as noisy as a bowling alley on a Saturday night. Soon, arguments broke out with Gary defending Tom and calling me a liar. Teddy objected to the latter while Stephen ranted about the moral depravity of our group. I turned on the news to drown them all out. In no time, they were arguing about the war. I'd had enough. I stood and clapped my hands four or five times and the room went still.

'It's after ten. Time to clear out. We're all tired and need some rest. Why don't we all gather here again tomorrow after lunch and plan our next steps.'

Gregg was the first out the door. He'd barely crossed the threshold when he turned and said, 'Libby, did you leave a note out here for Tom?'

'No. But I can.'

'Then this must be a note from Tom.'

'Bring it in,' I said.

I unfolded the paper and read Tom's message out loud. 'I just can't do it with all those people here. You and one other person of your choosing. No one else. I'll try again tomorrow just after it turns dark.'

Every pair of shoulders slumped. My little band of warriors all looked as drained as a pack of toddlers after a day at the park. If they didn't move soon, they might fall asleep on their feet.

'Listen up. This is what we're going to do,' I said. 'No meeting tomorrow afternoon. Dennis, you'll come over before dark and the rest of you can wait until you get further word.'

'I'll be here a couple hours before dark just in case,' Dennis said, nodding in agreement.

'That's fine. I'll make dinner for both of us.'

'Wait a minute, that sounds a lot like a date. Maybe I should be here, too,' Teddy said.

'Don't say another word, Teddy. You will regret it,' I snapped.

Teddy drew up his shoulders and let them collapse as he exhaled an exaggerated sigh.

'Why doesn't everyone else come up to my house after dinner. That way we'll all be together and Dennis or Libby can report to us all at once about the night's developments,' Charlie offered.

Murmurs of agreement zig-zagged through the room. 'That settles it then,' Charlie said. 'Now, go home. Libby looks exhausted and I'm tired, too.'

The last man remaining was Teddy. 'I'm sorry, Libby. It's just Dennis . . .'

'No more, Teddy. If we are going to last, you're going to have to accept the fact that I will probably always work surrounded by men – not by choice but because of the profession I've chosen. If that's going to be an eternal problem between us, there just can't be any us.'

'I accept that logically, Libby. My heart is just a slow learner. Forgive me,' he said, flinging open his arms.

I fell into his embrace that led to a long, satisfying and stimulating kiss. I did love that guy – he's the only one that has come close to accepting me as an equal. I knew my life would be better with him in it. I hoped that we could make it work.

THIRTY-FOUR

Sunday afternoon, I mixed up a meatloaf using the recipe I got from the woman who tried to kill me a couple of years ago. She was a two-faced, selfish, evil person but she was a fabulous cook. I cut up potatoes and left them in a pan filled with cold water until it was time to put them on the burner.

I slid the meatloaf into the oven and heard a knock. I didn't realize how edgy I was feeling until I jumped at the sound. Fortunately, no surprises – Dennis had arrived, just as he said he would.

Our conversational attempts stumbled into dead ends until we managed to find a path to a theoretical topic about fusion and fission. And Teddy was worried that our time together would be romantic?

When I went into the kitchen to mash the potatoes, Dennis followed me offering to help. I directed him to the flatware drawer for the eating utensils and the cupboard for napkins. He laid them on my little table for two and returned to the kitchen. He set the plates on the kitchen counter and slid the meatloaf on to a platter while I made gravy. It all felt very domestic – maybe that's what worried Teddy.

Over dinner and clean-up, we talked about the man whose arrival we anticipated. Dennis touched on Tom's chauvinism. 'He can't really help it, Libby. He was raised without an important woman in his life. I had a mother and two sisters. All Tom had was his dad.'

'Still, it's not as if he were living in a monastery.'

'Really, Libby? Pretty close. I don't remember any girls with an interest in science in my high school and Tom went to a private all-boys school. There weren't any women majoring in chemistry, physics or math in my university and I imagine they were absent where Tom got his degree. Working or living with females when you're younger teaches you the wisdom of treating women as equals. Tom never had those influences growing up but I've seen changes in his attitude since you joined our group.'

'Granted. He has gotten better but sometimes he still uses his bias against my gender like a cudgel,' I said.

'True, but you need to emphasize the positive side instead of always assuming the worst about men. For instance, who did Tom turn to with his problems? Not one of the guys.'

'Of course not. For centuries, women have been busy cleaning up the messes men make.'

Dennis sighed. 'For that matter, Libby – and I can't believe I'm saying this – you're too hard on Teddy at times.'

For a moment, I just stared at him and then I asked, 'In what way?'

'Teddy has two older sisters and has great respect for them and for his mom. Sometimes he wants to protect you because he loves you, not because you're a woman whom he sees as incapable of taking care of yourself – just because he cares about you. But you always suspect him of wanting to belittle you. You need to give him the benefit of the doubt. Listen, I was raised by a very intelligent woman. She was an R.N. before the children came along. She returned to her nursing career as soon as my younger sister entered kindergarten. Dad was very supportive. Whenever one of us kids were too sick to go to school, Mom and Dad would discuss their responsibilities for that day and decide whose work would be least disrupted by staying home. Honestly, my dad stayed home and tended to us more than my mom did. Nonetheless, whenever Mom mentioned one of the doctors showing disrespect for her and other women nurses, my dad offered to pop a few of them on the nose. My mother never assumed my dad was telling her she was not competent enough to take care of herself. But you often make that assumption with Teddy.'

I almost objected but stopped and looked hard at the many instances when I did just that. I had not been fair to Teddy, but I didn't know how I could still the little voice inside that pointed to suspicions that seemed baked into my brain. 'You're right, Dennis. I need to be more conscious of that and try not to allow my biased perception color my reactions.'

'Phew, you took so long to respond, I thought I'd really cheesed you off.'

I grinned. 'Can't blame you for that, Dennis.'

Dennis was washing the dishes and I was drying and putting them away when we both spun around. 'Did you hear that?' Dennis asked.

'Yes, it sounded like the front door.'

We peered out of the kitchen and there was Tom. In the lighted room, his clothes looked filthy, his hair matted and his eyes exhausted. Nonetheless, his mouth split into a grin. 'Here I am!'

'I have leftovers from dinner. Are you hungry? I can heat everything up,' I said.

'That would be great – shoot, I'll eat it all cold if warming it up is too much trouble.'

'Not at all. Have a seat. Talk to Dennis. I'll have it ready in a jiffy.'

I brought out a steaming plate of food and set it down on the table. Tom threw his leg over the back of the chair and started shoveling forkfuls into his mouth before his rear hit the seat. Dennis and I sat on the sofa fascinated. Tom resembled a famished bear fresh out of hibernation – we couldn't take our eyes off of him.

The plate was nearly clean before Tom stopped for a breath. With gravy smeared on his lips, he turned toward me with a grin. 'Sorry for my horrible manners. I was ravenous and this is delicious, Libby. It's the best meat loaf I've ever had. I'm surprised that you can cook like this.'

'Following a recipe in the kitchen is a lot like following procedure in the lab. One step at a time until you're done. I'm glad you're enjoying it.'

'If you say so,' Tom replied and dug back in until every remaining morsel had disappeared into his mouth.

'You want seconds of anything – or everything?' I asked.

Tom patted his stomach and said, 'I couldn't eat another bite. First hot meal I've had in a long time. Thank you.' He carried his plate into the kitchen.

'Just leave it in the sink, Tom. I'll clean up later,' I said.

Tom returned to the living room and slouched into the chair.

'Dennis explained your plan, Libby. I have a few concerns. First of all, how can you be sure that Crenshaw won't lock the two of you up when you mention that you know where I am?'

'I'm not, actually.'

'And then he could come and drag me out of your house?'

'He could.'

'And even if he agreed to any of the terms of an arrest, can you be certain that he will abide by them?'

'No, I can't.'

'But like I said,' Dennis interjected, 'Libby has the connection with General Groves that trumps anything Crenshaw can do.'

I didn't expect Dennis to say that to Tom. For all I knew, Groves wouldn't even remember my name any longer. I almost said so but when I looked into their faces, I realized that their belief in my ability to pull strings from on high was something they needed to have, but I wouldn't lie. 'I will use that avenue if I need to do so but there is no guarantee of its success.'

'You're just being modest, Libby,' Dennis said with a wave of his hand.

'I'm still not sure,' Tom said. 'Even your most optimistic outcome will keep me locked up for years, if not for the rest of my life. It'll be like being down in the mine and everything caving in on you and knowing no one can ever set you free. I know I deserved to be punished but I don't know if I can handle that.'

'I say that we all sleep on it,' Dennis suggested. 'I'll stay out here on the sofa. If anyone comes in the middle of the night, I can stall them, Libby, and you can get Tom out of the window.'

'That's crazy, Dennis,' I said with a laugh. 'Whatever makes you think someone would come here tonight?'

Before he could respond, a hard pounding on my front door echoed through the flat-top.

THIRTY-FIVE

I started toward the door but Dennis stepped in front of me and said, 'Get back from the door, Libby. Tom, go to the bedroom and open the window.'

The pounding stopped. Once Tom was out of sight, Dennis looked at me and I nodded. He jerked open the door.

Ruth stumbled inside as if she'd been leaning against it to listen.

'Libby, thank the dear sweet Lord that you are here,' Ruth said.

'Ruthie, what is wrong?'

'They came back. This time they wanted to know about some red-headed scientist named Tom. I told them I didn't know him and didn't think I'd ever met him. They said that I was lying. I told them I'd swear on a Bible if they brought one along. Of course, they didn't. But they said, "Libby Clark told us you've been dating him." Now, Libby, I know you'd never tell them anything like that but do you even know who they're talking about?'

'Tom,' I shouted, 'you can come out now.'

As Tom's head came into view, Ruth's jaw dropped, she wiped her hands on her dress and shifted her weight from one foot to the other.

'Ruthie, this is Tom, the red-headed scientist. Tom, this is my good friend Ruthie.'

'Maybe I'd better go. They could have followed her over here,' Tom said.

'Aw, shucks,' Ruth said. 'Nobody followed me. Big Sally took care of that – she was my lookout. You know Sally, right, Libby?'

'I don't think I remember her,' I said.

'Oh, sure you do, Libby. She's that big girl that can stick two fingers in her mouth and whistle loud enough to raise the dead.'

I nodded my head. 'Now, I remember. I think my ears were ringing for a week.'

'She watched till I was around the bend. If she saw anything suspicious, she was gonna whistle.'

'What if she whistled and you didn't hear it?' Tom asked.

'Libby, tell him. You could hear that whistle at least halfway to Knoxville,' Ruth said.

'She would have heard Shirley's whistle, Tom. Trust us on that. Sit down a minute and please try to relax.'

'Yea, well, can we trust her?' Tom asked.

Dennis jumped to Ruth's rescue. 'Tom, don't you remember her? Ruth is the sister of Irene – the administration and military tried to cover up her murder to protect a scientist. You can't have forgotten what we did. It was only three years ago.'

'So, what's the point?' Tom asked.

Dennis threw both arms up in the air and turned in a circle. Face-front again, he said, 'Tom, you sure make it difficult for anyone to help you. Libby and I are going out on a limb to negotiate a bearable surrender to authorities for you. If we say you can trust Ruth, then accept it as a fact.'

'I trust no one,' Tom said, with an outward thrust of his chin. 'There's probably a reward you're hoping to collect.'

'That's it. You're talking gobbledygook, Tom,' I said. 'You want to spend the night and let us negotiate for you in the morning, fine. If not, just leave. Right now, I need to get over to Charlie's house and let everyone know that the situation is going according to plan.'

'No,' Tom said, 'you will not inform anyone.'

'Tom, don't be ridiculous – these are your fellow Walking Molecules. If we don't communicate with them soon, they'll be storming the flat-top wanting to know why.'

Tom scowled and shoved his hands in his pockets and paced around the constricted space. When his feet came to a rest, Tom said, 'Okay. Fine. They need to be told. But if you leave, Libby, I'm leaving, too.'

'I'll go, Libby,' Ruth volunteered.

'Thank you, Ruthie. But it needs to be me or Dennis – otherwise they might think it's a trick. It would be unproductive for me to leave, Dennis. You're going to have to run over but you can use the car.'

'I really don't—' Dennis began.

'Hush, Dennis,' I said. 'You can get there and back in no time at all. We'll be able to handle any problems that arise, won't we, Tom?'

Dennis didn't look very pleased with the idea but he went anyway. As soon as the car pulled away, I said, 'Tom, you are filthy and you look tired. Go take a shower and climb into bed. There's shampoo in there – feel free to use it.'

'But what if . . .?'

'Leave the bedroom window open a bit – it'll be easier to slip out if the need arises. We won't let you down, Tom.'

He gave us both a distrustful look before turning away and going into the bathroom. In a few minutes, I heard the shower running. Once he was cleaned up and settled into bed, I grabbed my night clothes out of the room and returned to Ruth.

'Oh, Libby! You look exhausted. Why don't you turn in for the night, too?'

'Not until Dennis gets back – I need to know there were no surprises at Charlie's place.' I was really too tired for conversation. I just leaned back in the chair and listened to Ruth talk about her friends in the dorm. I heard someone bounding up the steps and jumped up to answer the door.

'No, you don't, Libby. You go back in the bedroom and let me see who's there.'

The steely resolve in Ruth's voice made me do as she said without argument.

I came out of the bedroom when I heard Dennis say, 'Ruth! I'm so glad you're still here. I was hoping to talk with you for a little while.'

'I hate to be a poor hostess but I'm going to bed. Night, Ruthie. Just let yourself out. Pick a night when you can come over for dinner and we'll do it. Night, Dennis. Feel free to use the car to take Ruth back to the dorm. Night, all.'

G.G. was already sprawled on my pillow when I walked into the bedroom. I scooped him up and climbed into bed and he purred me to sleep.

I woke up in the middle of the night thinking I heard a bear, but no, it was Tom sprawled spread-eagle, mouth wide open in the other bed, making more noise than quarreling squirrels. I drifted back to sleep and didn't stir till dawn.

I sat up, stretched and looked over to the other side of the room. Tom had already risen. I pulled on my robe and walked into the living room where Dennis sipped on a cup of coffee.

'Fresh pot in the kitchen, Libby,' Dennis said, lifting his cup in the air as if making a toast. 'I like your friend, by the way. She's a salt of the earth type, a refreshing antidote to all the secrets and subterfuge around this place.'

'Is Tom in the kitchen?'

Dennis jerked to his feet. 'I thought he was in the bedroom with you.'

'No. Did he leave?'

'If he did, it was before I woke up. Ruth left a note in the kitchen for you before she left. But it can't be about Tom. We were both laughing at his snoring when she went out the door.'

I rushed into the kitchen anyway and picked up Ruth's note. Underneath it was another folded piece of paper with my name on it written in different handwriting. I opened it and saw it was from Tom and read it out loud.

> I know you mean well, Libby. But I don't know if staying at your place while you two are negotiating is a good idea and I didn't want to argue about it. Crenshaw could prolong the discussion while he sends soldiers out to pick me up and then laughs in your face. Just negotiate with him and tell him I'll be back in touch with you. And don't waste your time looking for me at that old shack. I won't be going back there again. Thank you and Dennis for everything. The Running Molecule, Tom.

Dennis and I stared at each other for a moment without saying a word. I broke the silence. 'Let's see if we can catch Crenshaw before he leaves his house this morning.'

'Yeah, I think he'll be more cooperative there than in his

office where soldiers will be at his beck and call. But we have to hurry.'

'We'll take the car. I'll get dressed as quickly as I can.'

THIRTY-SIX

Lieutenant Colonel Crenshaw opened his front door, shaking his head. 'What now?'

'We've been in communication with the person responsible for the train derailment and the lab pranks,' I said.

Crenshaw's eyes shifted between me and Dennis. 'How long has this been going on? How long have you had this knowledge?'

'We saw him yesterday,' I said, dodging the whole truth.

'Where is he now?'

I shrugged and Dennis said, 'We don't know. He said he'd be back in touch.'

'Are you claiming you don't know how to initiate communication with him?'

'Yes, sir,' we said in unison.

'Why are you here if you can't deliver him to the authorities?'

'He's given us the responsibility of negotiating the terms of his surrender,' I said. 'And he'll get that information from us at a time of his choosing.'

Crenshaw sighed. 'Come in, sit down, I'm sure you remember how to get to the living room, Miss Clark. I'll get my wife to bring in some coffee.'

Dennis followed me over to the sofa. Crenshaw walked in and Mrs Crenshaw placed a tray on the coffee table. We fixed our cups and sipped while we waited for Crenshaw to begin the negotiations.

The lieutenant colonel shifted back and forth in his chair as he opened and shut his mouth a few times before speaking. 'Let's start with what, to me, is obvious. This person committed murder and, at the very least, needs to be locked up for the rest of his life.'

'Actually sir, he is guilty of manslaughter but not murder,' I said.

Crenshaw ran an open palm across his face. 'Nothing is ever simple with you, is it, Miss Clark? You see everything as gray when realists like me know that the black and white are clearly defined. I imagine your opinion is based on the information the killer gave you. So why don't you tell me who he is and what he had to say. I need to know what I'm dealing with before I can agree to any conditions.'

'I'm sorry, sir, but until we reach some accommodation on our requests, I can't give you his name but I can tell you his story.' I explained about the death of Tom's father and the stranger he met on the train on the way home.

'Wait a minute. Who was this stranger?' Crenshaw asked.

'I don't know, sir,' I said.

'I don't think he knew who the man was,' Dennis added.

'Sounds like an espionage agent to me. Was the stranger German or Japanese?'

'We don't know, sir. He didn't say,' I answered

'Did he give you any description of that man on the train?' We shook our heads.

'Of course not,' Crenshaw said. 'Go on with his story.'

I went through the sequence of events and his failed attempt to get the train to stop before anyone was injured or killed.

'You expect me to believe, that the person responsible is a fine, upstanding, patriotic citizen – an adult, not a child – who lost control of his own mind when his father's death made him an orphan. What is he? A scientist or a wounded grizzly?'

Dennis and I sat quietly, hoping it was a rhetorical question. I certainly didn't want to confirm that Tom was a scientist but I didn't want to lie, either.

Crenshaw made an upward gesture with his hand. 'Go on. What do you want me to do with the treasonous killer?'

'We want you to keep him here on the reservation for the duration of the war.'

'I probably would have done that anyway. What else?'

'We want him to be able to have visitors every day,' I said.

'No. You are asking far too much,' Crenshaw said.

'How often are you willing to allow him to have visitors?'

'I didn't say he could have visitors,' Crenshaw protested.

'You implied that, sir. Didn't he, Dennis?'

'Sounded that way to me, too,' Dennis replied.

'We'll table that for the moment,' Crenshaw said. 'What else?'

'We want him to get his meals from the officer's mess.'

'He'll get fed. Let's leave it at that,' Crenshaw said. 'Anything else?'

'Just one more thing: we want any criminal charge reduced from murder to manslaughter.'

'That's one promise I cannot make because I won't be able to keep it. Whether he faces a military tribunal or a criminal court, the disposal of his case is out of my control.'

'But you do have influence, Lieutenant Colonel Crenshaw. Will you advocate for a lowering of the charge?' I asked.

'I can't say right now. I'd have to question him about his story and make my own decision about its credibility.'

'I don't know if he will accept that condition,' I said. 'Back to the visitation . . .'

'I don't think I can do that,' Crenshaw said.

'Can't do it or won't do it, sir. We both know that it is totally within your power to grant that request.'

'Every day would be too disruptive.'

'We can accept every other day,' I suggested.

'Until I speak with him, I will not make any determination on the frequency of visits, Miss Clark.'

'You're agreeing to set up a visitation schedule, correct?'

'I will allow some visitors. But I will not commit to a plan ahead of the apprehension of the perpetrator.'

'I expected more flexibility from you, sir,' I said. 'You've only agreed to one out of four of our requests. After all, at this point in time, you do not know with certainty who was responsible. And even if you think you do, you have no idea of where to find him.'

'I assure you, Miss Clark, we can deploy enough assets to hunt him down. If you want to make this a voluntary situation where your friend is not at risk of losing his life in a capture, then those are my conditions. He stays here for the duration and I will establish a visitation policy after he is in custody. If you can't accept that, I will have you both arrested for obstructing justice.'

'The two of us are willing to accept those terms, sir. But the final decision is not for us to make. We will present it to him and proceed from there.'

'You do that, Miss Clark. I need to get to my office. You can let yourselves out.'

THIRTY-SEVEN

B efore anything else that morning, I hoped to find a note outside of my front door under the Mason jar on my landing. No luck. Where are you, Tom O'Malley? I began to wonder if I'd misjudged him. Was he really as distraught about the deaths of the railroad workers as he said? Was he so twisted about his father's death and the stress of our jobs that he had descended into madness? Would that mean that he was manipulating us for a nefarious purpose?

I walked to work in the rays of a rising sun that turned the treetops on the opposite horizon to gold. Spring in this part of Tennessee stirred up nostalgia for the carefree days of April and May in the hills of Virginia before my stepfather came into my life. The images of my mother from that time resembled the faces of the beautiful women Botticelli created on canvas. How did she let it all slip away?

Does she think of that life sitting behind bars suffering with cancer and knowing each day might be her last? Or is she haunted by the bad years since my father's death? Not long ago, I wanted her to suffer, but now I hope she's focused on the former. I pray that she dies in peace. I shook these worrisome thoughts away as I entered the lab.

The most important task for me today was the preparation and delivery of another shipment of crystals to the rendezvous point. Never again will the word 'rendezvous' stir up romantic fantasies as it once did. Now, it elicited the dark specter of death sealed in each container. I wondered if I would ever know the ultimate destination for my deadly cargo or if the information would remain eternally top secret.

As I stepped up into the military jeep next to the uniformed driver, Tom thundered through my mind. If he was determined to postpone the development of the gadget, would he assault us along the way? I needed to talk to Dennis to see if he was having the same doubts about Tom as me.

Despite my fears, the exchange was seamless and uneventful. All my driver wanted to discuss was the war in the Pacific and how much he wished he had joined the Navy to be part of the action. He nattered on and on about the fighting in the Philippines and on the island of Okinawa. I, on the other hand, had grown weary of hearing tales of combat and death with each passing day.

At lunchtime, I waited in front of the building for Dennis to emerge from the Alpha lab. Unlike the rest of the chemists in my area, I still had security clearance to the other lab but I drew the line at using it for personal reasons. I didn't have a long wait.

We walked to the cafeteria, side by side. 'Dennis,' I asked, 'are you worried about Tom's story or his motives?'

'I hate to say this, Libby, but I've been concerned ever since he skipped out on us yesterday morning. His actions make me question everything. But, at the same time, my suspicious thoughts raise feelings of guilt that I am betraying a friendship. Is there any chance that Crenshaw was just playing with us and he already has Tom in custody?'

'How, Dennis? I can't believe they could slip into the house and spirit him away while we slept. One of us would have heard something.'

'They could have been waiting outside and took him away when he was leaving.'

'That's true, particularly if they followed him for a while before confronting him. Still, he left willingly. Why?' I asked.

Dennis shrugged. 'I should have paid more attention in psychology class.'

'You took a psychology class?'

'Yeah, everyone said that Miss Browning's class was an easy A and I wanted to pump up my GPA.'

'That's why I took art appreciation,' I said with a chuckle. 'Did you get that A?'

'That's the worst part – I got a B. Libby, I have a question for you: would you mind if I asked Ruth out to dinner?'

'Ruth? Absolutely not.'

'Do you think she'll want to go out with me?'

'Yes, I do.'

'Oh, look, Teddy's coming this way.'

'Do you mind?' I asked.

'Not at all.'

'Wave him over.'

'You two look cozy over here in the corner,' Teddy said.

'Teddy—'

Dennis patted on the tabletop. 'Libby, Libby! Once again, you won't mind if Ruth and I go out together?'

I could tell by the begging look in Dennis' eyes that he was trying to save me from myself. He knew I was about to jump on Teddy's comment and he didn't want me to go there. He was probably right. 'Not one bit, Dennis. I think you and Ruth will get along well.' I thought I saw a flash of relief on Teddy's face but I might have imagined it.

While Teddy ate his lunch, Dennis and I updated him on what had happened with Tom and Crenshaw. He looked back and forth at us after we finished talking. 'So tell me,' he asked, 'what's bothering you?'

'Are we that obvious?' I asked.

Teddy nodded. 'You are to me.'

We summarized our uncomfortable thoughts as Teddy cleaned his plate. When we finished, Teddy pushed his tray aside and said, 'The big problem here as I see it is simple: you don't know who Tom talked to on that train.'

'Why would that matter?' Dennis asked.

'If it was just some ordinary guy, Tom's over-reaction doesn't make a lot of sense,' Teddy said. 'The man could have been an agent of the Japanese government.'

'Tom would have said something if the man was oriental,' I objected.

'Besides that,' Dennis added, 'I think he would have been skeptical if the man was Japanese.'

'The Japs aren't stupid,' Teddy said. 'They would recruit spies that looked like ordinary white men. Someone trained in psychological warfare techniques, perhaps armed with a drug from the Orient that makes people more suggestible. Maybe he was staking out the train station looking for someone in a vulnerable state of mind.'

'How would they know about our installation here?' Dennis asked.

'The Russians know. Why not the Japanese? For that matter, maybe it was a Soviet spy. America is being credited with winning the war in Europe. Maybe Stalin feels threatened by that. Maybe he'd want us to get our comeuppance in the Pacific. What better way to do that than to slow down the development and ultimate deployment of the gadget?'

'But still, it seems so convoluted,' I said.

'Yes, it does,' Teddy admitted. 'Maybe it's far simpler. Tom has been trudging through life filled with lots of anger and negativity. At a time when he was experiencing loss and guilt, it might not take much for him to crumble psychologically.'

'Sounds like you studied psychology at school,' I said.

'Sure. Intro to Psych was an easy A. You'd have to try not to succeed in that class.'

'So, Dennis,' I said with a grin, 'did you try to fail?'

'No but . . .' Dennis said.

'You took Intro to Psych and didn't get an A?' Teddy asked. 'What did you get?'

'We've gotten way off track here,' Dennis objected.

'Tell me, please, you at least got a B,' Teddy said.

'Yes, okay, I got a B. Can we change the subject now?'

'Yes,' I said, 'we need to get back to work.' I stood and disposed of my trash and placed my tray and plate in the returns. On the way back, we talked about the current situation with Tom.

'Do we have any way to contact Tom?' Teddy asked.

'Aside from leaving another note under the jar, I don't have any idea of how to reach him. Although that's something, it's not much and it would require him to take the action to come and pick it up,' I said.

'Is it possible that he's still at the shack and told us he wouldn't be there to keep us away?'

'Anything's possible at this point,' I admitted.

THIRTY-EIGHT

I started the analytic process on new samples from Alpha lab and was interrupted by Charlie. 'Libby, you have a phone call in my office.'

'Let me finish up the next step, first, Charlie.'

'No, Libby. I've been told it is urgent. It's a person-to-person call from beyond the fence. I think you'd better take it now.'

For a moment, I forgot how to breath. I picked up the receiver in Charlie's office and said, 'This is Libby Clark.'

'Please hold for a person-to-person call from Dorothy Clark.'

I willed my imagination to remain still as I waited for the sound of my aunt's voice.

'Libby dear, I hate to inform you but your mother has passed away.'

I closed my eyes and threw my hand over my mouth.

'Libby, are you there?'

'Um, yes. Yes, I am. I . . .'

'That's okay, dear. If you are near a chair, sit down. I know it will take some time to absorb the news. She slipped into unconsciousness for a few hours before she died. The last thing she said before that was, "Tell Libby and Ernie I love them".'

A sob jerked out of my throat. Words, however, could not form.

'Libby, I wish I didn't have to turn your thoughts to practical matters while you are still shocked by the news, but it is necessary to make arrangements right away.'

I nodded but realized she couldn't hear that movement on the phone line and croaked out a 'yes.'

'I am bringing your mother's body back to the farm to bury her next to your father. I plan to have the funeral service and burial on Thursday, as long as everything with transportation goes smoothly. Do you understand?'

'Yes.'

'I've spoken to Mrs Early and she will deliver the sad news to Ernie when he gets home from school. She expressed a desire to have you there as soon as possible. She thinks Ernie will need you. Can you leave tomorrow?'

'Uh, yes.'

'Good. I've already purchased your train ticket. You can pick it up at the ticket counter. You might not be able to reach me for a while. I am taking an overnight to Richmond and traveling with your mother's casket to Bedford early tomorrow morning. If you need to talk to anyone, Mrs Early said she would welcome your call any time of day or night. Listen, Libby, you can rest easy. Yes, you pushed your mother away for a long time but you made your peace with her before she died. You did the right thing – take comfort in that.'

'Thank you, Aunt Dorothy. I'll see you tomorrow.'

Charlie had hovered near the doorway while I was on the phone. As soon as I set down the receiver, he rushed in and placed a palm on each of my upper arms. He bent down and looked me straight in the eye. 'Are you okay, Libby?'

I nodded.

'Was it news about your mother?'

I nodded again and said, 'Yes, Charlie. My mother is gone.'

He wrapped his arms around me and I burst into tears. 'Cry it out, Libby. One of the most painful moments of anyone's life is when their mother dies.'

I wallowed in my self-pity for a bit, then my thoughts turned to Ernie. I had to keep it together for his sake. I straightened my posture and stepped back from Charlie. 'Thank you, sir. I need to get back to my analysis. And I need to leave tomorrow morning to be with my little half-brother.'

'Go to the ladies' room first and throw some cold water on your face. You can have as much time as you need to deal with this situation. Just let me know your plans when you know them.'

Sniffling, I said, 'I plan to return on Friday and be back to work on Saturday.'

'There's no need to rush, Libby.'

'Yes, there is, Charlie,' I said, forcing a smile on my face. 'We got a war going on and it's all hands on-deck.'

'You don't have to be a brave little soldier all the time, Libby. You can show vulnerability and still be strong.'

'Ideally, I know that is how it should be, Charlie. But I don't think it is an option for women. Someone's always looking for the chink in our armor.'

'The people who care about you will always allow you that latitude. You don't need to put up a false front for us.'

'Thank you. I will try not to test your hypothesis too often.'

THIRTY-NINE

Teddy and Gregg volunteered to stay at my house while I was gone in case Tom attempted to contact me again. Teddy drove me to the train station and kept my car to pick me up when I returned. I didn't think I'd forgotten anything but, of course, as I traveled east, I worried that I'd missed something that I'd later regret.

The second I stepped down on the platform in Bedford, Ernie threw himself into my arms and blocked the egress of those behind me. I walked sideways with him to get us out of everyone's way.

Justine Early gave us a couple of minutes for Ernie to sob his sorrow on my shoulder before she spoke. 'Ernie, grab your sister's suitcase and let's head off for home. We've got livestock to feed before dark.'

Ernie stepped back and dropped his arms. 'I'm so glad you came, Libby.'

On the ride out of town, I sat on the front seat next to Justine. Ernie hung over the back of our seats pummeling us with questions.

'Miss Justine, why aren't we waiting for Aunt Dorothy to arrive?'

'We talked about that Ernie. Your Aunt Dorothy preferred to meet the undertaker at the station without the distraction of our presence. The funeral director agreed to give her a ride out to the farm.'

'Whose farm?'

'Your farm, Ernie.'

'So, when are we going to see her?'

'After we finish the chores at our farm. I already told you, I'll take you and Libby over then. Your Aunt Janice is over there now straightening up and airing out the house. She'll make supper for the three of you and you can spend the night there with your sister and your Aunt Dorothy if you want,' Justine said.

'Aunt Janice?' I asked. 'Your side of the family or your husband's?'

'She's my sister. She lives over in Radford. She only planned to visit for a couple of days but when we heard the news about Annabelle, she offered to stay longer to help out.'

'So, Libby, are you sad?' Ernie asked.

'Ernie,' Justine reprimanded, 'that is a rude question. Don't let Libby think that's how I'm raising you. Of course, your sister is sad. She lost her mother, too.'

'It's okay, Justine,' I said. 'I don't mind.' Turning to Ernie, I added, 'Yes, I am very sad. It's not easy to lose a mother no matter how old you are.'

'Aren't you happy you went to visit her?'

'Yes, I am, Ernie. I'd feel a lot worse if I hadn't.'

'Aunt Dorothy said that, too. She said it was the best thing we could have done.'

I thought about the impact of loss on one so young. I was close to his age when my father died and the pain of that grief drove me to my knees. Because of the experience, I knew the death of our mother was worse for him but I didn't want him to feel all alone. His relationship with her was much less complicated than mine. He still had her on a high pedestal while I had seen all her weakness on full display, and yet, I still loved her. Knowing she was gone left a dark abyss in my heart.

Ernie changed the topic without warning. 'Have you ever tasted Aunt Janice's cooking, Libby?'

'No, Ernie, I've never even met her before.'

'Oh, she makes the best chicken 'n' dumplings. Is she going to make that for dinner, Miss Justine?'

'I told her that is what you wanted and she said she would.'

'Oh, goodie! I can't wait. She makes the best dumplings in the world.' As he finished that sentence, he choked. I looked at him and saw tears spilling from his eyes.

I twisted in my seat and grabbed one of his hands in mine. 'I'm so sorry, sweetie. I wish I could make it better.'

'I'm an orphan now, Libby,' he said through loud sobs.

'I know, darling, so am I. We'll make it, I promise.'

'Miss Justine,' he said. 'Can I call you Mom now?'

Justine's words strangled in her throat. She pulled over to the side of the road, got out of the car, flipped up the seat and climbed into the back with Ernie. Embracing him, she said, 'Yes, Ernie. Absolutely, positively yes. I would be honored.' She rocked him back and forth in her arms while I brushed away tears. Picking her to raise Ernie was most likely the best decision I'd ever made.

After we finished taking care of the animals, Justine and I sat on the front porch while Ernie packed his things to spend a couple of nights with me and his aunt. I asked, 'Do you think going back to the house might bother him?'

'Oh no, not any longer. He goes over there a lot. I once asked him why and he said, "I need to make sure nothing is being neglected. I have a responsibility to my Aunt Dorothy." A little while later, he added, "That's not the only reason. I spend some time just sittin' in the living room and kitchen getting used to knowin' that Mama will never be there again." I can tell ya, Libby, that floored me. In some ways, he's such a little boy and in others, he has more self-awareness than many people ever achieve in a lifetime.'

'Good. I was afraid I might be making a mistake.'

'Don't assume too much. I imagine just seein' his Aunt Dorothy will bring on another wave of intense emotion. It's going to be a difficult time but, in the end, Ernie will cope with the loss of his mother as well as he has every setback in his life. He's got a solid core.'

'Thank you, Justine.'

'Don't thank me. I should be thankin' you. He's been a joy to have around and he always says he wants to be strong and courageous just like you.'

'Me?'

'I know you think he's put his mother up on a pedestal and it's true. But the one he's erected for you is twice as high. I hope you don't ever fall off,' she said with a chuckle, 'you'd be sure to bust your head or somethin'.'

At the farm, Ernie insisted on carrying the bags into the house. He left them in the front hallway and escorted me back to the kitchen where he introduced me to his Aunt Janice. Even without being told, I would have known she was related to Justine. She had a little living-in-town polish in her hairstyle, dress and carriage, but she was the spitting image of her farmer-sister.

'Pleased to meet you, Janice,' I said.

'The pleasure is all mine. This boy talks up a blue streak about you every chance he gets.'

'I'll leave the two of you alone to get acquainted,' Ernie said, 'and I'll take your bag upstairs, Libby.'

Janice and I just stared at him as he left. 'He must have picked that line up from a movie. He sure didn't learn that from my brother-in-law. I do like the man my sister married but he's a bit rougher around the edges than your little brother.'

'He surprises me all the time,' I said.

'Your Aunt Dorothy told me she'd be here a little after 7 o'clock. So, I've timed supper to be ready about then. Would you like a snack to tide you over? I've got some homemade bread and some mighty fine cheese.'

'Did you bake the bread?'

'Did indeed. And my sister-in-law made the cheese.'

'Really? I haven't known many cheese makers around here.'

'And she churns her own butter, too. She's a marvel. But the farm women in my family work so hard day after day. I'm sure glad I married a city man. I doubt I'd have the energy to be a farm wife. But then I heard about you running this place when you were just a kid. I don't know how you managed.'

'I don't know either. And I couldn't imagine spending the rest of my life tied to the countryside, tending livestock and crops and making jelly.'

'Not me either. When my husband enlisted, I got a job at the Radford Ammunition Plant. It keeps me busy all day and gives me less time to worry about Sonny.'

'Is he overseas?'

'Yes, darn it. He saw some fighting in France and when that war was over, I thought he'd be coming home. He did for a short leave but then he got orders to ship out to the Pacific. I'm getting mighty tired of spending every day wondering if he got his head blown off,' she said, punctuating her remarks with a sigh. 'You do war work, too, I hear.'

'Yes, I do. But I'm not allowed to talk about it. In fact, I'm not supposed to let anyone know where I am. My aunt figured out my general location thanks to her connections, but she doesn't know exactly.'

'That must be hard. My big sister Justine would throw a fit if she didn't know where I was. Even if I was sent to a secret place, she wouldn't give me a moment's peace until I let her know.'

FORTY

I was amazed at the turnout for my mother's funeral. It seemed as if every farm family in the county was represented in the audience. Many stepped up to say a few words about her, mostly anecdotes that dated back before my father's death. Although more than a few mentioned my father, not one person mentioned Annabelle's second husband, Ernest Floyd.

Then, Ernie stood up at the podium with a sheaf of papers in his hand. 'To me, my mother was the best mother that ever walked the earth. I know this is not true for my sister, Libby.

She would have been if not for my father, a despicable human being who deserved to die.

'Yes, he died at my mother's hand. But my mother took his life to protect mine. Some say it was not extraordinary, any mother would protect their child. It was, however, an act of incredible courage for her. For years, that man oppressed my mother, oppressed my sister and ran the farm into the ground. He tried to oppress me, too. When he went too far, my mother stood up to him and refused to be bullied any longer.

'I ask you all to keep a close eye on the women in your lives: your mothers, your sisters, your daughters, your neighbors. If you see them under the thumb of an angry man, speak up and act before it's too late. Don't let another woman be forced to go to the extremes my mother did.

'I love my mother. And I miss her. I am just grateful that there still are three strong women in my life who I know will be there for me for as long as they live. My Aunt Dorothy, my sister Libby and my foster mother, Justine Early. Thank you.'

Ernie bowed his head, gathered his notes and looked down at the floor as he returned to his seat. The chapel was hushed – not a whisper, not a rustle, not a cough. A moment later, it erupted. Everyone jumped to their feet and applauded. I was impressed and shocked speechless by my little brother's performance. I sat down beside him and wrapped an arm around his shoulders. He turned, looked at me and burst into tears.

I stood next to Ernie in the receiving line at the back of the church. Listening to the comments from the attendees, I could tell the community would rally around Ernie once he was old enough to run the farm on his own. He was anxious to do just that but I hoped he would see the value in furthering his education. Virginia Polytechnic Institute had an excellent agricultural curriculum that would serve him well in the future. I made a mental note to talk to Justine and Aunt Dorothy about that before I went back to Tennessee.

Saying goodbye, the next morning, was difficult. Aunt Dorothy and Justine were emotional but nothing topped Ernie.

'Please, please, don't go, Libby. If you stay, I'll give you my share of the farm as long as you'll let me help you work it.'

'Ernie, I'm sorry I have to go and I wish I could say that I want to stay and run the farm, but it's just not where my heart is. Yours is here and I understand that and think it's wonderful. I hope you will try to accept that it is different for me,' I said.

'It's not fair,' Ernie said.

'I really don't know what fair has to do with it,' I said, 'but I will make you a promise. I will apply for a visitor's permit for you to come and visit me when school is out for the summer.'

'Really? That's a gas. I don't understand why I have to get a permit to go to your house. I'm your brother.'

'It's war time, Ernie, and I'm in a secret facility where things like that are necessary.'

'Are you a spy?'

'No, Ernie, I am not. I am a scientist.'

'So why is that a secret? What do you do?'

'After the war, I'll explain it all to you. But right now, I'm not allowed to tell anyone.'

He gave me a sidelong glance as if he thought I were making it all up. 'Well, whatever you say. Just let me know as soon as you get permission, okay.'

I assured him I would and gave him a kiss on the cheek which made him blush and squirm. I waved as I boarded the train. Alone, I brooded about what might have happened at Oak Ridge while I was gone.

The dining car was nearly full when I arrived. I was seated at the last empty table. After I ordered, the waiter approached and asked if a gentleman could join me. I agreed, hoping conversation with a stranger would pull me away from anxious thoughts.

He was of average height for a man but his intensely blue eyes with long dark lashes were hypnotic. As he slid into the seat opposite me, he asked, 'Are you sure you don't mind me sitting here. I can wait if you do mind.'

'No, please, have a seat.'

After he ordered, he asked, 'Are you headed for Knoxville, too?'

'Yes, I am. Do you live there?'

'I live everywhere. I'm a traveling salesperson. Do you work at the city behind the fence?'

'Why do you ask?'

'Just curious. Do you?'

Was that just a lucky guess because of my lack of a Tennessee accent? Or was this the same man who spoke to Tom? Unless I admitted to the truth, I could never find out. 'Yes, I do.'

'I thought you people weren't allowed to leave the area.'

'We don't do it very often because of the work demands but they do make exceptions.'

'What was yours?'

'The death of my mother.' I looked away from him and out on the passing landscape, not interested in continuing the conversation or gazing into his penetrating eyes.

He muttered his condolences – for what they were worth – and then said, 'What do you do there?'

'I am a scientist.'

'Really. I doubt that there are many lady scientists there.'

'I don't know another one but I wouldn't necessarily be aware of anyone working outside of my immediate area.'

'What kind of science work do you do?'

'I am not at liberty to discuss that.'

'I think I have a general idea of your work and I hope you are as concerned as I am that the decision to implement its use is now in Truman's hands.'

That confirmed it for me. He was either the same man or one working from the same agenda. 'What's wrong with the president?'

'You have to ask? Roosevelt didn't trust him. He told him nothing about what you are doing at your installation. Truman will feel he has to prove himself and what better way than by dropping the biggest bomb ever created on a bunch of yellow savages. Because of that, people in your position have a moral obligation to prevent another human disaster in the East by slowing down production.'

I pushed my plate to the side, replaced it with my elbow

and leaned my chin into the palm of my hand. 'Tell me, who do you work for?'

'The Acme Button and Sewing Notions Company.'

'Who doesn't need a few buttons? Why don't you show me your wares?'

'Sorry,' he grinned. 'All in my checked baggage.'

'Who do you really work for?'

'Excuse me?'

'Are you a Soviet agent? Or are you working for the Japanese?'

He laughed hard, slapping the tabletop. 'You crack me up.'

'I do not see any humor in my question, sir.'

'You're serious? You've flipped your wig,' he said as he stood and hurried out of the car and through the passageway.

Was I delusional or was he exactly what I thought? I closed my eyes to cement the memory of his appearance and the sound of his voice in my mind. I would report him to Crenshaw. Something sinister was afoot or I should say something sinister was riding the rails.

Happiness and gratitude filled me when we pulled into the station and I saw Teddy standing on the platform waving for all he was worth. With him here, I wouldn't have to worry about that unpleasant man confronting me again when I disembarked.

Teddy threw his arms around me the second I was close enough. Out of the corner of my eye, I saw that man stepping down onto the platform. 'Wait, Teddy. Look. Look at that man in the gray suit who just got off the train.'

'What about him?'

'Just get a good look. You want to remember what he looks like.'

Teddy's eyes followed the other man until he disappeared into the station. 'Okay. Now why?'

'Let's get my suitcase and I'll explain in the car.'

I was anxious to find out if he and Dennis had seen Tom while I was gone but needed to answer Teddy's questions first. I described the encounter and explained how it closely resembled Tom's experience. Then, I asked, 'Have you seen Tom?'

'Phew! Yes, we did. It didn't go well.'

'Why what happened?'

'It's a long story.'

'Tell me.'

FORTY-ONE

According to Teddy, in my absence he and Dennis had got along far better than anyone aware of their recent conflict would have believed possible. They shared an innate curiosity about the world around them and spent most of their first evening together speculating about the inevitable scientific and technological breakthroughs they anticipated once the energy to win the war was channeled into peace time endeavors.

Cleaning up the dishes from their bachelor supper soon turned to horseplay with swats of the dish rag and towel turning both of them wet. It ended when they both slid to the floor, doubled over with laughter. They cleaned up the puddles on the counter and floor before settling down in the living room to listen to the news. They'd almost forgotten all about Tom when he burst through the door. He bounced back and forth on his feet, looking from Teddy to Dennis and back again. His eyes were in constant motion. He jerked his hand through his hair again and again with no noticeable result. 'You got any leftovers from dinner?' he asked.

Dennis exchanged a troubled glance with Teddy before saying, 'We just made grilled cheese and tomato soup. We've got enough bread and cheese and another can of soup if you want me to fix that for you.'

'Yeah, do it,' he said in a tone that reminded Dennis of that sour adolescent phase he witnessed his little brother going through a few years ago.

Dennis went into the kitchen and pulled out the supplies and materials he needed. He wasn't certain if Tom had regressed or was exhibiting symptoms of serious psychiatric illness. Placating those with mental breakdowns didn't seem much different than manipulating around an adolescent's bad attitude. With that realization, he treated Tom just as he had his sibling, knowing catering to it often worked better than agitating in hopes of altering his current state of mind.

Tom stepped toward the sofa and bent his knees as if he were about to sit down, then shot straight up. 'Where is the girl?'

'Girl? What girl?' Teddy asked.

'What girl? Are you pulling my leg? That girl you staked your claim to? Where is she?'

'I have made a commitment to a woman named Libby Clark, not a nameless girl,' Teddy said.

'Girl, woman, what's the difference? Where is she?'

'She's not here.'

'You sure?' Tom said as he rushed around the corner to check the bedroom and bathroom. 'Then what are you doing here?'

Dennis stepped into the doorway of the kitchen. 'Come on, Tom. Settle down. Go sit at the table. Your food is almost ready.'

Tom stepped toward Dennis and said, 'What are you doing here?'

'Libby asked us to keep an eye on her cat and look out for you while she was out of town,' Dennis said.

'Out of town? She abandoned me? She said she'd help me and she just ran off.'

Teddy walked up behind Tom and placed a hand on his shoulder. Tom jerked sideways and put up his fists.

'Easy, Tom,' Dennis said. 'Libby had to go to her mother's funeral . . .'

'She abandoned me,' Tom wailed, his arms falling useless to his sides.

'No, Tom. She and I spoke with Crenshaw before she left.'

'What did he say?'

'Go sit down. I've got to go take care of your grilled cheese before it burns. I'll tell you everything.'

Tom backed up, his eyes jumping from one man to the other as if he couldn't trust either one of them for a moment.

He sat in the chair sideways, his eyes moved as if following a game of tennis.

Dennis set the plate and bowl in front of Tom who gobbled half of the sandwich in three manic bites. To wash it down, he picked up the soup with both hands and slurped from the rim. Teddy and Dennis looked at each other, both shocked by the further loss of Tom's table manners.

'Okay, spill it, Dennis. What did Crenshaw say?' Tom ordered.

'Libby gave him a list of demands about housing, daily visitation and meals as well as lowering the charges against you down to manslaughter. Crenshaw said he would agree to keep you here for the duration and you would be allowed some visitors, but he wouldn't commit to how often nor would he agree to anything about your meals or his willingness to influence the criminal charges until he had talked with you.'

Tom jerked to his feet. 'Blow it out your barracks bag! Libby would never let Crenshaw get away with that. You got rid of her so that you two could make me your fall guy. You guys have had it in for me for a long time.'

'Tom,' Teddy said, 'you know that's not true. We can only make you a fall guy if one of us sabotaged that train and we all know that didn't happen.'

'And if you don't believe us,' Dennis added, 'we're expecting Libby to return Friday evening. You can ask her yourself when she gets back. She thinks you should still turn yourself in to the authorities. We can get her to go to General Groves if Crenshaw doesn't keep his word.'

Tom snagged the other half of his sandwich in one hand and pulled open the door with the other. 'Tell Libby, thanks for nothing.' He stepped outside, slamming the door behind him.

'Should we . . .' Teddy began.

'No, Teddy, just let him go,' Dennis answered.

FORTY-TWO

'That doesn't even sound like Tom,' I said.

'Dennis and I were rattled, too, when he left. Yes, Tom has anger issues and resentments against women in the workplace but that night was excessive even for him.'

'And he's usually so logical – maybe in a negative way, a lot of times, but still he used to think things through. I can't believe his "fall guy" accusation. It makes no sense at all.'

The conversation ended as they went through security at the gate. After that, they drove in silence until Teddy pulled up in front of Libby's flat-top. 'I'll carry your suitcase inside,' he offered.

'Thanks. I'm really exhausted from this trip and want to take a shower and go to bed soon. But I'll be making a cup of tea first, would you like to join me?'

'Sure,' Teddy said, opening the door for Libby before stepping inside behind her. 'Dennis moved his stuff out of here this morning but I'll have to retrieve a couple of things like my toothbrush but that'll only take a minute.'

'What's Dennis doing tonight?' I asked as I put the water on to boil.

'He took Ruth out to dinner. In fact, I dropped them off at the restaurant in Knoxville before coming to the train station.'

'Oh, dear! How are they going to get home?'

'That problem already has a solution. They're catching a ride back with another fella who went into town for something or another. Anyway, they're covered. And Ruth said, "Me and Dennis talked it over. What kind of friends would we be if we didn't let the two of you have some time alone together after she's been out of town?" I couldn't argue with that.'

'No, I can't imagine you would,' I said with a chuckle as I carried the tea tray into the living room.

'I'm glad they did, aren't you?'

Fear clutched my throat. Was I ready to be honest with

Teddy? I had to be. I put my legs under me as I curled up next to him on the sofa. 'Absolutely, Teddy.'

Teddy kissed the tip of my nose and asked, 'What are we going to do about Tom? And what are we going to tell Crenshaw?'

'We say nothing to Crenshaw unless he asks. If he does, we tell him that we are working out the timing of Tom's surrender, which isn't a total lie. As for Tom, we wait for him to come and see me.'

'For how long?'

'If he does want to ask me about the Crenshaw situation, he'll show up tonight or tomorrow.'

'And if he doesn't?'

'On Sunday, we go looking for him. I suspect he might have told us he wouldn't be at the shack because that is exactly where he will be. We'll start there.'

'In the meantime, I'm supposed to walk away from here and leave you all alone?'

'Yes, Teddy. I don't need a round-the-clock guard. I can handle Tom.'

'I'm not sure you'd say that if you'd been here the other night. He's angry, out of control and making no sense. Dennis is worried about your safety, too.'

'Oh, so why don't I let the two of you smuggle me into your dormitory for the night?'

'I'd be willing to try – and I'm sure Dennis would, too.'

'Oh please! Both of you are like over-protective mother hens. Now give me a kiss and get out of here. I need to get ready for bed.'

As soon as I put on the coffee pot and fed the kitty the next morning, I stepped outside to see if Tom had left a note under the jar. No note on my porch, but out in my yard, I spotted a pup tent. A hand stuck out and waved and someone said, 'Good morning, Libby!'

'Dennis? What in heaven's name are you doing out there?'

'Teddy, wake up,' Dennis said. 'Did you sleep well, Libby?'

'Both of you?' I asked.

'Yeah,' Teddy said. 'We took turns watching your house.'

'Are you trying to earn Boy Scout badges or something? You're both crazy. But if you want a cup of coffee, come on in.' I was annoyed and pleased at the same time. Despite the mental turmoil, I could not suppress the grin that trespassed on my face.

I served coffee and the three of us sat in the living room. 'Did you plan this ahead of time?'

'No,' Teddy said. 'I just got lucky. As I walked up to the dormitory, a car pulled up and Dennis and Ruth got out.'

'Ruth was insistent that you weren't left alone last night. She suggested that she should go over and spend the night,' Dennis said.

'But then I said that you were probably already in bed and Ruth would wake you and so . . .' Teddy added.

'So, I have a lot of camping gear. I went in and got my tent while Teddy and Ruth waited. We walked Ruth to her dorm and set up here in your yard,' Dennis said.

'And we didn't disturb your sleep, did we?' Teddy asked.

'No, that was good,' I said. 'But you're being over-protective.'

'You didn't see Tom the other night,' Dennis said. 'And besides, Ruth gave her blessing.'

'I guess I'll have to have a talk with her, too,' I said.

'Good,' said Dennis, 'she's coming over to spend the night after work today.'

'Well, gee, did anyone think of asking me first?' I griped.

'You were asleep,' Teddy said.

I shook my head. 'It is heartwarming to know you all care about me but sometimes you make me feel smothered.'

'Better smothered, Libby, than completely nuts like Tom,' Dennis said.

'Or here by yourself when an even further unhinged Tom comes calling,' Teddy added.

FORTY-THREE

The hours dripped by like a slow leak. I wanted night-time to descend and herald the arrival of Tom at my door. I knew that wasn't a given but I couldn't even hope until the sun went down. My constant glances at the clock made the day feel longer but I couldn't seem to stop myself.

Just the same, I spent a lot of time wrapping things up in the lab at the end of the work day, mostly due to my absence for a good chunk of the week. I arrived home a bit late and stepped inside to the smells and sounds of cooking emanating from my kitchen.

'Libby! Hope you don't mind. I was as hungry as a hog that ain't been slopped for a week. I messed around till I found fixins for supper. I've got spam and onions frying in the skillet, green beans heating and potatoes cooking on the back of the stove.'

'Mind? I'm deeply grateful. I'm hungry, too. Did you bring those green beans with you?'

'No, Libby! I found this jar in your pantry tucked behind some other canned goods. It might be the last one, though. Hopin' that don't bother you much.'

'Not at all, Ruthie. What can I do to help?'

I set the table while Ruth hummed songs I didn't recognize as she finished preparing dinner. I know my Aunt Dorothy would be appalled but although I turned my nose up at spam at the beginning of the war, I'd now grown quite fond of it. Still, I would never dream of serving it to Aunt Dorothy. She would instantly embark on a project to refine my palate.

After devouring our meal in record time and cleaning up in the kitchen, we curled up on opposite ends of the sofa to listen to the radio and chat. Ruth was over the moon about her date with Dennis.

'Libby, I know he's lots smarter than me, but I still think

he likes me. I mean, you're lots smarter and you like me so it's not impossible, is it?'

'I was delighted you two were going out, Ruthie, because I thought you'd be very compatible,' I said.

'You did? Really?'

'Yes, I did. And don't short change yourself. You might not have the education that Dennis and I do but you are very smart about life and people. And you are probably the most loyal friend I have ever had.'

'Aw, gee, Libby. You're gonna make me blush. But, still . . .'

'But nothing. If things got serious between you two, how would you feel about moving out west with him?'

'Honest, Libby, I'd follow him anywhere. But don't let him know that – at least not yet. Could you talk to him? See if he likes me a little? Could you? But don't let him know that I asked.'

'If the opportunity arises, I will be glad to talk to him, Ruthie. But I can't just blurt it out or he'll know you asked.'

Ruth sighed. 'I sure hope he asks me out again.'

A knock startled us both. Ruth was the first to recover. She bounced up and ran toward it. 'Must be Tom.' Instead, when she pulled the door wide open, two smiling faces looked in at us: Teddy and Dennis.

'We wanted to make sure you two were okay,' Dennis said.

'Come on in, fellas,' Ruth said.

Teddy sat down beside me and Dennis took the chair caddy-corner from Ruth. 'We brought a little surprise,' Teddy said as he pulled a pint of brandy out of his pocket.

'Brandy?' I said. 'Where in heaven's name did you get that?'

'One of our dorm buddies managed to smuggle in a case, don't know how he pulled that off,' Teddy said.

'And he was asking triple the price he paid for it, but considering he brought it down from New York, I guess he was entitled,' Dennis added. 'I'll get the glasses.'

Everyone sipped the first swallow without a grimace, except for me. I didn't think I'd ever get a taste for hard liquor. I swallowed my first three sips like cod liver oil. After that, it seemed to go down smooth.

We sat and talked and somehow it seemed natural that

Teddy's arm encircled me and Ruth cuddled up in Dennis' lap. Then the bottle was empty, the clock struck midnight and a round of yawns overrode all attempts at conversation.

After Teddy and Dennis were gone, I said, 'Ruthie, I think you have your answer. I don't think I need to ask Dennis about anything.'

'He kissed me goodbye.'

'Yes, he did.'

'Do you think . . .?'

'No doubt about it, Ruthie. He certainly didn't come over here looking for me.'

Ruth was still grinning when we climbed into bed. Although I had a terrific time tonight, now that Teddy was gone, I began to worry. Tom had not shown up. What did that mean? Was he still here in the woods or had he run away? We needed to send out a search party tomorrow.

FORTY-FOUR

I fixed breakfast for Ruth and I, planning how I was going to communicate with the men to gather a search team when I wasn't allowed inside the dorm. By the time I was dressed, though, they were all gathered in the street by my house: Teddy, Dennis, Rudy, Gary and Gregg. Ruth insisted on joining us and no one objected.

The light rain that fell overnight intensified the smell of the moss and rotted leaves beneath our feet. The air was crisp and fresh. We couldn't have picked a better morning for a walk in the woods if only we could forget why we were there.

Spots in the trail were muddy and some patches were overgrown making our forward progress a bit slow. Eventually, we made it to the shack. The path to the rickety door remained clear indicating that Tom or someone had been here on a regular basis. Inside, the wild unstoppable growth of vines over and through the walls dimmed the light and tinged it green.

We stood still for a bit allowing our eyes to adjust. Dennis was the first to spot the note nailed to the wall. He pulled it away, taking care to rip it as little as possible. He folded it open, stepped outside and read it out loud.

Libby, I didn't think I could fool you for long. I thought sooner or later, you would call my bluff and come back to the shack. Thanks for what you tried to do. I'm sorry, I just can't face losing my freedom for the rest of my life. Like I told you before, it would be like being trapped deep in the coal mine, always hoping for salvation but knowing it would never come. I don't know what's wrong with me but I sense something is. One moment I'm feeling energetic and optimistic about the future, the next I am consumed by dread, fear and a sadness that my father's death can't explain. I decided it would be better to pay a tribute to Marvin. Tom.

For a moment, I couldn't breathe. The world stood still and silent. Then, I once again heard bird song and the rustle of forest creatures. My lips moved but the words scrambled before I could utter a syllable.

'Does this mean what I think it does?' Teddy asked.

'I hope not,' Dennis said.

Gary said, 'What do you mean?'

We all turned and looked at him. 'Isn't it obvious?' Dennis asked.

'What?' Gary moaned.

'I guess we need to go that way,' Teddy said.

'I never wanted to revisit that spot again,' Gregg said.

'What? What are you talking about?' Gary asked. But no one could put it into words. Ruth, too, had a puzzled look on her face but wisely, she did not comment. She simply joined us as we walked toward the path that veered off to the tree where Marvin was tortured and killed.

We reached the turn-off and stopped. I didn't want to go up that trail and I doubted anyone else did. We stood rooted in the intersection. All except Gary who shoved through the crowd and ran like demons were on his tail.

Gary's high-pitched shrieks brought us around. We raced to his side. By the time we entered the clearing in the deadly spot, Gary had shimmed up the trunk and was easing out on the limb.

'Gary, come on down,' Dennis said. 'We need to contact the authorities.'

'No, no, he might be still alive,' he said as he reached the spot where the rope encircled the tree.

'It's too late, Gary,' Dennis said.

'No. You don't know that,' Gary screamed as he hung over the edge and slid his hands into Tom's armpits and tugged.

'Gary, listen to me. I'm going to be blunt. You must listen.' He described the length of Tom's neck, the swollen tongue hanging out of his mouth – the graphic details of the obvious signs of death.

Gary gave up his struggle, let his arms and legs hang down on either side of the limb and sobbed like a child with a broken heart. We gave him time to express his grief and then Dennis talked him down from the tree.

The effort took so much out of Gary that his knees buckled when he tried to stand on the ground. Rudy grabbed him before he fell, threw one of Gary's arms over his shoulders and wrapped both of his arms around Gary's waist. We hobbled down out of the woods, heading toward my flat-top.

By the time we reached it, we all agreed that Dennis and I would go speak to Crenshaw while the others waited at my place for our return. When we parted to go our separate ways, Teddy stopped us. 'What if Crenshaw won't let you leave?'

Dennis straightened his posture as if that effort would push the fatigue out of his body and into the ground. 'If I let Crenshaw keep Libby, Ruth would never speak to me again. I can guarantee you that I will never let that happen.'

Ruth let out an incoherent sound that blended joy and terror in one utterance. She certainly had her answer now.

FORTY-FIVE

On the way to Crenshaw's house, Dennis and I decided that I'd do most of the talking and he would be there to back me up should Crenshaw doubt anything I said. I hoped that he could get me out of Crenshaw's grasp but the man could be unpredictable and he was in charge and never let anyone forget it.

I knocked on the door and it jerked open. 'Again. Can't I get through one Sunday without you disturbing my peace. Have you no respect for the Sabbath?' After that outburst, he paused and studied our faces. 'Oh, for heaven's sakes, come in. You two look like gray clouds on this otherwise sunny day.'

We sat down in the living room as Crenshaw leaned through the kitchen doorway. 'Coffee for three, Mother, as soon as possible, please.'

'Well, what is it?' Crenshaw said as he sat down.

'I suppose the best place to start is with the most urgent concern,' I began.

'Which is?'

'We found a body in the woods.'

Crenshaw bowed his head, placed two fingers and a thumb on his forehead and spread them apart hard enough to leave white marks in their wake. 'I don't want to hear this.'

'I don't want to say it, sir.'

'Why, Miss Clark, do you always find bodies? Why you? A line of thought endorsed by many investigators is that there are no coincidences. If I subscribed to that theory, I could only assume that you've been responsible for all of them.'

I looked down at my hands as I folded them primly in my lap. I could feel the vibrations of Dennis' anger in the cushions. I darted a look over at him and sharply shook my head.

'Let me see how that coffee is coming,' Crenshaw said as he rose to his feet and disappeared around the corner.

Dennis hissed, 'If he keeps this up, I'm going to punch him.'

'Stay calm, Dennis. You can't blame him for that reaction.'

'Oh yes, I can.'

'It doesn't help, Dennis.'

Crenshaw returned and his wife followed carrying a tray with a silver coffee server, three cups, three spoons, a creamer and a sugar bowl. 'There you go,' she said with a smile as she set it down on the table.

'Thank you, Mother.'

She flashed a smile at us and said, 'Let me know if you need anything else. I've got coffee cake and cookies and—'

'Thank you, Mother. That's all for now.'

We prepared our coffees in silence. After settling back into the chair, Crenshaw said, 'Where? Where did you find this body? And whose body is it?'

'Tom O'Malley, sir. We found him in the same tree where Marvin lost his life.'

'Please tell me he didn't die the same way.'

'He didn't, sir. It appears to us as if it were a suicide by hanging.'

'Was there a note with the body?'

'He left a note but it wasn't with the body. It was in the shack where he was hiding out.'

'Do you have it?'

'Dennis, you have it, right?' I asked.

'Right here,' Dennis said, pulling it from his shirt pocket and handing it to Crenshaw.

Crenshaw read it over and asked, 'What is he talking about? What does this mean?'

'Tom was responsible for the pranks in the lab and for the sabotage of the train,' I said.

'I thought you were going to get him to surrender, Miss Clark.'

'That was the plan. However, when he learned you wouldn't agree to meet all the demands, it seems he found an alternative solution.'

'Are you trying to say I'm responsible, Miss Clark?'

'No, it's not . . . it's more than that . . . it's—'

Dennis interrupted, 'Sir, Tom O'Malley was not of sound mind when he committed those acts of destruction nor when he took his own life.'

'That's a flimsy excuse,' Crenshaw said.

'Science is working hard in the field of mental health, sir. One day, we will have a clear understanding of these forms of illness. Look at men who go to battle – some come home emotionally and mentally damaged. One day scientists will understand how to take care of that.'

'Any man who can't take the rigors of the battlefield is a weakling. They just need to grow a spine,' Crenshaw declared.

'Actually, sir,' Dennis continued, 'scientists are focused on those problems and believe it is far more complicated than that. We can only hope they have a solution one day for the soldiers psychologically injured in the war.'

Crenshaw pushed upward and paced across the room. 'Do you have any idea of how sick I am of scientists? How tired I am of waiting for science to find the answers to end this war once and for all?'

Dennis and I sat in silence, not wanting to agitate him any further.

Crenshaw stopped and stood in front of us with his arms akimbo. 'What are you waiting for? Go. You delivered your bad news. My men haven't forgotten the last body – they won't have any trouble finding this one. Your services are no longer needed. Now, just go.'

'I have another development that I need to tell you about, sir,' I said.

'Of course, you do,' Crenshaw said and slumped into his chair.

I told Tom's story of meeting a man on the train when he was on his way to his father's funeral. I continued relating the conversation I'd had with the man I'd encountered on my way back here.

'Was it the same man?'

'I have no way of knowing, sir. I had planned on talking to Tom to see if it might have been but I never had a chance.'

'This could be important. I need you to come in with me and give a statement about your meeting to an agent. Once you do that, I'll get a private to drive you home. You,' Crenshaw said, pointing at Dennis, 'you can go now. I'm sure your little friends are gathered together somewhere waiting for news.'

'I'm sorry, sir,' Dennis said. 'I cannot go back without Libby.'

Crenshaw strode over and hovered over the seated Dennis. 'You think I'm going to do something to her, Mr Jance?'

Dennis slowly straightened his knees and towered over Crenshaw. 'No, sir. But if I go back without her, no matter what I say, they will believe the worst.'

'Oh, for heaven's sakes. Then come along. Scientists!'

FORTY-SIX

Crenshaw's decision to sit next to me in the back of the jeep invoked a keen sense of discomfort and apprehension. My unease expanded when he acted human. 'I understand you've recently lost your mother, Miss Clark.'

I certainly did not give him any credit for caring but, at least, he was trying. 'Yes, sir. I returned Friday from her funeral.'

'I'm surprised your stay wasn't lengthier – there must be many matters needing your attention, most particularly the needs of your half-brother.'

Disturbed that he knew details of my private life, I reached the conclusion that he wanted me out of the way for an extended time. Logic or paranoia? 'The needs of my country are of paramount importance to me in this time of conflict. Sublimating my personal desires is a sacrifice that many Americans make every day.' I knew my answer sounded stiff and wooden but with Crenshaw, I always felt as if every word I spoke brought me a step closer to stamping on a land mine.

'I'd like to believe that, Miss Clark, but some of your

actions and your reluctance to answer all my questions completely and fully make me doubt your expressed sentiment.'

'Could you ask the driver to stop? I'd rather walk the rest of the way.'

'Don't be childish,' Crenshaw snapped.

I focused my gaze on the passing scenery. Fortunately, he was not obtuse enough to continue the conversation.

When we arrived, Crenshaw told Dennis to wait in the lobby area while I gave my statement. Dennis, however, would have none of that. He stood and said, 'I'm sorry, sir. I made a commitment. Miss Clark will not leave my sight for one moment.'

Crenshaw glared at him. 'Corporal, secure that man.'

I rose to my feet and interjected. 'Lieutenant Colonel, if you want my statement, you will retract that order and allow Mr Jance to accompany me.'

With a sharp jerk of his head, Crenshaw turned the malevolent look on me. 'One day, Miss Clark, you will push me too far. When that happens, I will make sure that you will be unable to communicate with anyone. What General Groves does not know will eliminate any possibility of his intercession on your behalf. And if you think one of your co-conspirators can reach him, think again. The general's aide de camp will never let those calls go through. Corporal, take them both back to the interview room.'

The soldier latched onto my upper arm. Dennis stepped forward and laid a hand on the man's shoulder and in a quiet, yet firm, voice said, 'Let go of her.'

The corporal raised his head, sized up Dennis and released me. Dennis wedged between the two of us and placed a hand on my shoulder blade for the walk down the halls.

Once we were alone, I said, 'Dennis, don't push your protectiveness too far. You're putting yourself at excessive risk.'

'What a nice, cheerful room,' Dennis said.

'Cheerful? It's dull. It's boring. And you're changing the subject.'

'Ah, but you have not seen the rooms in the basement. This

one is freshly painted. It is clean. It doesn't smell like mold. And it has a window to the outside world. I think our status has risen.'

'Okay, Dennis, if it will make you happy, I'll agree: it's a lovely room. Now, back to the point I was making . . .'

'Alright. You deserve a full disclosure of my motivation. In my mind, there is nothing excessive about the risk I'm taking to stand up for you, Libby. Admittedly, I have a strong affection and great respect for you but, to be honest, it is more than that to my dogged persistence. And that is Ruth Nance. I will never, under any circumstances, back down on standing up for you because Ruth would never forgive me if I did. That is a risk I cannot bear to take. Nothing that the army could do to me is more frightening than the specter of Ruth's disapproval.'

What a delightful surprise – I didn't know matters between them had progressed that far, I thought but only asked, 'She means that much to you?'

As his mouth opened, so did the door. Crenshaw stepped inside, followed by a WAC stenographer and a major. The first two sat at the table with us and the nameless officer leaned against the back wall.

'Start at the beginning and tell us the whole story of your involvement with Tom O'Malley,' Crenshaw ordered. 'I will only interrupt if you make an unclear or incomplete statement.'

I chose to begin my narrative with the night I fed Tom, offered to negotiate on his behalf and provided him a place to sleep. I related his disappearance in the middle of the night but never mentioned the Mason jar notes or the involvement of anyone else. I wrapped up with the discovery of Tom's body by me and unnamed others.

'We need the names of those who accompanied you in the woods when you made the discovery,' Crenshaw said.

'No. You don't need them. You simply want them. I have no intention of satisfying your curiosity.'

Crenshaw turned to the stenographer and said, 'Thank you. Please transcribe your notes and bring a copy back for Miss Clark to sign.'

She closed the door behind her as she left and Crenshaw

turned to Dennis. 'I suppose you were also there. Am I correct?'

'Yes, sir,' Dennis said.

'I understand that westerners take great pride in their strong sense of patriotism unlike the effete attitudes in the northeast. I expect, therefore, that you will want to inform me who else was in the group that discovered the body.'

'Then, sir, you have made a mistaken assumption.'

'If you were military, I would have grounds to throw you both in the guard house.'

Dennis and I looked at each other but said not a word. The silence that followed felt bigger than the room itself as if the slightest pressure would make the walls explode outward, obliterating us all.

Finally, a timid knock at the door broke the spell. 'Enter!' Crenshaw barked.

The WAC slipped in and slid a piece of paper on the desk in front of the lieutenant colonel. 'Is that all, sir?'

'Yes. You're dismissed.'

Crenshaw scanned the document and pushed it in front of me. The major stepped up and handed me a pen. I was halfway through reading it when Crenshaw interrupted. 'Just sign it, Clark.'

I looked up at him. 'I will, sir, as soon as I have finished checking it for accuracy. And not until I do.' I continued to stare at him until I got a response.

'Read then. Read, read, read,' he said with a dismissive flip of his hand. 'Just be quick about it.'

His impatience caused a momentary surge of pleasure but I was as anxious to get out of there as he was. I bent my head to the document and read it to the end before reaching for a pen, signing it and passing it over. Crenshaw had the major and Dennis sign as witnesses and then he added his flourish at the bottom.

'Major, arrange for their transportation, please,' Crenshaw said and left the room.

Back at my place, the cacophony of questions ended only when Dennis boomed, 'Sit down and shut up! Give Libby a chance to explain.'

The roar faded to a murmur and then to nothingness. I related the events of the evening emphasizing Dennis' strong support. I did not, however, repeat what he said about Ruth to the group. I asked for follow-up questions.

Rudy spoke first. 'Did Crenshaw send out a recovery team to bring back Tom's body?'

'I assume so,' I said.

'But did either of you hear him order anyone out there?'

'I didn't,' I said. 'Did you, Dennis?'

'No. But what else could he do? He certainly wouldn't just ignore what we told him.'

'I agree with Dennis,' I confirmed. 'He wasn't with us every moment. I assumed that he was doing just that while we waited in the room for his arrival. Frankly, my big worry now is about Tom's aunt. I'll have to call her tomorrow and I'm dreading it.'

'Shouldn't an official be doing that?' Gary asked.

'I doubt that they will but even if they do, Gary, Tom's aunt deserves a more personal contact from someone who cares about her nephew.'

'Why even bother to tell her? They won't send the body home for burial. Knowing could only be a source of pain,' Stephen said.

'Strong pressure on the authorities made it possible for Irene to come home,' Ruth said.

'Good point,' Dennis said. 'How can we pressure them, though? Tom, by his own admission, is guilty of serious crimes and he committed suicide.'

'His aunt can apply the pressure – not us,' Gregg said. 'Once she knows what happened, there's no security reason not to release the body to her.'

'But then there is another problem,' Joe said. 'Tom's family is Catholic. Suicides cannot be buried on church ground.'

'Why can't we tell her it was an accident? Why can't we say he fell from a tree? I mean, that's not a lie – that's precisely what broke his neck,' Teddy said. He looked around the room at an array of shocked faces. 'What? Wouldn't that be an act of kindness?'

'Yes, it would,' Joe said. 'We would, however, need to get

Crenshaw's blessing. He could throw the truth in her face if he wanted to do so.'

'But why would he?' Dennis asked. 'Doesn't he always want to conceal ugly facts? We've just offered him an easy out. He can cover up Tom's activities and bring peace to a grieving family.'

'He can't cover up the train incident. People died,' I said.

'You underestimate Crenshaw, Libby,' Joe said. 'He can say the stories about explosives being involved in the derailment are nothing but idle rumors and irresponsible speculation. He can weave a tale about the heroism of the men who died – who gave their lives for the soldiers in their care. The situation is abounding in propaganda potential. For all we know, he could be engineering just that as we speak.'

'Okay. Here's my plan. I call Tom's aunt. I'm sure I can do that from Charlie's office tomorrow morning. I'll tell her that Tom's body has been found. I will insist that I can't tell her anything more until I learn more. It skates so close to dishonesty, it repulses me but it seems for the best at this moment. As soon as I can tomorrow, I'll go see Crenshaw and try to persuade him to go along with this deception as being the best for everyone involved.'

'Make sure when you're making that last point that you do a little flag waving – he certainly does that with us often enough,' Dennis said.

'And find out about Tom's body. Make sure it's been collected. And be clear that you want Tom sent home for a proper burial if he wants the truth to be buried with him,' Joe said.

'That sounds like a threat,' Teddy objected.

'I sure hope it does. A plea to his finer principles does not affect him as much as a veiled threat,' Joe said.

After that, the room went silent for a few moments until Gregg asked, 'All in favor of Libby's plan with the added provisions, raise your hand.'

Every palm stretched to the ceiling including Ruth. A couple of the men looked surprised that she was still in the room but no one objected to her vote. 'The ayes have it,' Gregg said. 'Go with God, Libby. Now we need to clear out and let these two ladies get some sleep.'

Dennis and Teddy lingered after the others. Ruth and I gave our respective fellas a kiss goodnight and soon they were gone.

Ruth was over the moon when I told her what Dennis had said about her. She sighed herself to sleep in record time. I tossed and turned for a few minutes before I remembered my father's long-ago advice: 'Tomorrow will take care of itself, girl.' I smiled, too, at that memory and joined Ruth in dreamland.

FORTY-SEVEN

I stood in Charlie's office, staring at the black phone on his desk. I felt mildly nauseous and my heart raced. I picked up the receiver, realized the only name I knew for Tom's closest living relative was Aunt Gertrude. I returned the phone to the cradle. I wracked my brain but although I knew the woman's maiden name was O'Malley, I didn't recall ever hearing her married surname.

I'd have to call her Gertrude. It felt rude and overly personal but I had no other choice. I began the call again, connecting with the switchboard and listening to the far away ringing of Gertrude's telephone.

When Tom's aunt answered, I said, 'Ms Gertrude, I finally have some news for you.'

'Is this Libby? From Tom's work?'

'Yes, ma'am.'

'The tone of your voice does not sound as if you are calling with good news.'

'No, ma'am. I am sorry. Tom's body has been found.'

'His body? He's dead? No. It can't be true. Please, tell me it's not true.'

'I wish I could, ma'am. Sadly, your nephew Tom O'Malley has passed away.'

'What happened?'

'Again, I apologize but I cannot tell you anything more

about what happened. The military is recovering the body. After they have, we should all know more.'

Gertrude sobbed, blew her nose and cleared her throat. 'Thank you, dear. I know this had to be difficult for you. Please keep me informed. Do you know who I need to call to bring him home? I want to bury him next to his father.'

'I will call you back with as much information as I can obtain.'

Gertrude thanked me again and I muttered my condolences one more time and disconnected the call. I hung my head and blinked as quickly as I could to stop the tears that wanted to fall.

When I looked up, Charlie was standing across from me. 'I just talked to Gregg, Libby. He told me about your plan and the need to talk to Crenshaw to get his agreement. Why don't you go up there now instead of waiting until the end of the day? I'll fill in for you at your station while you're gone. I won't be as quick at the procedures as you are but I will plod away.'

'Are you sure?' I asked.

'Yes. Go, Libby. Resolving this matter as soon as possible will be a good thing for all of us.'

An hour later, I was still sitting in the waiting area. The intercom buzzed and Crenshaw asked his aide to step into the office. I stood at his return.

'Sit, sit, sit, Miss Clark. Not yet. The lieutenant colonel knows you are here. He assured me that he would see you just as soon as he wraps up a pressing matter. I need to take care of something for him on another floor but I'll only be gone about ten minutes. Can I bring you a glass of water or a cup of coffee when I return?'

'No, thank you,' I said, sinking back into the chair. I listened to the aide's fading footsteps as he walked away. I jumped up, glanced down the hall to make sure that he was gone and then approached Crenshaw's office door, wrapping a sweaty palm around the knob.

I took a deep breath and rushed inside. 'Lieutenant Colonel Crenshaw, I am sorry to interrupt but I have an urgent matter—'

The man in the chair in front of Crenshaw's desk turned and stared at me. He was in uniform with no badge of rank but the star insignia worn only by officers sparkled on his shirt collar. His blue, penetrating eyes turned on me in surprise. I knew those eyes. I'd seen them on the train. I swallowed hard and clutched my hands together in a vain attempt to hide their shaking.

'So, we meet again,' the man said with a chuckle.

'Lieutenant colonel, sir, arrest this man.'

Crenshaw wiped an open palm across his face. 'Sit down, Miss Clark.'

'I don't know how he's managed to manipulate you, sir,' I said as I walked backwards. When I felt the door frame against my back, I stepped sideways to stand in the open entry, ready to run.

'Miss Clark, for heaven's sake, have you lost your mind?'

'Call the MPs now, sir. This man is dangerous.' I kept my eyes on Crenshaw's face praying for his look of incredulity to fade. All the while, I could feel the heat of the other man's stare burning on my skin.

'Miss Clark, you are being hysterical. Come in, have a seat and we'll talk this out,' Crenshaw said.

I didn't like the look in Crenshaw's eyes. It felt as if he were humoring me, trying to lull me into a false sense of safety. 'No sir, please listen to me.'

'Miss Clark!' Crenshaw's aide said from behind me. He grabbed my upper arms in a firm grip. To the lieutenant colonel he said, 'Sir, I'm sorry, sir.'

'Stevenson, I told you I was not to be interrupted,' Crenshaw barked.

'But sir, you sent me—'

'No excuses, soldier. Escort Miss Clark to the chair on my right, place her in it and then leave, closing the door behind you. We will discuss this matter later.'

I twisted my body trying to escape the aide's grasp, throwing him a bit off balance and loosening his hold on me for a moment – but not long enough. He latched on to my waist, lifting me in the air and swung me around. Before I touched ground again, I landed a sharp back kick in his shin.

He cursed under his breath but his grip grew painfully intense.

'Miss Clark,' Crenshaw shouted, 'for God's sake, I simply want to talk to you.'

Stevenson plopped me into a chair and I popped back up. He pushed on my shoulders and pressed down. I slid forward and did a prat fall on the floor.

'Perhaps, you need to call G.G.,' the man said, 'and let him know that his pet monkey is out of control.'

'Shut up, Cooper. You're not helping,' Crenshaw said. 'Will you please just talk to me, Clark?'

'I will not be willing to stay in the same room with the man who killed Tom O'Malley as surely as if he put the noose around his neck.'

'I've heard that there's only a thin line between genius and madness but I've never seen it demonstrated before my eyes,' the man said.

'Agent Cooper, give us a moment alone,' Crenshaw said.

'Really, Crenshaw—' Cooper objected.

The lieutenant colonel stepped up to the man. 'I cannot pull rank on you, Cooper, but I know who can. Leave us.'

As the look of disbelief on Cooper's face mutated into acceptance, he shook his head. 'Crenshaw, these scientists are not good for your health.'

'This way, sir,' Stevenson said, gesturing toward the doorway.

When the knob clicked shut, I rose from the floor and brushed off my skirt. 'Who is that man, sir?'

'He is an agent of the United States government.'

'Have you considered that he might be a double agent and that his loyalties lie elsewhere?'

'Clark, I'm not the enemy here,' Crenshaw said.

'Maybe not, sir, but it seems to me that you are fraternizing with the enemy. That man inspired Tom O'Malley to commit the destructive actions including the damage to the railroad tracks and that makes him responsible for those deaths as well.'

'It was a mistake, Miss Clark – an ugly, misguided mistake. I would like to explain everything to you but I need you to understand that what I am going to tell you cannot leave this room. You can't tell your group. You can't tell your supervisor. No one.'

'But, sir—'

Crenshaw waved away my words. 'You can tell them that what happened to Tom was a mission gone awry. You can tell them not to talk to strangers on trains. Any general information like that you can share. But I need your solemn word that you will not repeat any of the details of what I am about to tell you.'

I nodded, feeling my jaw tighten. I needed answers but I also wanted to share them. I'd have to settle for what I could get.

'I understand because of your past experience, you would be prone to see spies everywhere. It is only natural. Similarly, it is to be expected that the military intend to increase their plans to uncover potential spies before they do any damage. When you stepped into this room, I was discussing one such program with Agent Cooper. I told him that what he was doing was not working and had demonstrated the potential for unexpected consequences. I intend to go up the chain of command with my concerns with the hope I can bring all of this to an end.'

'I don't understand. What program are you talking about?'

'I imagine you would agree with the initiating premise that the spies that can do the most damage are turncoat scientists.'

'That's logical,' I said, the questions in my mind bouncing around like ping pong balls in a wind storm.

'The next premise was that an individual is most likely to be turned when they are at their most vulnerable.'

I sucked in my breath. 'As in when they are facing a personal loss?'

'Exactly. I was not aware of what the agency was doing until last night. However, they were targeting scientists, like Tom and you, who had lost a family member recently as well as those who lost sons and brothers on the front since the beginning of the conflict.'

'Sir, I want to end this war as much as anyone but, to me, those men are as predatory as snake oil salesmen.'

'Agreed, that is why I wanted it stopped immediately. Agent Cooper, who is with the Counter Intelligence Corps, strongly disagreed. He is tasked with rooting out any subversive elements and he feels that he is doing just that.'

'No. He's preying on our sorrow,' I objected.

'Think a minute, Miss Clark. Did you fall victim to his ploy?'

'No, but I was protected, in a way, because I was forewarned by Tom. But Tom had not made peace with his father – his emotions were so conflicted. He had a breakdown or the onset of some deep psychological disturbance. That agent destroyed him.'

'I agree, Miss Clark, but nonetheless, I do not think you would have succumbed as he did. You're made of sterner stuff. Now, I hope you will be open and truthful with me. I want to know every detail of your interaction with Tom O'Malley.'

'Sir, I've told you I will not name names,' I said, bristling anew.

'No. I don't expect you to do so. Just say "we" or "they" when required. I want an explanation to better understand what happened to that young scientist. I had a long talk with the chaplain and I've come to the realization that some of my preconceived notions have colored my perceptions in a way that is detrimental to my command. I am trying to broaden my outlook and I want to stop what they are doing but I need a better understanding of what happened to Tom O'Malley.'

'Only if you will agree not to do anything to besmirch his memory.'

'Agreed,' Crenshaw said with a nod.

I detailed every aspect of my communications and interactions with Tom, only interrupted occasionally with questions from the lieutenant colonel. When I had finished my tale, I asked, 'Has his body been removed from the woods?'

'Yes. It is in the morgue.'

'What are you going to do with it?'

'That decision has not been reached. It's a complicated situation with many factors to consider.'

'I think I have a solution for you.' I ran through our plan to label Tom's death an accident.

'No one will contradict that account?'

'No one on my end, sir. Your soldiers are out of my control. It does tidy up the situation and makes it all a bit easier for Tom's family.'

Crenshaw crossed his arms and rested his chin in his palm before spinning his chair and staring out the window. I bit my tongue a hundred times before he turned back around. 'Agreed. Accidental death. He took a walk in the woods before going to the train station and suffered a horrible accident.'

He stood up and stretched his hand across the desk. I wrapped my fingers around his and shook. 'Thank you, sir.'

'Don't make me regret it,' he warned.

FORTY-EIGHT

I ran down two flights of stairs anxious for a quick escape from the oppressive atmosphere in the administrative building. Outside, I took several deep breaths before I felt free of the miasma. The web of lies spun in the name of security soiled everything it touched. Whatever my future held, I knew that I never again wanted to perform any work involved with weapon making or with the military brass.

As I walked, I was amazed anew at the monumental changes and growth of our little isolated community. In three short years, the population had exploded as had the number of buildings, stores and amusements now available right here. No longer did any of us need to go beyond the gates for any of life's necessities. But was the price we paid too high? After the war, will the mail censors go away? Will our phone calls be private again? Will we be able to leave our community without passing by armed guards? If all that remained here, I don't think I could bear it.

Entering the lab, I brushed aside the greetings and questions and went straight into Charlie's office. He joined me there moments later.

'Did Crenshaw approve your plan, Libby?' he asked.

'Yes, he did. But I feel soiled and corrupted by enabling yet another lie.'

'It's for the best.'

'I know that, Charlie. But I don't like living in a place where truth is so readily sacrificed for the greater good. It eats at me every day – I fear my character bears a taint that will never be erased.'

'It's the war. War corrupts everything. When it is over, everything and everyone will return to normal. You'll see,' Charlie said.

'I wish I could believe that,' I said. 'Now, I have to lie to you – well, not exactly lie but conceal the truth, which seems morally equivalent to me.'

'See,' Charlie said with a chuckle, 'no irreparable harm to your soul. You're still bothered by it. What's at issue?'

'Crenshaw imparted information to me on the condition I do not share it with anyone and he made a point of telling me that includes you.'

'He mentioned me by name?'

'Yes,' I said. 'I have been instructed that I am permitted to tell you and the group that the official cause of Tom's death is accidental, that it was precipitated by a mission gone awry, and that all scientists should take care not to talk to strangers on trains.'

'Why?'

'That, I cannot tell you. I do know but I can't utter a word about it.'

'You're going to have a small rebellion on your hands.'

'I know. It's why I'd like you to be with us when I explain. I was hoping to gather everyone together at lunch time and explain it then. When the badgering starts, I am hoping you'll be willing to intervene.'

'I'll do my best. Do you want me to go over to Alpha and inform the others in that lab to join us? If so, I'll need a list of names.'

I scrawled out the names on a piece of scrap paper and handed it to Charlie. 'Please destroy this after you've talked to them all. I don't want it falling into the wrong hands. I'll call Tom's aunt while you're gone.'

I sat down, attempted to banish my feelings of dread and picked up the phone. The call went smoother than I thought it would. Gertrude was composed and her voice cracked only once. She accepted the accident explanation without question. I provided her with information I had received from Crenshaw's aide to enable her to bring Tom home to lay for eternity beside his father. I wiped away tears and walked out of the office.

Every pair of eyes seemed to turn to me as I emerged. The faces of the Walking Molecules members appeared concerned and quizzical. The expression of the others was baffled antici-pation, as if they knew something was happening but had no idea of what it was. 'I'll be coming around to each of your stations to get a status report. Be prepared to tell me where you are in the process and the length of time you think it will take you to complete what is at your table right now.'

I went around, jotting down that information and making no comment to the others. With the members of my group, I informed them of the informal lunch get-together with Charlie.

At noon, Charlie and I led the crew from our lab outside. The guys from Alpha lab exited, too, and flocked together with us. Charlie came to a halt in front of the cafeteria. 'Maybe this isn't the best place to talk. Why don't we all get something to carry away and convene at my house. We will be able to talk more freely there.'

I wasn't sure if I agreed. If we were in the corner of a crowded room, perhaps the criticism of my lack of openness would not be as intense but I went along with the others who agreed with Charlie.

Lunches in hand, we gathered around the Morton's dining room table. Charlie pulled out folding chairs from a closet and added the extra seats needed. I explained to them the situation using exactly the same words I had used with Charlie, but their reaction was far different.

'We are supposed to be able to share within this group anything and everything,' Dennis complained.

'I'm Tom's best friend, I deserve to know the whole truth,' Gary yelled.

I lost the remaining comments in a cacophony of discordant voices. It all blended together with the fury of a storm.

Charlie rose to his feet and tapped a fork on the side of a glass. 'Don't any of you realize how difficult this is for Libby? Don't you think she wants to tell you?'

Hostile murmurs rose around the table until Gregg and Teddy stood. Teddy, understanding his personal bias, had the good sense to defer to Gregg.

'Charlie is right,' Gregg said. 'If she had not made a commitment to Crenshaw, she would not have learned anything and she would not have been able to get the assurance that Tom's body could be returned to his family. And that he be laid to rest on the church grounds beside his father. Our sense of deserving to hear more has to be sacrificed to granting peace to Tom's family. We owe them that.'

Nearly every head looked down at the table and nodded. The notable exception was Gary who held his head high, moving a harsh glare from me to Charlie to Gregg and back again.

Rudy raised his head. 'One question, Libby. Are you saying that the mission that went wrong involved manipulating Tom to the point of madness?'

'I did not say that, Rudy. However, I can understand why you would find that a logical hypothesis.'

'But, is it in alignment with what you know?'

I glanced at Charlie as I struggled for an answer. He simply shook his head. 'Rudy, I'm sorry, but I cannot answer that question.'

'I'll take that as an answer,' Rudy said.

'That is your right, Rudy, and the right of everyone at this table. Reach your own conclusions as best as you can, just don't expect me to confirm any of them.'

A heavy silence descended but it was soon replaced by the sounds of chewing and multiple one-on-one conversations. I could not wait to get back to the lab. The walk back was no happy stroll. Teddy, of course, tried to inject a lighter spirit into the afternoon. He attempted to make me laugh, but it didn't work. I was ready to go home, pack my bags and cocoon myself in the safety of Aunt Dorothy's home until the war was over.

FORTY-NINE

My legs felt like two tree stumps as I plodded home after work. I had no reason to remain here any longer. The majority of the men in the lab did not know what was going on but they clearly picked up on the new negativity in attitude toward me from the members of the group. I felt as isolated now as I had done when I was the newly-arrived alien in the midst of an all-male world.

The camaraderie I had established with my lab mates proved to be as ephemeral as fog. I felt like nothing more than an annoying presence and an unneeded pair of hands. The war in the Pacific would be won with or without me. It would be a relief to no longer be torn between my patriotism and my moral qualms.

I had arrived here with the idealistic notion that I could make a difference in the outcome of the conflict – I had long ago abandoned that belief. I should leave and let it all go on without me. I could wait the war out in seclusion at Aunt Dorothy's home. After that, I could resume my professional life.

First, I'd announce my plans at the beginning of the next regular meeting of the Walking Molecules, and excuse myself. Then, I'd formally resign to Charlie. But, wait. I would have to tell Teddy first – I couldn't surprise him in a room full of people. I'd also let him know that I expected a visit when the war was over – that should cushion my departure a little bit for him. And I'd promise to write – often.

My steps felt lighter with the decision made as I approached my home. When I turned the final corner and my house came into view, I saw a woman waiting by the door. As I got closer, I realized it was Eleanor Stanley, dressed to the nines in white gloves and a stylish hat as if she were visiting the queen. She had asked me to think about what I was willing to do to improve conditions at the hutments. A wave of guilt washed over me – I had not given another thought to her request.

I walked up the steps and stretched out my hand. 'Mrs Stanley, won't you please come inside.'

'It's Eleanor, please. I hope we will be seeing a lot more of each other. Right now, I would love a few minutes of your time,' she said with a smile.

'Certainly, Eleanor,' I said, a bit wary about the intimation of a future relationship. 'Should I put on the tea kettle?'

'That would be delightful, thank you.'

While I worked in the kitchen preparing the tea service, Eleanor talked about the heat and humidity of summertime in the south and her longing to be able to return to Maine for the season as she did growing up. The way she described the fresh air, cool breezes and the invigorating chill of the water in even the hottest months, I yearned to escape with her.

When we settled in the living room with our cups, Eleanor said, 'You are probably wondering about the timing of my arrival on your doorstep, Libby. There are two reasons why I am here today. First of all, I did not want to bother you immediately after the death of your mother – I am so sorry for your loss.'

'Thank you. How did you hear about my mother?' I asked.

'Oak Ridge might have exploded in growth, but in many ways, it's still a very small town. The grapevine moves information around faster than a hungry bobcat chasing down dinner. I imagine you're not as aware of the gossip machine since you are working with men all day.'

'Men do gossip,' I said, 'but mostly about the women they've been dating and in ways that bore me.'

'Oh yes, boy talk,' she said flapping the air with one hand. 'I explained to you previously about our desire to improve the living conditions for the colored laborers here in Oak Ridge and, well, I want to inform you about what we have learned this week, but I really need you to agree to keep what I say confidential.'

'Of course,' I said, inwardly groaning about more secrets in my life.

'First, I want to make sure you understand, none of our husbands are telling us about the work they do. Most of what we learn from them is intuitive. Some of us have been married for a long time and that gives you a sense of knowing when something is wrong – when they are facing a dilemma that makes them uncomfortable. Lately, more of us sense self-doubt in our spouses. We can tell they are troubled, in some way, by the end goal of their labors. I don't want you to reveal your personal concerns but are you battling any ethical or moral questions?'

The question startled me. Was this a test? Was she sent to pry information out of me to destroy me? I shook my head, but remembered – it really didn't matter since I was planning to leave anyway. 'Quite simply, yes I am.'

'I expected as much. We also have a network that reaches out to other secret facilities. One of us has a sister whose husband works at another place. She doesn't know where her sister is located – just that it's drier and not as green as here. Her sister doesn't have to contend with mud but she does have to fight an unending battle with dust. Another woman has a connection to a different installation with lots of trees like we have here.

'We've all been soaking up hints and clues as best we can. One thing that seems universal is the belief that something big is in the air. That whatever you all are doing, it is about to be used in some way. We assume it is a weapon. What else could be so top secret? If we are correct, it must be something that they are certain will finally end the war. You don't need to confirm or deny this – we know you can't do that.

'However, we believe that when the war ends, we will need to move quickly. Everyone will be celebrating and in that exuberant mood, we will be more likely to have our demands met.'

'And just what are your demands, Eleanor?' I asked.

'We want all the residents at the hutments to be installed in housing with windows and proper heating before winter. We want all married colored couples to be able to live together with their families just as the rest of us do. And, yes, we know some white folks are living in tacky little trailer homes but, at least, their families are together and they are protected from the elements. We want the colored employees to be treated as equals not as livestock. We are in the south but we are not of the south and it's about time we started acting like it.'

'I agree with you, Eleanor, but what makes you think I could make a difference?'

'You'd be surprised, Libby. To have a professional woman in our midst will make it far more difficult for the powers that be to push us aside as a bunch of silly hens. You can encourage your male peers to support our efforts, you can speak for us in settings where a mere wife would not be allowed entry. You could make a difference not just for us but for all the oppressed out there living in those primitive conditions. I am not flattering you when I say that we think you are the key to our success.'

'I might be a scientist, Eleanor, but I'm still just a woman to many.'

'You are much more than that to the rest of us. You are a role model to all our daughters. You are an example to all our sons. And your reputation as someone who stands up for the right things has spread inside this fence like wildfire. As a matter of fact, when I told my husband dinner would be a bit late this evening because I would be talking to you, he was impressed. Told me that Charlie Morton said if he was ever in a fight, he'd want you on his side. Then my husband insisted that I treat you with respect because you've earned it.'

I could not have stared harder at her if she sprouted a foot in the middle of her face. 'I'm surprised enough that Charlie said that about me,' I admitted, 'but I don't think I even know your husband.'

'You two have never met but he has heard a lot about you. And I think, Miss Libby Clark, that the only person here that doesn't think you are unstoppable is you. You place far too little value on your importance.'

'Then this is not your standard gung-ho recruiting speech?' I said, hoping that she'd laugh and admit I'd caught her. But she didn't.

'No, Miss Clark, not hardly. You are the only person whom I think is capable of making all the difference in the world to our cause. With you by our side, we can get the laborers out of those hutment hovels and reunite families.'

'I am flattered and I would like to help but my work – the time it takes is always so unpredictable.'

'We don't expect you to do the time-consuming work and we don't expect you to be the public face, but we would like to have you on board as our secret weapon. No one, however, would have any hesitation to deploy you when needed.'

Her analogy made me squirm but it also made me rethink the plan I'd formulated on the way home. Perhaps I could still make a difference here – not on the world stage but on my little corner of the planet.

'Well, I've taken enough of your time, Libby. I do not expect you to make a snap decision but just let me know—'

I surprised both of us by interjecting, 'You can count on me, Eleanor. Anything I can do outside of work hours, just let me know.'

Eleanor threw her arms around me, thanking me again and again. 'One little thing, I know you said, "outside of work hours," but would you consider getting signatures for our petition inside the lab?'

'I'll see how it goes with the group of scientists I meet with every week. If I have any success there, I'll take it to the lab as well.'

'Bless you, dear. I'd better rush off now. My husband might not be as pleased about this meeting if I don't get home and get dinner on the table before bedtime. Talk to you, soon.'

I closed the door, still a bit stunned that I'd made that commitment with impulsive fervor. I had to admit, though, I was pleased with myself. I was certainly going to stir things up at the next Walking Molecules meeting – just not in the way I originally thought.

FIFTY

I walked to work still trying to absorb yesterday's zigs and zags. Too much change for one day. I also worried about the significance of Eleanor's intuitive revelations regarding the imminent use of our work product. I knew it might just

be the result of long-term exposure to the secrecy of this
project that built a wall between spouses.

I entered the lab prepared for the worst. The room went
silent. Goosebumps raised on my arms as if I were chilled.
From a distance, I spotted clutter at my lab station and my
apprehension grew. I want to turn and run as I drifted back to
the comfort of my decision to resign last evening.

I walked softer with every step forward, expecting an
unbidden emotional explosion that I knew I must suppress. I
choked back tears as I recognized the source of my discomfort.
A tin of coffee, a chocolate candy bar, jar of jam, a box of
cookies and two books – one I'd already read but that was
irrelevant. I swallowed hard before turning around. 'Thank
you, one and all. I hope you understand how deeply I am
touched by this gesture and how desperately I needed it.'

Gregg stepped toward me with an empty potato sack. 'We
thought you'd need something to carry it home in.'

I nodded my thanks because I didn't dare speak for fear of
losing control. The lump in my throat caused pressure that
threatened to push the tears out of my eyes. I swallowed hard
as Gregg helped me load everything up and stick the bag under
my station.

Gregg shouted, 'Okay, everybody, we have work to do.' He
smiled, gave my forearm a squeeze and walked back to his
work area.

An hour later, Charlie informed me he was heading to a
meeting at the administrative building before he left the lab.
For another hour, we worked in near silence except for the
clink of lab glassware, the whir of equipment and the shuffling
of feet.

Charlie's quiet clearing of his throat was loud enough to
break the spell. We all looked up at his furrowed face. 'All
personal leaves and pre-arranged early departures are canceled.
Sundays off are terminated. We will work seven days a week,
ten to twelve hours a day, until further notice.' Charlie ran his
gaze around the room where stunned faces greeted his without
comment until a cacophony of protest erupted.

'Why, Charlie?'

'What's going on?'

'We'll run out of product from Alpha lab within the week.'

Charlie raised his arms and silence descended again. 'Alpha has the same instructions. Engineers have been asked to seek methods to speed up the output from the Calutron. If I knew why, I would tell you.'

'Does it mean they're about to deploy the gadget?' Stephen asked.

'Not to my knowledge,' Charlie said. 'However, I do acknowledge the logic of your deduction.'

'And even if you knew, you probably couldn't tell us,' Stephen added.

Charlie sighed and seemed to shrink as if deflated. 'You're probably right, Stephen, but I honestly do not know what it means. I did ask but got no answer. Does it mean they are ready to deploy in a surprise maneuver? Or does it indicate that they want to have everything operational before they deliver a threat with force behind it? Or just maybe, the design is flawed and they need enough material to test alternative designs. I simply don't know.

'The length of our days will depend on the industriousness of our output. I will have to track incoming from Alpha and if we're exceeding that, we can stop in as few as ten hours – otherwise, we keep on going. Get busy. We have no time to dawdle.' He sighed again, before crossing the room to his office.

Throughout the day, Charlie emerged from his paperwork, checked on Alpha's input and helped anyone who was lagging or encountering a problem on our lab floor. He seemed in a state of constant motion. Even when I stopped in his office to present a purchase order, he was standing behind his desk, moving back and forth between the piles of documents needing his attention.

Eleven hours into our day, Charlie walked to the center of the room and announced, 'Wrap up what you're doing, it's time to call it quits. We're running ahead of Alpha – they'll need to work an hour longer but all of you can call it a day. In the morning, try to get in a little early and we can get a head start on tomorrow.'

I finished up the procedure I had started and moved on to

help others still hard at work finishing their tasks. Charlie was busily engaged assisting at different stations. Soon, they'd all straggled out and we were the last two in the lab.

'Got a minute, Charlie,' I asked.

'Sure. Come into my office – I need to get off of my feet.'

Charlie sat behind his desk and pulled a bottle of bourbon and two glasses out of the bottom drawer. He waved the bottle at me but I shook my head. He poured a small dribble into a glass and upended it down his throat. 'Okay, what's up?'

'Someone shared information with me last night that I didn't take very seriously until you made your announcement today.' I continued to relay what I had learned from Eleanor.

As I spoke, Charlie leaned forward on his desk. 'Who told you this?'

'The wife of a scientist.'

'Which one?'

'Charlie, you know I can't betray that confidence. I'm telling you because it seems to fit with what happened here today.'

'What conclusion have you reached?' Charlie asked.

'That they've got one gadget ready to deploy and they want enough material to build a back-up. Have you heard any rumors about testing?'

'Not one,' Charlie said. 'But somewhere, someone has to have been doing testing. I've heard a lot of talk about the fear of a blood bath if we invaded Japan. Many expect more deaths there than we've experienced throughout the rest of the war. If that's an official assessment, then they have to use whatever else we have to end this conflict before we reach that point.'

'What are we unleashing, Charlie?'

'I don't really know, Libby, all I can say is God help us all.'

FIFTY-ONE

I stood outside near the exit for the Alpha lab waiting for Teddy to emerge. By my calculations, they had about a half hour or less of their workday remaining. I jumped at the first clap of thunder. Looking over at the ridge, I saw a bright bolt streak through the sky and braced myself for the next rumble. It arrived along with the first big, wet drops of rain.

I raced for the laboratory entrance, grateful that my badge displayed my clearance for entry. I stepped into the mud room vestibule and leaned against the wall opposite the sink.

One by one, chemists started to file out. They glanced at me without comment but their curiosity put inquisitive scowls on their faces. Those expressions were soon replaced by dismay when they opened the exterior door and saw the deluge sluicing from the sky.

Teddy walked in and shot me a quick double take. 'Libby, what are you doing here?'

'Waiting for you. I was outside but then the skies opened up.' At that moment, a monstrous boom of thunder confirmed my observation.

Teddy cracked the door open. 'Whoa! You're not kidding.'

'Are you ready to make a run for it?' I asked.

'No sense in delaying the inevitable,' he said with a sigh.

'You can come to my place if you want or you can veer off at the dorm.'

'Your place, it is.'

We grabbed hands, shoved open the door and took off. Streams rolled down the roads forming deep puddles in every pothole and rut. The sky churned with angry clouds, flashes of light and thunder that shook us down to the soles of our shoes. We moved as fast as we dared, slowing when one of us slipped a bit on the wet surface. Even though it was a treacherous journey, we were laughing by the time we arrived at the steps to my flat-top.

We shook off the best we could and went into the kitchen where the linoleum floor was impervious to water damage. We slipped off our shoes and bent over the sink. I squeezed water out of my hair and Teddy brushed the water off of his shorter cut with his hand.

I threw the tea towel at him and said, 'Wipe off your face. I'll get more for both of us.' I returned carrying the stack of every bath towel I owned and set them on the kitchen counter.

'Libby, go get out of your wet clothes. I'll stay in here and drip.'

I didn't argue but I did have another plan. I grabbed my robe in the bedroom and went back to the kitchen. 'Here, you can take off your clothes and put this on. As soon as I make some coffee, I'll turn on the oven and lay your pants and shirt on the stovetop. I don't think they'll get completely dry but at least they won't be dripping when you put them back on.'

'This looks a little small . . .' he said, holding up my robe.

'Wear it anyway. It will cover enough,' I said as I left to change my clothes. Once I was in dry clothes, I hung my wet things in the bathroom before I returned. Teddy looked trussed. His shoulders stretched the seams. The waist line crossed the middle of his chest and the tie was barely long enough. The hem barely tickled his kneecaps.

He scowled and said, 'Don't you laugh.'

I threw a hand over my mouth and squeezed my lips tight but it wasn't enough. I burst loose a huge guffaw at the ridiculous sight.

'I told you . . .' he complained.

'I tried. Honest. I tried,' I said and collapsed into his arms.

He held me while we laughed and gasped for air.

I stepped back. 'Coffee?'

'Please. And wipe that smirk off your face.'

I fixed a cup for each of us, turned on the oven, arranged his clothing on top and we retired into the living room. When Teddy sat down, he draped a towel over his midsection.

My lips rebelled at the restraint as another titter bubbled up.

'Don't you start,' he said with a barely suppressed chuckle.

We collapsed on opposite ends of the sofa and sighed in unison. 'Actually, I didn't ask you here to laugh at you. I had something to discuss,' I said.

'Good. That makes my ego feel a bit soothed. What is it?'

'How would you feel about staying right here after the war?'

'Here? In Oak Ridge?'

'Yes. I have something to do here that I think is important.'

'Another job?'

'No. Not a job. A volunteer opportunity that I think really matters. Would you be okay continuing to work here for a while after the war?'

'Will there be any work here for us?'

'I doubt they'll need all of us – but some won't want to stay. Surely, they wouldn't erect these buildings and facilities and then abandon it to ruin. Someone will need to find a way to pound the swords into plowshares for peacetime applications.'

'Probably. But why do you think the war is about to end. Everything I hear is that the invasion of Japan will be a difficult, costly and lengthy operation.'

'I don't think we'll need to invade,' I said.

'Why not? What did they tell you in Beta that they didn't say in Alpha?'

'It was nothing that was said there – Charlie told me that both labs were given identical messages about the work to deliver to their chemists and nothing about the reason.'

'Then what makes you so certain?'

'I'm sure you know of the research that's been going on since before the war at the University of Chicago, but did you know there are at least two other facilities connected to ours that were created out of nothing at the start of the war?'

'I've heard some rumors but how do you *know* that? Do you have connections there?'

'No. But I've met someone who does.'

'Who?' Teddy asked.

'The wife of a scientist here.'

'And her contacts are other wives?'

'Yes.'

'How would they know more than we do?'

'Men have always undervalued women's sense of intuition – no surprise that the military has done the same. You can keep information secret but you can't hide the energy behind it. Women at all three facilities have picked up on an increased level, a rising sense of urgency – they've smelled the change in the air. They are all convinced that something big is about to happen.'

'Given that I accept that premise, what do you think is about to happen?' Teddy said, setting down his coffee cup and leaning forward with intensity lining his face.

'I think the gadget will soon be deployed.'

'Exactly what is the gadget? Do you know?'

'I don't know. But I expect that it is a bomb – the most powerful the world has ever seen. I believe it will split atoms and release horror into the earth's atmosphere.'

'If you're right, what will be the after-effects?'

'I don't know. I doubt that anyone knows.'

Teddy slumped back into the sofa. 'And we will bear responsibility for it.'

'Some of it, yes.' My fears and anxieties danced a jitterbug in my chest. I leaned back and breathed deeply to try stilling the rapid tattoo of my heart.

'My God . . .' Teddy whispered.

We sat there stunned by the possibilities that lay ahead – voicing them made it feel more real. Our hands, seemingly of their own volition, moved together and squeezed tight. We listened to the pounding of the rain on the roof, each lost in our own thoughts.

Teddy broke the silence. 'This volunteer opportunity? Does it have something to do with the scientist's wife you met?'

'Yes. A group of wives have recruited me to join in their effort to transform the hutments.'

'The hutments?'

I explained to him what we knew about the lives the colored workers were required to live. 'Even after the war, we are going to need them as laborers, as cafeteria workers, as maids

– they are a vital part of our society. It's about time we treated them like humans instead of livestock.'

'But, Libby, this is the south.'

'The south is out there,' I said waving a hand in the air. 'This is federal property. They are citizens of the United States – just as we are – citizens who made sacrifices to win the war. We need to show them the respect they deserve as fellow human beings.'

'But they still segregate the military. How can you possibly think your efforts will succeed?'

'We're not going for integration – not yet. But we do think we can change their deplorable, un-American living conditions. And even if that is a quixotic goal, we have to try.'

'What can I do to help?'

'First of all, you can sign the petition I'm bringing to the next Walking Molecules meeting. We will present it to the administration and the military the moment that the war is over. We will be demanding immediate action.'

'You can count on me, Libby. You can always count on me. And if you want to stay here and work – I want to do the same. No strings. No obligations. I'll be here waiting for you to make a commitment or chase me away.'

AUTHOR'S NOTE

I n May 1945, time was drawing nigh for the deployment of the uranium-based bomb. Unbeknownst to the scientists at Oak Ridge, their July 25th shipment of Uranium 235 arrived at its Pacific Island destination on July 27th. There, every available bit of the U-235 they had sent was incorporated into Little Boy. On August 6th, the *Enola Gay*, piloted by Colonel Paul W. Tibbets, Jr., dropped that bomb on Hiroshima, Japan. Three days later, Fat Man, the first plutonium bomb, fell on Nagasaki. Those two were the only atomic bombs existing in the US arsenal at the time but Truman told the Japanese to 'expect a rain of ruin from the air, the like of which has never been seen on this earth.'

The Japanese fell for his bluff. Emperor Hirohito ordered the war council to accept the terms of surrender laid out by the allies. They announced their intentions on August 15th. Representatives of the Empire of Japan formally signed the Instrument of Surrender on board the *USS Missouri* on September 2nd.

Although military experts believed that more than 100,000 American lives and several times that amount of Japanese lives would have been lost in a physical invasion and credited the use of the weapons for preventing those deaths, many scientists still agonized over their role in the creation of the bombs. Oppenheimer, director of the Los Alamos facility, condemned the sins of the physicists and said, 'There is blood on my hands.'

Code named Fu-Go, the fire balloon was a real weapon launched by the Japanese during World War II. It was a hydrogen balloon that carried an anti-personnel bomb or incendiary devices designed to take advantage of the jet stream over the Pacific Ocean to drop bombs on American and Canadian cities and rural areas. This Japanese weapon was the very first with intercontinental range, albeit without any targeting ability. The sole purpose was to terrorize the populace of the two countries. Balloons were found floating off the coast of Los Angeles and landing in the states of Wyoming, Montana, Oregon, California, Kansas, Iowa, Washington, Idaho, South Dakota, Michigan and Nevada as well as the Canadian provinces of British Columbia, Saskatchewan, Manitoba, Alberta, the Yukon and the Northwest Territories. One of the more menacing landings was near the Manhattan Project's production facility at the Hanford Site, in Washington state, causing a short circuit in the power lines there.

Despite the widespread distribution of these weapons, the incident mentioned in this book was the first and only time a fire balloon caused any fatalities in the North American continent.

Because of the housing shortage caused by the population explosion at Oak Ridge, some white workers were also housed in the crude hutments, however, all of them were moved to more suitable structures by 1945. Much of the black population continued to reside in the segregated shacks until 1950, despite efforts by many wives of scientists. Nonetheless, when the Supreme Court decision in Brown versus the Board of Education was announced in 1954, Oak Ridge was the first community in the south to desegregate its junior high and high schools beginning in 1955. Segregation continued at the elementary schools for another decade.

Finally, I want to express my appreciation to my dependable support team: my excellent agent Jane Dystel; author and friend Betsy Ashton; and my first reader and biggest cheerleader, Wayne Fanning.